THE DIVORCE PARTY

M.M. DELUCA

BLOODHOUND
— BOOKS —

Copyright © 2025 M.M. DeLuca

The right of M.M. DeLuca to be identified as the Author of the Work has been asserted by them in accordance with the Copyright, Designs and Patents Act 1988.

First published in 2025 by Bloodhound Books.

Apart from any use permitted under UK copyright law, this publication may only be reproduced, stored, or transmitted, in any form, or by any means, with prior permission in writing of the publisher or, in the case of reprographic production, in accordance with the terms of licences issued by the Copyright Licensing Agency.
All characters in this publication are fictitious and any resemblance to real persons, living or dead, is purely coincidental.

www.bloodhoundbooks.com

Print ISBN: 978-1-917705-10-3

*Sometimes you don't feel the weight of something you've been carrying
until you feel the weight of its release.*

Unknown

LAS VEGAS
SUNDAY SEPTEMBER 2ND

She fumbles with the key card, takes a few shallow breaths, then holds it in front of the scanner, praying it works.

A moment of dizzying panic before the green light flashes and the door opens onto the penthouse suite. Dimmed lights glow softly from an oversized chandelier dripping with crystal tears. She picks her way across the carpet past a silk sofa, a gold-trimmed bar top stacked with bottles, and on into the bedroom. Someone's lying on the king-sized bed. Sleeping.

Waiting.

For her.

He'd slipped the extra key card into her hand in that rooftop club where colored strobe lights played like rainbows across the night sky. She was dancing, arms raised, and he pulled her close to brush his lips against her neck. They'd just finished another bottle of bubbly, and all her cares, all the secrets and regrets, had melted away.

She was that party girl again, and after so many years it felt sweet.

Now this is the payoff. The prize. And she's the winner. Too bad for the others.

She slips off her silk minidress. Tiptoes across the carpet and slides onto the cream bedspread. He's been waiting for her and she doesn't plan on disappointing him. It was always meant to be. Last night was proof – the way their bodies moved together in perfect synchrony, the way he traced the line of her lips with his finger and looked at her as if she was the only woman in the world.

She crawls across to him.

He doesn't move.

She touches something wet and sticky. Metallic-smelling. She flips herself off the mattress and looks at the reddened palms of her hands, and the crimson sheet that's supposed to be white.

His eyes are open. Fixed vacantly on the ceiling. Staring from a pallid, lifeless face.

Now she's panting, breath rasping from her throat as her eyes fall onto a note propped against his head and written in red marker – *or is it blood? His blood?* She retches as she reads it.

YOU WANT HIM, YOU CAN HAVE HIM.

She stumbles backwards. White sparks splinter into darkness, her knees buckle under her, and she's falling.

Her cheek smacks onto the floor as she passes out.

THE INVITATION

Popular lines for divorce party invitations:

"I do – I did – I'm done."
Pop the champagne, I got back my last name.
Single and ready to mingle.
He put the 'ick' in 'prick'.
Straight outta marriage, let freedom ring.
Take a shot, I untied the knot.
Divorced A.F.

TWO WEEKS EARLIER

DAISY

Daisy tries to open the back door, hold her travel coffee mug upright and keep her bag strap balanced on her shoulder. A cascade of reedy notes emerges from the kitchen, like someone scraping rusty nails across a bandsaw. She glances back into the kitchen where Wade is perched at the counter studying a *Master the harmonica in 20 days* handbook.

Starting today she'll be the sole breadwinner in the house. Again. Wade's unemployment has finally run out. Again.

She should have kicked his lazy ass out long ago. He's been in and out of work their entire marriage. And since their son, Ethan, won an architecture scholarship and headed west to Seattle, Wade's dropped all pretense of job hunting. She knows for a fact he's been hanging around local pool halls and bars instead of searching for job leads. As a result, her credit cards are all maxed out and there's no way she can beg the bank for another overdraft extension while Wade tries to crack the music scene.

Anxiety squeezes the breath from her. *If things keep going this way, she'll have a heart attack. At thirty-seven.* A sick, woozy feeling engulfs her, and she lets go of the screen door. It slams shut, knocking her elbow. Her coffee mug smacks onto the patio and shatters into tiny pieces. A pool of freshly dripped brew oozes across the concrete. *Goddamn it. She needs that caffeine.*

Tears of frustration sting her eyes. She kicks the coffee cup into the dogwood bush and heads towards her car, a ten-year-old Dodge Caravan with silver paint job and powder-blue upholstery. Wade gave up his car a year ago. Couldn't make the payments on his Mazda Miata.

She drives to work on auto-pilot, anticipating the day ahead. Eight hours spent subbing at her local high school, a prospect that now seems worse than having multiple tooth extractions without the freezing. She's never been able to land a permanent teaching job. Can't understand why. She's pretty, personable, creative. So what's the problem?

One school principal suggested she has trouble staying focused. That she can't seem to follow directions or stick to the basic school rules. But how can she help it when the lesson outlines left by the regular teacher are so boring they'd put an insomniac to sleep, and the school rules way too archaic for the twenty-first century? So what if she'd smoked up in her car during lunch hour. Any sane person would need a pick-me-up after three hours with a bunch of kids who haven't cracked a book open since their mom read them *The Berenstain Bears*.

She drives the final mile up the road and pulls into the school parking lot behind a candy-apple-red Mustang convertible carrying members of the football team plus girlfriends. That car is worth at least three times as much as hers. A sobering thought.

She walks like a robot towards the front door, and ten minutes later, she's just started today's PowerPoint presentation on persuasive techniques. It's like doing stand-up in front of a hostile audience. She looks towards the window, which glows

THE DIVORCE PARTY

blue and shiny like a celluloid movie frame. A voice in her head says *leave this room now or be eternally screwed.*

Fidgeting bodies, gaping yawns and pen-poking displays merge into a blur and her once-lucid words become nothing more than a monotonous *blah-blah-blah*. A verbal fog enveloping everyone, including herself.

White light explodes across her line of vision. She switches off the overhead projector, collects her bag and walks towards the door. On the way out she picks up a balled-up Kleenex, throws it into the wastebasket, then nods to the class. "Have a nice life," she says before pulling the classroom door shut.

Downstairs, in the entrance hall, the principal, who's usually holed up in his office, is checking the Coke machine as he does twice every day. He loves his machines. They're so *cooperative. Unlike his students.*

She walks past him just as he drops a can of Coke. Stooping, she picks up the little varmint. He breathes a sigh of relief, nods and wipes it off, then carries on loading. She passes by him, invisible. He's oblivious to her coat, packed bag and the potted rubber plant she's been nurturing in the prep room.

Nobody comes after her as she walks out into the fresh air.

Only a couple of pale faces are pressed to the window of her ex-classroom.

On the drive back home, she passes rows of shops and coffee houses and bakeries, all appearing brighter, shinier and more colorful than before. She's almost dizzy with her new clarity of thought – coasting on a dream that ends abruptly when she lets herself back into the house, wondering what she's going to tell Wade now she's quit and they're both out of work. That ought to shake him from his torpor.

But the house is deserted. Wade's bowl of Cheerios sits half-eaten on the dining table, a dead fly floating in the milk. A small network of rings surrounds his coffee cup as if he'd moved it around until he found a spot where he could prop the little white note that sits against it. She feels a flutter at the top of her stomach when she reads the message.

> I don't know who I am anymore and I sure as hell don't know who you are. Gone to seek the truth...

The writing tails off into an indecipherable squiggle. He couldn't even summon up the energy to finish his goodbye note. Typical. And Wade was never one for penmanship. Or studying, for that matter. *But what the hell is he talking about? Finding the truth? What does he know?*

She stops herself. *Don't panic.* Everything is a-okay. *Maybe he's finally seen the light and gone to make things right with his parents?*

She stops and takes a few deep breaths, then notices a crisp, cream envelope leaning against the cereal box, her name embossed in gold on the front. Inside, an invitation. A gray card with a silver border. Tasteful, expensive-looking. Silver embossed writing.

I do

I did

I'm done

Please join me, Evie Cummings, for a divorce party weekend, to celebrate my new status as an independent woman

Aria Hotel, Las Vegas.

Evie Cummings, used to be Evie O'Sullivan. Unofficial leader of The Party Girls. Daisy, Evie, Savannah and Zoe. The four of them united by their messed-up, deprived childhoods, an anomaly in the top-tier university they'd managed to squeeze into, like gate-crashers at a high-society birthday party.

Daisy was a bridesmaid for Evie just after graduation, but that was supposed to be the last time they'd see each other. They'd all agreed. Considering what went down around that time.

Heart racing, she scans the date of the party. It's in two weeks. Hell, she has to go. Has to know what all this is about. Even if she has to sell Wade's precious vintage album collection to get the money. Christ, she'll sell the house. It's in her name anyway. There has to be some equity left in it. And she doesn't give a damn about Wade's sudden disappearance. Good riddance and good luck to him. He can go to hell for all she cares.

On the positive side, she's never been to Sin City, but always dreamt about going. Entertainment twenty-four seven. Shows, pool parties, spas, shopping and gambling. Maybe she can win a life-changing jackpot. After all her years of sacrifice and self-deprivation, she deserves a lucky break.

But something still nags at her. Why, after all this time, has Evie chosen to bring the four of them together? That time is done. Finished with. And surely, she has a host of wealthy country club buddies who'd be happy to chip in on a luxury suite and maybe bankroll the oversize liquor bill?

Does Evie know something she's not letting on about? How would that be possible?

Daisy picks up the phone. Her hand trembles as she remembers that name: The Party Girls.

Back together again. Good news or bad news? Doesn't matter. She has to find out.

SAVANNAH

Sequins sparkle on her slim, black sheath. Six piles of chips are stacked at her fingertips. An ice-cold mojito stuffed with mint leaves arrives. She's up forty grand and the wheel just keeps on giving.

This whole life is a gamble. You're dealt a certain number of chips and it's up to you to place them at the right time, in the right spot. She's done okay up till now. Taken risks and used her analytical skills for maximum profit. No reason to think her run of luck is going to dry up anytime soon. She's here, in the best high-limit room in Vegas – a paradise of gilded walls and glittering chandeliers, and she gets a sexy adrenaline rush every time she steps through the velvet door that reminds her of a decadent bordello.

Then she thinks of the invitation she received yesterday, and for a moment loses focus. The wheel stops on red and she's put her chips on black. *Damn you, Evie.* Just the thought of that name brings bad luck. Maybe it's time to call it quits – cash out, head to the bar and enjoy her drink. Her run is over. But only temporarily. Tomorrow she'll be red hot again.

Leon is bartender tonight. He's gorgeous. Tall, gold-skinned, caramel eyes. A law student during the day, he has plans to enter the corporate field. She's told him many times he's got the charisma for big trial cases, but he claims he's too paranoid. Doesn't want to worry about looking over his shoulder for some ex-client nursing a grudge about a bad verdict.

She gets that. Vegas has been a sanctuary for her. A place where the past is irrelevant, and all that matters is *now*. A person can disappear here amongst the tourists and convention delegates, the pro-gamblers and the wannabe high-rollers, the scammers and their unsuspecting marks. Shady types skulking around the casinos, but she's learned how to avoid them without pissing them off. She's also an expert at spotting the good ones.

Leon's one of them.

She rests her elbows on the bar. Nurses her mojito. Leon swoops over to wipe the counter beside her.

"What's up, Sav? Where's that smile tonight?"

"Ugh. Got a blast from the past. An invitation. Old friend from college."

"Unwelcome, by the looks of it?"

She shrugs. "Meh. I'm one of those people who thinks old memories should be left in the past, where they belong. They stink like dead leaves if you start raking them up."

"So you're one of those glass-half-empty types?" says Leon bundling the cloth in one hand.

"Nostalgia sucks. I prefer looking ahead."

He tilts his head and grins. "Me, I love going home to see my folks. Gives me a chance to reconnect with my buddies and catch up with the latest news. And besides, roots are important. Our past shapes us into who we are, which means we can never truly leave it behind."

"I disagree. Sometimes you have to lose your past so you can start fresh. Unless you had a mom and dad, a brother and sister, and a dog named Spot?"

Leon smiles the warm, sunny smile of someone raised with a secure foundation. "Our dog was called Marley. My mom and dad were huge reggae fans. And I had two older sisters who spoiled me rotten. Pretty sweet childhood, I guess. What's your story?"

"Heavy drinking widowed mom. Lonely, deprived childhood. What more do I need to say?"

"Sorry for prying. I get why you don't want to talk about your past. But tell me about the invitation."

Savannah swirls mint leaves around the ice cubes. "It's from an old college friend. A group of us were really tight there. She's getting divorced, so this is some kind of weird celebration."

"How long since you last saw her?"

"Maybe sixteen years ago. Just after we graduated college. I was actually supposed to be in her wedding party, but something – I mean things got in the way. A family emergency. I had to leave."

"So that makes you..."

"Yes, I'm gonna be thirty-seven this year. Don't remind me."

He grins. A sweet grin. "I find older women incredibly sexy."

"You're just being kind." She drains her mojito and pushes the glass towards him. Sighs. "I can't believe she doesn't have anyone else to ask. After all this time she must have a whole new set of friends, so why the hell would she ask me? We haven't talked in years."

He sorts out lime and a sprig of mint. Starts to muddle it in a fresh glass. "Could be sentimental. Maybe you remind her of a more innocent time, when she had no baggage. After all, I hear these divorce parties are all about celebrating new beginnings. I've talked to plenty of people who have them here."

More innocent times? Savannah almost chokes on a piece of lime. So many guys here mask sly, hidden agendas with their fake tans and bleached porcelain smiles, but Leon is an innocent, an optimist. Always sees the best in people. How could he know the truth about their college years? That her entire life is tainted with secrets and lies?

Tears press at the back of her eyes. "You're such a sweetheart. Why didn't I run into you when I was a freshman?"

"What did you study?"

"Chemistry."

He pushes the sweating drink towards her. "Strange, I never pegged you for the scientific type."

She takes a sip. Tastes like a double. "Don't you know you never can tell a person's real story just from their appearance?"

"Did you ever work in the science field?"

"Briefly. I did a placement at a toxicology lab. Couldn't take another day discovering how many sad alcoholics and addicts there were in town."

"Pretty depressing."

"Let's just say it took an entire weekend to get over a week of work."

"Sounds like hell."

She nods. "That's why I came here to heaven. Followed my true passion. Became someone else."

He opens his mouth as if to ask another question, but she shakes her head just as a text *pings* onto her phone. She starts, always wary of unexpected messages. Her heart drops when she sees the name attached.

Evie.

She still hasn't figured out how Evie tracked her down when she's been so careful to stay off social media.

For a moment she considers deleting the message. Just blocking her.

But she can't.

Her breath comes in shallow gasps. She glances up and

Leon's watching her, brows knit in concern. She wipes a thin trickle of sweat from her temple and reads.

> Hey gorgeous. Just working on the itinerary. Hope you're up for a jam-packed party weekend.

Damn, she doesn't need this. Not now everything's been going so smoothly. She downs her mojito and is about to stow her phone away when another text comes in.

> Zoe and Daisy are coming. Can't believe we'll have THE PARTY GIRLS back together again.

Just seeing those words knocks the breath from her. The phone pings again.

> And in Vegas. You know they say what happens in Vegas stays in Vegas.

Leon taps the bar in front of her. "Everything okay?"

She picks up her purse. Climbs down from the stool and backs away. "I'm fine. Just gotta sort some stuff out."

Leon smiles. "As long as you know I've got your back if you have any problems." He tilts his head. "I mean it."

"Appreciate that," she says, frowning as the next text arrives.

> Hope you remember the rules. Not like last time.

She feels like throwing up.

> What do you mean?

A pause. No response. She taps again.

> ???

She waits. Nothing. Seems like Evie's left her hanging. *Deliberately, knowing her. Damn.* Why did she have to show up again? Now she'll have to take half a sleeping pill just to get a few hours' sleep. Rehearsal's early tomorrow, and her legs are already protesting.

"Sure you're okay?" says Leon.

"Just tired. Gotta go. See ya."

She tries to think of the fat cashier's check in her purse. A nice addition to her dance studio fund. But it's not working.

A hot belt of air hits her as she walks out into the back parking lot. She remembers the air conditioner at her apartment has been acting up.

Dammit. Trouble usually comes in threes. Evie's invitation was as welcome as a corpse on a beach. Why can't she leave the past where it belongs? Like they all agreed.

They swore to each other, that once Evie was married, they'd never see each other again.

So what's changed now?

ZOE

Zoe's stuck at a red light, in a long line of cars waiting to enter Lakeshore. It's rush hour, the sky is a sheet of gunmetal and a storm is about to blow in. That means a miserable drive back to Oakville with rain slashing across the steamed-up windshield, and a late start to her weekend. She should have taken the train but then she would have missed the estate sale in Rosedale. She would have missed *this*. Her finger idly traces circles on the pink satin ballet slippers lying next to her on the passenger seat. Child-sized and dainty, they conjure up images of small girls clad in leotards, twirling in endless pirouettes across a stage. She had to buy them. Probably won't ever need them, but then again, who knows?

She blinks and focuses on a mother holding the handle of a stroller at the other side of the crosswalk. Inside sits a tiny wisp of a child. An insubstantial little boy, just inches away from the thundering tires of semi-trucks and cars. So vulnerable. Zoe holds her breath, wondering if the mom is going to forget the kid is at least a foot in front of her, and push him out into oncoming traffic.

Zoe holds her hand over the horn as the mom goes to step off the sidewalk. A half-ton truck runs the final seconds of the amber light and the mom yanks the stroller back onto the curb. Zoe falls back against her headrest, panting. She can't even contemplate what might have been.

The light turns green and she pulls onto the main road, and tries to merge into the procession of cars that swish by on their desperate commute home.

Switching to cruise control, she finally relaxes. As a pediatrician, she's seen her share of good parents. The ones who'd move heaven and earth to do the best for their sick kids. But she's also seen the suspicious bruises on pale, skinny backs, and the unexplained broken bones. The kids whose grimy hair stinks of second-hand smoke, or the ones whose toenails are so long they have trouble walking.

Those cases make her blaze with the injustice of it all. She's been trying to get pregnant for seven years. A year of soul-crushing fertility tests followed by long, excruciating periods of waiting. But it turns out that they both have problems. Marcus, her husband – fifteen years her senior – has lazy sperm or low sperm motility. Probably caused by his penchant for wine, weed and cocaine, which he refuses to give up. And she has some serious cervical scarring. Luckily Marcus was too laid-back and squeamish to question her hurried explanation of endometriosis, so her secret is safe. For now.

The doctor says there's a tiny percentage chance that they can harness those sluggish little swimmers and do something *in vitro*, but it's a long haul and she's already thirty-seven. Besides, Marcus would rather spend a day at the golf course than an hour trying to oblige her with a cup of sperm on demand. Truth is, the childless life is a perfect fit for his brand of self-centeredness, and now she's starting to wonder if she's mother material after all.

She feels the usual catch in her throat when she thinks of

her own motherless childhood. Her mom passed away from an unexpected bout of viral pneumonia when Zoe was just six, leaving her alone with her dad, a bus driver, who usually passed out from exhaustion as soon as he came home, from taking on extra shifts to keep things going.

Still, she hasn't gotten used to the idea that she can't control something that's dominated every aspect of her life for the past seven years. She's been in command of everything else so far. Even hooking up with Marcus whose high six-figure salary and seven-figure profit shares got her through med school when she was struggling to study and pay her fees. Marrying him saved her career. Moved her upwards socially to a life she'd always dreamed of.

The traffic grinds to a sickening halt. A crack of thunder rattles the asphalt, and lightning slashes across the sky. The rain starts to drum onto her hood. There's something else she almost forgot about. It's peeking from the top of her bag. The invitation to Evie's divorce party. Getting it was a real shocker. She hasn't kept in touch with Evie since the impromptu wedding sixteen years ago, when she and Daisy were bridesmaids, forced to wear gaudy yellow chiffon dresses that looked like something from a small-town sixties' prom, while Evie swanned around in her one-of-a-kind designer gown.

With her reckless swagger and her don't-mess-with-me bravado, Evie was the unofficial leader of their foursome, a group of street-smart kids, united by their dream of clawing their way out of their miserable, impoverished lifestyles. Zoe shudders to think of that time in her life. It's over. Done with. They'd all agreed to forget about it. Hadn't they?

And why the hell is Evie getting divorced? She got everything she wanted. A GQ-type husband, holidays in St Kitts, a designer home and top-of-the-line furnishings, the infinity pool overlooking a lake. It's the life they all dreamed of back in college. Seemed so perfect. But is it? Zoe feels a sudden chill. Checks to see if her window is open.

It's closed.

So why is her skin crawling? Maybe Evie finally realized the truth about her husband.

But that's another story. One she thought she'd left behind after the wedding when the four – or was it three – of them vowed never to contact each other again.

But the more she considers it, the more she feels this whole divorce weekend thing feels *off*. She wonders if Evie's invited Savannah, who mysteriously dropped out of the wedding party and disappeared a couple of weeks before the big day.

Traffic starts up again and soon she's clipping along the rain-drenched freeway, spray flying up around her, spattering the windshield. She's actually dreading the idea of seeing her old college friends now that she's reinvented herself as a respected and successful pediatrician.

She was someone else then. Why not let things be? They've all done fine since then, haven't they?

But maybe Evie's experience has been different. Is that any surprise?

Considering who she'd married.

Suddenly Zoe feels nauseous. Especially when she rereads the last line of the text Evie sent earlier.

Time to get The Party Girls back together. Reminisce about old times.

No way does she want to even consider that. But maybe she'll have no choice.

SAVANNAH

Savannah groans on the ninth hamstring stretch. After four hours of sleep, her muscles are screaming. She stayed up until one playing blackjack. Couldn't step away because the cards were going her way all night.

The other dancers are raring to go. Smiling and fresh-faced, they welcome the early morning grind. Not surprising. Their average age is barely twenty-five. Twelve years her junior, and she feels every millisecond of those years in her creaking knees and aching joints. These kids are probably pumped up with scrambled egg whites and vegan protein drinks topped with chia seeds, while she barely had time to grab a double-shot espresso and chocolate glazed donut at the coffee shop on the way in. Now she's having a massive sugar crash.

On the plus side, her face is still youthful. People have always pegged her at ten years younger, but with all the late nights and added stress, it can't last. She dreads the onset of crow's feet or the risk of tearing a ligament or dislocating her hip. That's why she has to stay with the cards when luck is on her side. Grow that retirement fund until she can quit the variety show and pursue her true dream of becoming a choreographer.

Who would have guessed her high school dance classes would actually get her a paying job one day? Certainly not her mom who'd said *all that prancing around* instead of studying was a total waste of educational opportunity. In between her bouts with the bottle, she'd forced Savannah to apply for college and aim for a *real job*.

"Dreams aren't for people like us," she'd said once, on her way out to work a late shift cleaning at the hospital. "I thought your dad would always be there to support me, so I never finished my education. But you'll be different, Sav."

Eventually they'd made a deal. If Savannah maintained an A academic average, she was allowed to stay in dance. And she did it, because dance was already in her blood. The sheer elation of letting go, of moving her body effortlessly through space became her only escape from the hunched precision of the chemistry lab and the endless pages of formulae. She kept up her part of the bargain. Maintained impeccable grades and stayed in dance from tenth grade until graduation.

Her dance teacher, Viv, who'd appeared in a major touring production of *The Phantom*, said Savannah was a natural, with her long legs and flexible body. After grad, they met for coffee and Viv encouraged her to keep up with the dancing. Said she was way too talented to give up, and there were scholarships to be had in New York and LA. Savannah took her advice and ended up at UCSD on a scholarship.

"Are you actually sleeping upright, Savannah?" someone says.

She blinks and looks up, realizing she'd drifted off and hasn't warmed up. The others are assembled at the perimeter of the dance space, ready to run through the Rat Pack routine. Tia, their choreographer, glares at her, hands planted on her slender hips.

Savannah grins sheepishly. "Rough night. I couldn't sleep."

"Take a few minutes to shake out your legs and loosen your joints. The rest of you, ready?" She claps her hands and the young dancers segue smoothly into the sixties' showgirl number. The guys follow behind, holding imaginary top hats and canes.

Savannah stretches her arms behind her back then extends them. She'll have to find a way to clear her mind during practice. She isn't ready to lose this gig. It's steady and pays the bills. It's also had a long run, billed as a *wholesome family show* with plenty of glitz and old-style Vegas glamor, not to mention the theater is situated in the heart of the Planet Hollywood Miracle Mile Mall, at the center of the Strip.

In her time on the show, she's seen so many girls come and go, and not always willingly. They'd either slacked off with their fitness routines, or fallen into a hard-partying lifestyle, then gained a flabby midriff or sprained an ankle and drifted off to a burlesque show or one of the many strip clubs dotted around the seedier parts of town.

She won't let that happen to her. The sparkle of the spotlight, the snappy routines, the smell of the greasepaint and glittering costumes still make her heart beat double time. She's even started to think about choreographing her own show. Maybe starring in it. Of course, only in small theaters at first. Quirky indie places. Maybe even Off-Broadway. She's not too old. Martha Graham was still dancing in her sixties. So, she still has some good years ahead, and she's been taking a quality modern dance class twice a week, studying the intricacies of the Graham technique. All preparation for the next move, which will be inevitable now that Evie's tracked her down. She'll find somewhere wholesome and family-oriented to hide.

"I'm ready," she calls, and Tia gives her a nod, allowing her to merge in with the moving chorus line.

After rehearsal she decides to splurge on a massage and facial at the hotel spa. While she's stretched out on the soft leather bench, waiting for the masseuse, a text comes in from Evie.

> I bought a penis piñata. Looks kind of like this. LOL.

Savannah stares down at the large pink paper mâché penis, complete with swollen blue paper testicles. A cheeky face with cartoonish eyes and a lolling tongue, grins from the protruding tip.

> Friday night freakout. Are you up for it?

She doesn't answer and is about to lose the phone when prickles of dread creep across her skin. The latest text glares at her.

> ??? I'm counting on you, and you know why.

The masseuse clears her throat. "You know, if you want to get the most benefit from the session, you should be free from distractions."

Savannah gulps and punches in a message.

> I'll be there.

Evie replies with a thumbs-up.

> I knew you'd come through.

Savannah clicks off the phone and buries her face in her arm – tries to clear her head. Stifle the cold stab of fear, and give herself over to the masseuse's punishing hands, but thoughts of her first meeting with Evie, sixteen years ago, keep coming to mind, like a bad dream.

Savannah was shoplifting in Walmart.

Oblivious to the dark-haired girl beside her, she'd just added a six-dollar bottle of eyeliner to the lipstick, mascara, and nail polish already stuffed into her coat pockets.

As Savannah tried to slip past the cashier, the dark-haired girl moved close to her, ripped some of the stolen goods from her pockets, and shoved them into hers just as a six-foot-seven security guard blocked her path. Next minute the guy clamped a hand down on the dark-haired girl's shoulder and demanded she follow him to the store manager's office. Baffled, Savannah followed along.

In the musty security office, Savannah gaped in awe as the girl who said her name was Evie, broke down in tears and confessed to the manager that her mom was dying of cancer and all she'd intended was to get her a last gift. Somehow, she persuaded him to allow her home with a caution. But the cops had already been called and, in their words, why waste a perfectly good ride? Besides, Evie said one of the officers reminded her of Zac Efron, so they huddled in the back seat and spent the entire ride back to UCSD staring at his blue eyes reflected in the rearview mirror. Savannah felt like crap when he suggested he'd send an envelope around at work to collect money for Evie's mom's treatment. He backed off only when Evie convinced him her dad wouldn't dream of accepting charity.

The cops dropped them off far enough from the school grounds not to make a spectacle. Facing Evie, Savannah struggled to find the right words.

"Why did you do that? I – I mean I was the shoplifter and you took the blame. You must be crazy."

Evie placed a hand on Savannah's shoulder. "I've been where you are, babe. I know how tough things can get. You needed a break, and besides I love helping people out. It's in my blood. I'm a kind person at heart."

They turned to walk towards the school. "So what are you taking?" asked Savannah.

Evie shrugged. "A little bit of this and a little bit of that. I like to keep my options open, you know. Liberal arts with a little bit of kinesiology sprinkled in. You?"

"Chemistry. I'm going to be a research scientist."

Evie whistled through her teeth. "Wow, I'm impressed. Hey, want to come to a party tonight?"

Savannah shrugged. "I have a pretty packed class schedule and studying takes up a whole whack of time."

"Don't worry. Everyone's gotta have some fun, and I kind of need a buddy to come to this party. You'd be doing me a big favor."

Savannah felt a small quiver of concern. She couldn't allow anyone or anything to interfere with her plans to graduate and get a dream job in a big research lab. Nothing could stand in her way, and yet, looking into Evie's steely brown eyes, she found it impossible to refuse this person who'd just saved her from criminal charges.

"Sure," she heard herself saying. "Gotta take a break from the serious stuff some time."

"Yay," said Evie, linking her arm into Savannah's. "Let's go and have a couple of drinks to get warmed up."

DAISY

Daisy tosses the empty wine bottle into the recycling bin and gets ready to crack the second. She pops the cork, pours out a big one, and cranks up Joe Bonamassa on the sound system.

She sits down and checks her voicemail. Maybe Wade's actually made an effort to contact her. No text messages so far, but then she suspects his phone's been cut off until he can find the funds to buy a pay-as-you-go plan. Right now, he's probably couch-surfing with his bandmates as they plan the *big tour* they've always dreamed about in Ray's funky-smelling, beat-up Dodge Caravan.

Scrolling through the messages, she mutes the music and listens. It's not Wade talking. Just a bunch of static and some phrases from an irate voice. Probably someone from the school board office – *"a serious breach of contract"* – *"gross negligence"* – *"professional counseling is called for…"* A forceful push on the number seven button deletes them. *Screw the school board.* They were paying her a pittance anyway. A final voice message is a bit more troubling. From some old *associates* of Wade that she'd rather forget about.

"Where is Wade? He didn't show yesterday. Now he's really screwed things up."

Her heart skips a beat and she sweeps that one into the trash where it belongs, then drinks until the tips of her fingers feel like firecrackers and her brain starts to whirl at warp speed along with the music, but when a slow, mournful song comes on, she slips into more maudlin thoughts.

Tears stream down her cheeks as she considers the sad state of her life. Her future stretches out ahead of her – an arid expanse of nothingness.

She squeezes her eyelids shut. Clenches her fists. This has to stop. She's got to view this opportunity from a different perspective. Concentrate on herself for a change, because now that Wade is gone, she can do whatever she wants. Now's her time. And that last text message is a sign that she needs to get out of town quickly. Maybe reinvent herself, and this Vegas party will be a good place to start.

Evie sent them all a penis piñata picture yesterday. Trust her to come up with something so raunchy. Who could forget her legendary party games in first year, like *Suck and Blow* and *Five Minutes in Heaven?* And everyone was shit scared if they were up against her in Truth or Dare. That thought causes a sinking feeling in Daisy's gut, because sometimes Evie's dares went way too far.

But they'd decided to bury all that stuff long ago. She hopes that's still the agreement, unless Evie has other plans.

A *ping* signals yet another message from Evie who's sent an update on the piñata event. The weekend's going to be a hoot. And she, Daisy, will be the first to bash that mega-sized piñata with the biggest club she can find. It'll be cathartic, destroying that object of male preoccupation. Wade was obsessed with the size of his dick. He was so insecure he stuck balled-up Kleenexes into his jeans at his rare out-of-town gigs.

She drains the glass of wine and feels a new surge of energy. She'll start by purging all the junk in the house. She moves into the living room and sweeps every cheap statuette, half-used candle and dollar-store knick-knack into a box along with Wade's shot glass collection, defunct CDs, and heavy metal posters.

Moving into the bedroom, she throws open the closet. Finally registers the bare wire hangers clinking against each other.

He's gone, for sure.

At one time she'd have broken down in tears at losing him, but life has hardened her and now she simply sweeps the hangers out of the way, giving her own clothes double the amount of space. But they're a sad and shabby collection. She'll have a garage sale at the weekend. Sell all her *teachery* pants, polyester blazers and sensible shirts. Afterwards she'll cultivate a whole new edgier look once she gets some money together. Get her black hair cut into a modern style, buy new makeup to enhance her sea-blue eyes. Everyone always said they're her best feature. Might as well make the most of herself before it's too late, and a makeover might just be her ticket to a whole new life. She's a pro at that. Did it once before. Right after college. She pulls out a UCSD sweatshirt. The only memento of her school days. She sniffs the worn fabric, detects the faint, musky scent of weed and patchouli caught in the fibers. It reminds her of Evie's dorm room and the first time they met sixteen years ago.

Daisy was in the dark dorm hallway passing a bag of weed to one of the sorority girls from Delta Gamma. The girl, a dead ringer for Haylie Duff, wore massive Oakley sunglasses and a black hoodie.

She shoved a wad of bills into Daisy's hand, stuffed the baggie into the pocket of her pink Lululemon leggings and took off without a word. Daisy was about to count the bills when someone tapped her on the shoulder.

"Hands up, kid. We got you."

Daisy's heart slammed into her throat as she raised her arms slowly, aware of the telltale bills grasped in her right hand.

"Now turn around and keep your hands up where I can see them."

The glow of light from an open doorway revealed a small heart-shaped face with black spiky hair about a quarter of an inch on top. The young woman was medium height, and slim, with the kind of face Daisy would call arresting – strong nose, defined cheekbones, bold brows and shiny, deep-brown eyes. She wore body-hugging tights and a pink sleeveless top. She was Daisy's height and didn't look like a narc, but then Daisy had never actually seen one – even at high school. She held Daisy's gaze with steely intensity, then doubled over in a fit of laughter.

"What the...?" said Daisy.

The girl straightened up. Her face was flushed. "Gotcha, didn't I? You were actually pissing yourself."

"Bitch," said Daisy, steaming mad. She turned to go. The girl grabbed her shoulder.

"Hey, I'm doing you a favor. Don't you know how risky it is to do deals here in the open?"

Daisy shrugged. The girl was probably right, but Daisy's judgment was flawed when it came to money matters. Risk was no obstacle to her when big money was a real prospect.

"C'mon in and meet my buddy, Savannah. By the way, I'm Evie."

They entered Evie's tiny room. Daisy leaned against the doorpost while Evie went to her desk and unearthed a book of *matches, lit an incense stick, then clicked on a lamp covered by a paper globe.*

Beyond her a tall, leggy, blonde sat on the window seat, sipping from her water bottle and occasionally directing her attention to an open textbook beside her.

Daisy always studied the way people looked, and measured it against her own attractiveness. Ever since a guy at junior high told her she had the face of an angel, she'd become caught up with the idea of physical beauty.

"So this is Savannah, or Sav as I call her."

The girl gave a brief, regal nod, then turned back to her textbook. Seemed like a real ice queen.

Daisy stepped towards Evie. "And I'm Daisy – Daisy Carmichael."

Evie shot a hand out. "Pleasure to meet you, Daisy. You're super pretty, but I guess you've been told that a whole lot."

Daisy blushed. Too right she had. A modeling agent had taken one look at her blue eyes, creamy skin, upturned nose and wavy black hair and told her she was breathtaking – Liz Taylor meets Snow White – with one damning caveat. 'You're too short for the runway. Maybe try the Sears catalogue.' Daisy hadn't bothered to follow that particular lead, instead choosing to dabble in a little dealing to supplement her living expenses.

"Never thought about it, really," she said, blushing. The quarterback on the high school football team had always said she blushed pretty, as if she had roses on her cheeks. He'd promised to take her on a fancy dinner date, but too bad he'd drunk a bottle of rye after winning the college championship and got the head cheerleader pregnant, then had to marry her. Lost his scholarship to Michigan State and went to sell used cars instead. It was probably better that way. Sooner or later, Daisy would have discovered some major flaw in his character, and then it would've been too late.

She'd seen it before. Her own mother always hooked up with losers, Daisy's dad being the original narcissistic egotist who gambled away his money on the horses, then took off when he couldn't pay the loan shark who'd subsidized his days spent at the track. Daisy was determined she wouldn't let her grim childhood define her, wouldn't fall into that same self-defeating trap.

"You tuning me out or something?" said Evie.

Daisy shook her head. "Sorry. You just reminded me of someone I once knew."

"You have an old-fashioned name. Does that mean you're an old-fashioned girl?"

Daisy's brows knit. What was her deal? "N-not really. Why?"

Evie inclined her head towards Savannah. "Me and Sav are going for drinks tonight at the golf club. You interested in coming?"

"Yeah – I mean – sure," said Daisy, thinking a golf club sounded like somewhere old guys and losers hung out. "But that's not really my type of place."

"Think you're not good enough?"

Daisy nodded. "Kind of."

"With that face you're good enough to go anywhere. So listen to Sav and me and come along."

"I don't have anything fancy to wear."

"You can borrow something," said Savannah, suddenly perking up. "I just went shopping."

"Yeah, she's a real pro shopper. Gets some crazy deals," said Evie, grinning. "Hey, you got any more of that stuff in your pockets?"

"What stuff? Oh – you mean...?"

"Yeah. The home-grown."

Daisy took out the remaining bag. "Help yourself."

Evie clapped her on the shoulder. "Hey, Sav. I like this one. I think she'll get along with us just fine."

ZOE

Zoe walks into the living room to find Marcus stretched out, comatose on the sofa, watching *Rear Window* through half-closed eyes. He has a thing about Grace Kelly. Loves that blonde, ice-maiden look. When they first started dating, Zoe bleached her tawny hair just to please him. She feels the slow burn of resentment. No doubt she's totally fried her hair. As an intelligent, professional woman, she can't believe she's kept up this ridiculous charade. It has to be insecurity on her part. Despite all her education and experience, that little flame of self-doubt burns deep in her soul, reminding her of where she came from and who she used to be.

He fumbles with the water pipe on the side table. "Hey, beautiful, want a hit?"

"You know I can't. I have patients who rely on me. They trust that I'll be clear-headed when they come to my office, and I could get called in for an emergency at any time. Then what?"

"Just say no, hun. You don't have to give me a lecture. It's just, I need to unwind. Crazy day and all that. And it is legal here, you know. Just like having a glass of wine."

"Can't you listen to classical music? Read a good book? Work out?"

He struggles to open his eyes. "That all sounds intriguing, but way too much effort and brain power required."

Her stomach growls. "And supper?"

Now his eyes snap open. "I've been in back-to-back bloody meetings since eight this morning. Talked the ass off a never-ending stream of faceless money managers and techies. How about you pick up the phone and order something? I could murder some sushi, and don't forget the yam tempura."

Zoe bristles as she heads upstairs to shower, punching in a quick order from Sushi Hon around the corner. He knows nothing about her day, and the packed schedule of patients, the heart-rending stories, the stress of juggling with difficult parents and life-or-death scenarios.

At least her bathroom is a sanctuary. Breathtaking with its bold, tiger-striped marble floor and walls. A freestanding tub sits in the center of the room beside a massive walk-in shower. Floor-to-ceiling windows look out onto a manicured garden complete with hot tub, extended deck and in-ground pool.

She turns on the hot water just as another text comes in from Evie. Earlier today, Evie's penis piñata text had arrived when Martha, the consultancy receptionist, had been standing over Zoe's shoulder as she signed some forms.

"Girls' night out?" Martha quizzed, her eyebrows rising to her hairline.

"Just an old college friend with a warped sense of humor," said Zoe, realizing details about the text would be all over the office within an hour, and *rabid party girl* is not exactly the professional, family-friendly image she wants to cultivate. She's worked hard to gain the respect of her colleagues and employees.

She glances at the latest text:

> It's going to be fun, fun, fun. We're booked into the Aria. Spend our daytime at the pool.
> Tickets for Chippendales at The Rio. Saturday.
> Check this out. So hot.

Zoe clicks the link and is immediately confronted by a row of rock-hard, gyrating abs. These guys have energy by the bucketful, unlike her sluggish husband who can't even move his little finger to tap out a food order.

She reads the promo material.

```
A mantastic, sex gods, abs party that
will make you lose your mind, welcoming
groups of all sizes and all ages for a
fierce and fabulous night of fun.
```

She strips off her clothes. Her hips are still slim and she has a taut midriff. Not bad for a thirty-seven-year-old. The jogging and stationary cycling have paid off. Maybe she could get into watching a bunch of hot, ripped guys strut their stuff onstage. But she stops herself. This is typical Evie with her seductive powers of persuasion, sucking her back into a lifestyle she discarded long ago. She isn't that girl anymore. The lean, hungry twenty-year-old wearing frayed jeans, cheap shoes and thick eyeliner. Lifting condoms and discount perfume from the drugstore. Now she has impeccable taste, high standards, and a moral compass that would have spun in circles at the things she did back in college. It had all seemed necessary at the time, but why can't she just leave it behind? Another text arrives.

> I know you'll come because we really need to talk. Something came up and I think you should know about it.

Zoe's mouth feels dry. She swallows. Punches in a response.

> What do u mean? Tell me.

She waits, her breathing coming in shallow bursts.

> Can't talk about it on the phone. See you in Vegas.

Damn her. She should have steered clear of Evie when she first came across her sixteen years ago. Life would have been way simpler.

She'd been working the bar at a high-end golf club to make ends meet. At the time, she was driven by a burning ambition to become a doctor at any cost. Nothing could stand in her way. Living in La Jolla had already given her a glimpse of the life she craved. A fun, beachy, high-class town, its many golf clubs were brimming with rich, eligible guys who could show her a good time and buy her a decent meal when she wasn't studying.

When Evie swanned into the Torrey Pines lounge, Zoe's first impression was of a compact, muscular girl with a pixie cut, wearing a sleek, black Lululemon tracksuit. Her two friends, a hot brunette in a tiny crop top and ice-blue jeans and a tall, leggy blonde in white halter top and shorts, made straight for the table beside the one with the three hot guys. Regulars from one of the biggest frat houses. The girls in her dorm had dubbed them The Golden Guys. Wealthy, popular and handsome, they acted like they owned the place.

The leggy girl wore white shorts and kept crossing and uncrossing her tanned legs so one of the guys couldn't help but get an eyeful of her toned muscles. A California-type blonde with sun-streaked hair, pale eyes and a knockout figure, she seemed more aloof than the dark-haired girl, whose knee was tapping the underside of the table as she gawked at The Golden Guys with the enthusiasm of a kid vying for attention.

Zoe was passing a card containing her phone number to an older guy who was a regular at the club. He'd taken her out for a few meals and bought her some nice clothes in exchange for a couple of overnight stays at a fancy resort hotel nearby. Zoe classified the arrangement as a friendship with benefits because nothing sexual happened. She'd accompany him to dinner and listen to him talk about everything from tedious business meetings to minor spats with his frigid wife to the miseries of growing old.

"Doing a little extra-curricular work on the side?" said a husky voice. Zoe looked up to see Evie's glinting eyes fixed on her.

"None of your business," said Zoe.

"You come from money or are you dirt-poor like I was?"

"Also none of your business."

"No need to be bitchy. I was just trying to make polite conversation." Evie slipped her a hundred-dollar bill. "Three Buds and keep the change."

Zoe shrugged. Her face flushed. "Are you sure?"

Evie nodded. "Certain. Now where were we? Oh – you were about to tell me about your crappy childhood."

Embarrassed, Zoe sighed. "Okay. Mom died of pneumonia when I was a kid. My dad was a bus driver. He did his best, but he was out a whole lot. So I was left alone for hours on end and basically had to fend for myself."

Evie smiled. "That's a real sad story. Hey – I get it. I'm from Fairfield, Alabama. My mom was a wrestler in the old WWF. She'd never tell me who my dad was, but I'm pretty sure it was her creep of a manager. Anyway, she was big news in the eighties. Then she had to quit when she had me. By 2000 she was a chain-smoking, has-been with a messed-up face. Now she works at a local gym and fights a few small-time matches, does a little mud-wrestling, just to make some cash on the side. Let's say, I was alone a whole lot too when I was a kid. Not much supervision. Hardly any friends to speak of. Guess they found me too edgy and all that. Gave me the cold shoulder at school. But I survived and showed them all when I got a wrestling scholarship."

Zoe's heart fell. She'd come all this way to La Jolla to escape types like Evie. Hungry, snarling types you couldn't turn your back on. But wrestling. There was something awesome about the sound of it.

"I'm gonna be a doctor," said Zoe.

Evie whistled. "A brainiac. But that costs big bucks. You got scholarships?"

Zoe nodded. "And this job helps."

"What about your little sideline?"

"Don't know what you're talking about."

Evie sighed. "Hey, what if you could make the same extra money without having to let old guys grope you?"

Zoe's stomach fluttered. "What exactly would I be doing?"

Evie grinned. "Knew you'd be interested. Come and meet my friends when your shift is over."

At the time Zoe prided herself on having street-smarts, but she was a neophyte compared to Evie. Because when Evie did you a favor, you were hers for life. She owned you; you owed her and she never let you forget it.

So what exactly did Evie want after all this time? Or did she have some warped idea that now she was single, they could be friends? Out of the question. It would never happen. And what about the pact they'd made about never seeing each other again?

Unless something had changed. They'd tied up all the loose ends, hadn't they?

She turns on the shower and stands under the warm water. It's pointless trying to say no to Evie. She'll have to go to Vegas, but nobody at the medical consultancy can ever find out about her weekend, because she'll make sure there are no selfies or candid shots or any picture of her anywhere in that damned place.

She sends a text back to Evie.

> Looks hot. I'm up for it. Let me know how much I owe you.

Evie replies with a thumbs up and a *will do*.

Zoe slips underwater, luxuriating in the warm bubbles.

She'll go, but this will be their final meeting. She'll make that crystal clear from the start.

The thought of it makes her body tremble.

What happens in Vegas, stays in Vegas.

And Marcus will never, ever need to know anything about it.

SAVANNAH

Savannah looks out of her apartment window at the rising sun as it bleeds into the morning sky, silhouetting the palm trees and high-rises against the jagged peaks of Frenchman Mountain. It's her favorite time of day. Coffee's brewing and her umbrella plant has grown up to the ceiling. It's the first time she's felt tied to a place in seventeen years.

She's just read Evie's text about her wild plans for the Saturday night Chippendales show. *Why on earth would Evie do something so crass as buying tickets for the Chippendales?* If anyone from the dance community sees her watching those muscle-bound hacks, she'll never live it down.

A more worrisome thought, however, is that Evie and the others don't know she lives in Vegas, let alone dances here.

Her Facebook and Instagram profiles are still centered around the last place she lived and worked as a toxicologist. She occasionally adds innocuous posts like *how to crimp the perfect pie crust* or *six great hacks for keeping vegetables fresh* or *how to get sweat stains out of T-shirts*. She doesn't want them to know about her showbiz career. Anonymity suits her, and she'd prefer it to stay that way. But how is she going to get out of doing her show this weekend so she can go to Evie's party?

She'll tell Tia she's sick and try to get someone to cover for her. The producers keep substitute dancers in the wings in case of emergency. She'll have to pay them out of her own pocket. But it's worth it not to worry about blowing her cover.

And yet, no one else knows her like those old college friends. They've heard every detail of her messed-up childhood and her lonely teen years. They understand the anxious, insecure person at the core of her being. But they don't know *everything*.

At least she hopes they don't.

Settling down on the window seat, she remembers how the four of them had shared the details of their pathetic backgrounds as if they were competing for the world's worst childhood.

Daisy went first. "Too bad my mom was a party animal, always hooking up with losers. Once when I was in tenth grade, she left a voice message telling me she'd taken off to Cancun for two weeks with her boyfriend of the moment and wouldn't be around. It was the week of my sixteenth birthday."

Evie wrapped her arms around Daisy, whose eyes had filled with tears. "How could she leave her little Daisy on her special day?"

"Cut it out," said Daisy, shoving her away. "I made my own cake from a dollar-store mix and blew out the candles alone."

"Oh my God. That is so heartbreaking," said Zoe. "I wonder if Savannah can top that one."

Savannah swallowed. She wasn't ready for painful personal revelations so soon. "I was also raised by a single mom."

"That it?" Evie said, perching on the edge of Savannah's bed. "We need details. We're gonna be spending a whole lot of time together. Gotta trust each other."

Savannah chewed the inside of her lip and sighed. "Okay. Here goes. Dad was a cop, mom a homemaker. When I was ten, some cranked-out junkie stabbed him outside our house for the few dollars in his pocket. I saw it all. He died, and Mom and I moved from suburbia to the grunge side of Evanston. Mom took up drinking and I basically had to fend for myself. I clawed my way through high school and now I'm here."

Evie's mouth compressed into a thin line. "Holy shit – that's crazy – I mean seeing your dad cut down in cold blood and all that, but hey – looks like fate brought us all together so we could finally get what's due to us."

Savannah moaned. This chick had such a giant chip on her shoulder. But she'd saved her ass at Walmart. Her heart seemed to be in the right place.

Daisy chirped up again. "Let's cut the sob stuff. Why choose UCSD?"

Evie perked up. "Now you're talking. It's California. La Jolla. There's so much money here and I mean to get my hands on some of it. What about you, Sav?"

"I always loved the ocean."

Evie grinned. "You interested in surfing?"

"Nah, I just love walking along the beach."

"Sounds like some lame Hallmark moment. I have something way more electrifying in mind for all of us. You know this place is running with rich guys? Trust-fund types with plenty of cashola."

"I – I kind of wanted to get ahead on my own. Don't need a guy to distract me," said Zoe.

"Chill – no pressure. There are ways to get good grades and

party too. I've specialized in that all my life, so don't worry. I'll take you all under my wing. You'll never look back."

Savannah was forced to avert her gaze, Evie's brown eyes glared intently at her through the thick lenses of her glasses that she only wore in private.

"So first thing I gotta do is get rid of these dumb glasses. Get contact lenses. Then I'll tell you about my brilliant idea to make money real quick."

Savannah sighed. That was exactly what she'd been afraid of.

She goes to pour herself another cup of coffee, still trying to figure out why Evie asked her to be in her wedding party. Especially after what happened at grad.

But she can't think of that right now. She has to find a way to stop them from probing any further into a secret that can never be uncovered. *But surely all of them have something to hide.* You don't emerge from the few years they spent together without a few skeletons in the closet.

Pulling on her rehearsal gear, she stops dead at the sound of a sharp knock on the door. She freezes. She isn't expecting anyone. The knock gets louder. She heads into the hallway and peers through the peephole. It's a delivery guy in a FedEx cap.

"Show your ID," she says.

He holds up a name tag, and she opens the door.

"Delivery for Miss Savannah O'Brien."

"I wasn't expecting anything."

He holds out a solid, square package. "Sign here."

She scrawls a signature on a form, and he scurries away. Closing the door, she studies the box for a sender's address. There's nothing. A sick feeling starts up in her gut as she rips the tape away to reveal a white box filled with red tissue paper.

Inside is a black lacy corset, and a small leather-handled whip and a slim length of rope. A note is nestled underneath.

> *Hey gorgeous. Long time, no see. Get ready for me. I'm coming to the party too.*

She drops the box as if it's burnt her hands. She's had notes like this before, but not for a long time. She moved apartments. So how did they find her new address?

Is this related to the divorce party? Or is it Evie's idea of a sick joke?

She'll have to act quickly. Get out. Get help. Go to the cops? No, she can't do that. Can't risk it.

Maybe Leon can help her. He's offered plenty of times.

She'll have to talk to him tonight. As soon as the show's over.

She runs into her bedroom and immediately starts packing a case. Tonight, she'll stay at the hotel. The next day, who knows?

DAISY

Daisy already has a prospective buyer for Wade's rare album collection. The sum he's offered will be enough for the flight and probably the hotel reservation. Also, she's hoping Clark County School District might be recruiting new teachers for the Vegas area, because she's decided to stay on there for a while, even if it means subbing.

If Wade can just up and leave, then she can too. After all, he made the first move, so what's she waiting for? And she doesn't even have to look for teaching jobs. She could do anything. Work in a casino. Do something in PR. Anything to keep a roof over her head and food in the fridge.

She sets to work lining up all the clothes and knick-knacks she cleaned out last night. She's even pulled some of the smaller pieces of furniture into the shed and set up a sign saying: *Moving sale. Larger pieces available for viewing inside the house.*

She's going to clean this sucker out. And she hopes one of the first things to go will be Wade's damn recliner. Covered in hairs from his rapidly balding head, it's an awful tweedy thing with a kickout footrest, an attached wooden swingout table stained with rings from the thousands of beer bottles Wade sucked dry, and a deep dent in the cushion left by his big, lazy ass. Christ, she'll give that thing away to the first person willing to haul it out of there. If not, she'll do a ritual burning right here in the carport area.

She'll give him a final chance before everything goes, so she shoots him a text.

> Don't know where you are, but I've had enough. I'm selling everything. House too, and taking off. Hope you find what you're looking for.

She presses send and waits a few minutes. Nothing. So she sets to unloading more junk onto the picnic table, just as the sun breaks through the cloud cover. In minutes, cars start to pull up. A couple with a stream of kids exits a beat-up Dodge Caravan, and an elderly woman climbs out of a white Buick. Her heart pounds with anticipation.

Three hours later, the picnic bench has only a third of the items left. Business has been brisk and she's made one hundred and sixty-five dollars. Not exactly a fortune, but not bad for a bunch of garbage. Even the cursed recliner went for ten bucks to a guy who's furnishing his man cave. A fitting home for that chair. She felt such an incredible surge of relief when the guy finally loaded it onto his half-ton truck, she almost forgot to take the money. Still, she hasn't made enough for Vegas hotel bills. She needs a big sale. Like the record collection or the guitar. The guy called and said he was on the way to check out the albums sometime in the afternoon and he still hasn't shown. She chews on her carrot sticks and waits.

Soon enough, after a rush of customers who buy most of her books for a dime apiece, a glossy white pickup pulls up. The guy is a hipster type with full beard and shaved, manicured hair. Dressed head to toe in black, he sidles up the driveway, smiling.

"I'm here for the record collection. Mind if I check it out?"

She tries not to appear too eager. This guy looks like he has money. Lots of it, judging by his Blundstone boots and the heavy gold rings on three of his fingers. "Sure. It's inside. I'll get it."

A black car pulls up. An older man and a younger one step out.

"Or maybe you could just go inside and look. The box is on the kitchen table."

"You don't mind?"

"Be my guest."

He crosses through the shed, up the wooden steps and into her kitchen. The door slams as the two men stand by Wade's Fender guitar.

"How much you want for this?" the older one asks.

"My husband paid eight hundred and fifty for it just three years ago."

The younger guy smirks. "Must be a sucker. Someone scammed him. You can buy a made-in-Mexico Fender Stratocaster for five hundred bucks."

"That figures." Wade was useless when it came to money matters. He'd grown up with wealthy parents, got everything he wanted, but had no clue about budgeting.

"Give you a hundred," says the old guy.

"Three hundred."

"Two fifty."

"Two seventy-five."

"Deal," he says, and she watches him peel off bills from a thick wad.

"Pleasure," says the old guy as he takes the guitar and heads off towards the black car. The young man hovers.

"Just want to check out this amp." He squats down and starts turning knobs, just as the hipster pokes his head out of the door.

"I have a couple of questions for you."

"I'll be back," she says to the kid as she climbs the wooden stairs.

The hipster is sorting through the albums, checking every label. "You've got some great Stones albums here, but does your husband happen to own the red vinyl Carnaby Street Limited Edition of Goat's Head Soup?"

Daisy shakes her head. "I'm more of an R&B person, so I wouldn't know. If it isn't there, I guess he doesn't."

He flashes a brief smile. "I'll keep looking, if you don't mind."

She feels the comforting roll of bills in her pocket. A good haul, but it's still not enough to pay for the weekend. "Sure. No problem."

The garage is empty when she gets outside and the black car is gone. *At least they took the guitar,* she thinks, glancing over at the empty spot. *Guess the kid didn't want the amp.*

But the space below the table where the amp had sat, was also empty. The kid took it. Stole it, actually. How could she be so stupid to leave him here alone with it? Tears burn the back of her eyes. When will she ever get a lucky break?

The door opens behind her and the hipster guy walks out, empty-handed. Her heart drops. "You don't want them?"

He smiles a tight-lipped smile. "Sorry. I have most of those vinyls. Maybe someone else might be interested."

She kicks the table legs. "Maybe."

He thrusts his hands into the pockets of his jeans. "Have a good day."

She nods and watches as he swings up into the truck and accelerates away in a cloud of dried-up mud. A fine drizzle has started up again and it's turned chilly. She'll need a jacket. She heads inside and grabs the rain jacket hanging on the banister. Deciding to get a new cup of coffee, she heads into the kitchen and stops dead at the sight of the empty kitchen table. The box of albums is gone. *How the hell did he take them?*

Her eyes are drawn to the front door. She's sure it was locked, but it swings ajar, letting in a swarm of flies. Then it all becomes clear. They set her up. The hipster and the guys in the black car who swung round to the front of the house waiting for the hipster guy to carry out the albums while she was busy in the garage.

She flops onto the kitchen chair and cradles her head in her hands.

Stupid. Stupid. Stupid. I'm such a pushover. A doormat.

How can she get to Vegas now? She'll have to sleep on the street or worse still, beg her friends to lend her money.

ZOE

Dark storm clouds are rolling in across a clay-colored sky by the time Zoe jogs up her tree-lined driveway.

She keys the code into the garage pin pad and lets herself inside. Marcus was still sleeping when she left, but she sees a light on in the kitchen. It's not like him to be up so early on a Sunday. He usually stays in bed and watches Netflix on his laptop for at least an hour or two, but it's only eight thirty and he's already sitting up at the breakfast counter, resting his forehead on his hand and scanning some documents. Something about his demeanor tells her another storm might be brewing.

She's disoriented as she rounds the doorway and enters the kitchen, wiping the sweat from her forehead with a towel. He looks up, his eyes puffy and moist. He's been crying. This is bad. She's only seen Marcus cry once when he loaned his vintage Corvette to a buddy who got wasted on Iron Curtains – vodka and Jägermeister – and threw up all over the seats. The stink lasted for weeks and they were still digging out half-digested bits of chunky salsa from the crevices, even after the deep clean. He ended up selling it at a loss.

Did someone die? Did he lose at poker? She feels weak and shaky.

"What's happened?" Her nerves are quivering. That's all she needs. An unexpected crisis to throw a wrench into her plans for the coming weekend. A sudden pang of guilt reminds her she's being self-centered, so she places a comforting hand on his shoulder. "Are you okay?"

To her horror, he buries his face in both hands and starts snorting in a moist, snotty way. She's never seen Marcus lose control, and she recovers her poise in time to grab a wad of Kleenex and hand them to him.

He blows his nose and wipes it with a flourish. Is he going to hand her the wet tissue? She recoils.

"I've been lying to you. I'm so, so sorry." He looks up at her with reddened eyes, and for a moment her heart leaps. Maybe he's been unfaithful? Does that mean she can finally get out of this train-wreck of a marriage, with a clear conscience and firm footing on the moral high ground – a great position to engineer the most favorable divorce settlement?

"Lying? About what?"

He shoves the papers towards her as if expecting her to immediately understand what's got him so flustered. The top sheet looks like a financial report. She picks it up and scans the tables of numbers that mean little to her, except the one, very large, very bold, red figure at the bottom of the page that has an ominous-looking minus sign in front of it.

"What is this? One of your funds?"

He starts up with a weird groaning sound, as if he has gut ache, and she's sure she can hear his teeth grinding. "It's a new one. A new cryptocurrency."

"For Christ's sake, spit it out. Are you bankrupt or something?"

There's a long, pregnant silence. Long enough for her stomach to somersault one way and back the other.

"Jed was so stoked about it. Said it would be the same story as Bitcoin. Remember back in 2011 when it was a buck a share and he told me to buy, but I blew him off, and now he's loaded. This time I trusted him, and he got me to sink a whole bunch of money into this piece-of-shit currency. It tanked a week ago."

"Why didn't you tell me?"

Marcus's nose is as red as his eyes. "I couldn't find a way. That's why I've been high every night since I found out. I tried to numb the pain, but I can't hide it anymore. I think I'm gonna have a heart attack or something."

Zoe grinds her teeth and turns away. She can't bear to look at him. "How bad? How much did you lose?" There's another long silence. Too long for her liking. "I said how much, Marcus? Tell me. Rip off the Band-Aid. I prefer it that way."

At first, his mumbling is inaudible, but she catches the phrase, *about seventy-five percent of everything.*

"And the house?"

"We can remortgage it."

She's doing quick calculations in her head. Figuring out how much of her money is tied up with his, trying to remember if her name is on the house, or if everything's in his business name. Wondering if she's going to have to do some quick transfers to hide her assets. Save herself and preserve the lifestyle she's accustomed to. Then she feels his hand clamp down on her arm like a claw.

"I know I'm a worthless loser husband. With the baby thing and now this. But do you still love me, honey?" His mournful, swollen eyes fix on her with a weak, pleading expression she detests. She could knock him right off his stool and smash the cursed water pipe he's always sucking on, into a million tiny pieces. He's a spoilt entitled weakling. He's never known what it's like to be really penniless. Totally destitute. Down to your last dollar so you can't eat. Zoe clearly remembers a terrible period in her life just after Evie's wedding, when she started med school. Often her nightly supper menu was a choice between two flavors of instant noodles.

"Now's not the time to ask me that. I need space. Time to think." She wrenches her arm away. To her horror, he claps a hand over his mouth and starts blubbering again.

"Don't give up on me, Zoe. Please don't leave me. I'm nothing without you."

"You should have thought about that before you sunk our money into some two-bit scam. Jed has money to burn. He doesn't give a damn if he loses a few million here and there."

Her words unleash a fresh torrent of moaning. Zoe's not sure how much more she can stand. He's always been such a prick about his business dealings. Never listening to her advice. Always acting like a hotshot when he boasts about how *men have God-given instincts with money, while women just don't have the balls for business.*

She takes a deep breath, throws her shoulders back, and uses the firm, assertive voice she reserves for the parents of her more challenging patients. "I'm going away next weekend to meet some old girlfriends, and to consider my options. I'd appreciate a full picture of the damage and how it will affect us and, in particular, me, by the end of the week."

He sits up, suddenly alert for the first time in ages. "You're going to leave me. I knew it."

He's not responding the way she hoped. There's no hint of an apology. She has to maintain control of the situation. "Don't jump to conclusions. It's just a weekend get-together with old friends."

"I know you, Zoe. It's damage control. You're looking for a way out. You can't outsmart me. What kind of get-together?"

A divorce party will set him off again, so she lies. "It's a college get-together. We were all buddies at UCSD."

"You mean a reunion?"

She nods, hoping her cheeks aren't flushed. "Sure." It's scary how quickly she slips back into her college survival mode, where barefaced lying is the default setting. Just shows you can take the girl out of the street, but you can't take the street out of the girl. "It'll be a fun weekend with the girls."

"Can I come?" He looks desperate.

"Absolutely not. No men allowed."

He's calmed down a bit, so she grabs a glass of water. She's parched. Her heart's racing.

"Well, as long as you're not lying to me," he says, shuffling the papers into a neat pile. "I mean we're in this together, aren't we? We're a team, baby? Right?"

A wave of nausea threatens to send her hurtling upstairs. "I need to take a shower." She clamps the towel over her mouth to hide her derision. He's like the extra guy trying to climb into the lifeboat, clinging on so hard they all sink.

"Want an omelet, hun?" He's slipped into his repentant husband act. She's seen it enough times to know it. It's not working.

"I'm not hungry right now," she says, crossing the kitchen and heading for the stairs.

"I'll make it anyway. There are some nice porcini mushrooms in the fridge. You might have an appetite once you've showered."

I'm never going to feel better, she thinks, climbing the stairs to the distant sound of cracking eggs and Marcus actually humming a tune. She needs out of this house so badly; she could pack a bag and leave today. She detests this clingy, whining version of him, and wishes she'd never, ever complained when he was laid-back and cool, or high and out of her hair. She should stay in a hotel. Get some peace and quiet, away from this broken marriage.

Away from Marcus.

Suddenly she's glad she'll be seeing Evie, who was always so good at *looking after things*. Steering them out of awkward situations, and sometimes getting rid of troublesome people who just happened to be standing in your way.

She opens the bottom drawer of her bedside table and takes out a crumpled envelope. Pulls out the snapshot inside. It's the four of them – Evie, Savannah, Daisy and Zoe posing in their blue-and-gold wrestling kits. Zoe has a medic's badge on hers. Evie's holding the silver trophy showing they were runners-up at the California State championships. The university had never seen anything like women's wrestling before, but when Evie got something into her head, nothing could stop her.

They were hanging out in the gym between classes watching Evie work out when she first suggested the idea of the wrestling team. Evie had just wrapped up a session on the rowing machine. She stood in front of Savannah, Zoe and Daisy, her muscles pumped up and glistening.

"Hey, losers – ever thought about wrestling?"

"Can't say I have," said Zoe, flipping through her anatomy textbook. "It's pretty aggressive – isn't it?"

Evie tapped a finger to the side of her head. "You think it's just a slugfest?"

Zoe shook her head.

"What about you, Sav? Ever watched it on TV?"

Savannah shrugged. "Guess not."

Evie began to pace back and forth.

"So – wrestling is just like dancing. It's about athleticism, choreography, strength. And, boy is it sexy."

"I'd never thought of it that way," said Daisy. "But you might be onto something."

Evie jumped up and ran to the door. "Check this out," she said, stretching her arms up into the air. She focused quickly on the opposite wall and took a quick run then flipped into a lightning-fast handspring before landing in a splits position on the ground, just below their feet.

Savannah's mouth gaped open. "Holy shit."

Evie scrambled to her feet and dusted her tights down. "Told you. I'm planning to set up a women's wrestling club. Shake this tight-assed place up a bit. And if you're a dancer you'd be a natural fit, Sav."

Zoe grimaced. "Looks risky. I don't want to get injured."

"You like to meet guys?"

Zoe hesitated. "Not sure how the two are connected."

Evie stood over Zoe. "Listen, dummy. We're not following them around on the golf course like lovesick caddies. We're gonna show them that we're smart, sexy and strong. In my books that could be a real turn-on. Hey, if you're too chicken, you could be the team medic. We can definitely use your expertise."

Relieved, Zoe exhaled. No way would she risk some life-threatening injury to her head or body. "Sounds good. I'll do it."

Daisy's eyes were almost bugging out of her head. "I've always wanted to try something badass like that. Can you teach me?"

Evie whirled around. "Sure, but don't you have class right now?"

"Screw that," said Daisy, throwing down her books. "This looks way more fun."

"Guess I'm in," said Savannah. "I have a spare now. Let's do some warm-ups."

"Gotta go to class," said Zoe. "But I'll brush up on my first aid."

Evie clapped her hands. "Then I'd say we got us a team. We're gonna be ready for our first meet in a month's time. Oh – and I'll let you know about the little sideline I have planned once we've won our first meet."

Zoe puts the picture back into the envelope, her heart pounding. So many things changed when the wrestling club started up. That's when they met The Golden Guys and found out more about Evie's little sideline.

SAVANNAH

Savannah goes back to Leon's apartment after the show. He didn't hesitate when she asked if she could stay there. *Thank God there's one guy in this world I can trust,* she thinks as she sips her takeout coffee and watches the lights on the Strip transform the night into a neon rainbow. The show played to a packed house tonight. Better still, her feet felt like they had wings when she tap-danced across the stage in the Rat Pack routine. All she needs now is a little nightcap and a lucky streak at the casino. More winnings to add to her retirement fund.

After the divorce party she'll make serious plans to move away from Vegas now that Evie's found her. She thought she'd covered all her tracks, but it's next to impossible to stay incognito these days. But something nags at the back of her mind. Is it just sheer chance that the delivery of the surprise package coincided with Evie's divorce party? Surely it couldn't be her idea of a sick joke? Come to think of it, what does Evie really know and what exactly has her soon-to-be ex-husband, Blair, told her?

She has no other choice but to go through with this damned party, find out what's on Evie's mind, then get out of town and break all contact with everyone. She feels a tug of regret when she thinks about Leon and how kind he's been. But getting sentimental always lands her in trouble. She has to be practical. Accept her screwed-up life for what it is.

Maybe she'll find some sweet little place up on the West Coast with quaint coffee shops, artisan bakeries and streets of remodeled vintage homes. Maybe an artsy college town where she can set up her own private dance studio, and do teaching and choreography on the side.

Just another hundred thousand bucks would do it. Doesn't seem much to ask, she thinks as her phone buzzes with another message from Evie. Christ, she's almost forgotten about the fact that she has to find a replacement for Friday and Saturday night.

The first message contains an image of a wedding cake. White with pink rosettes piped around it. A happy bride stands on top. The tuxedo-clad groom beside her is turned upside down, his head plunged deep into the icing.

> How do you like the cake? It's for the 'burn the dress' ceremony we're having after Chippendales? Then we're going to get blasted and do some freedom karaoke!! Lol.

Savannah's not sure she'll be able to get into all these crazy activities. Burning a wedding dress? In Las Vegas of all places. And where exactly are they going to have this bonfire without attracting attention? The cops are swarming all over the place, and they won't welcome an open fire in this tinderbox of a city.

But then, Evie was always the reckless one in the group. The tough and sexy wrestler who crashed the frat parties where all the rich college guys hung out. That's where they first met The Golden Guys: Wade, Cal and Blair, Evie's soon-to-be ex.

But the setup of three guys and four girls was always going

to be a recipe for disaster. Someone inevitably had to play odd man out.

Evie had been right about the allure of the wrestling team. The Party Girls, Evie's unofficial name for the wrestling foursome that fought hard and partied even harder, was soon the hottest news around the school after they won their first meet. To Savannah the moves came naturally, and she couldn't deny the thrill of the fight. The sense of power when you had your opponent in a hold they couldn't escape. And Daisy was a tiger. Lightning-fast and deadly.

They'd crashed the frat house party after Evie promised to give a free bikini-clad demo of their wrestling moves as a little light entertainment for the upcoming Thanksgiving extravaganza. Sure enough, The Golden Guys zoned in on them like bees to honey.

Blair, the undisputed leader, was loud, brash and out to impress by throwing his money around and name-dropping about his mega-CEO dad and all his celebrity cronies. His dark, silky hair, pale skin and deep-blue eyes reminded Savannah of a hero in a Gothic romance. Wade was the pretty boy – all blond curls and limpid blue eyes. Shy and introverted, he was the follower in the group, while Cal, the rugged second-string quarterback on the football team was more enigmatic and standoffish than the others.

Savannah's stomach lurches. Her skin crawls at the memory of that time. Why is Evie counting on her? Has she changed, or even grown up? And what's so important that she needs to see them personally?

She considers getting in touch with Daisy or Zoe. Surely they'll know more about why Evie's marriage is over. At least then she'll be prepared. But she can call them later. Now she needs an hour or two listening to the comforting *swoosh* of the roulette wheel. That's always good therapy, and a great way to get her mind off all her worries.

An hour later she's back in the purple-and-gold room, a sweating mojito at her side. Leon's looking luscious behind the bar, she's ten thousand bucks closer to her goal, and the gut ache is gone. She's in her element. She flicks a drop of condensation from her white silk sheath dress and puts five grand on red. Got to speed things up if she's considering early retirement. Sitting back and looking around at this opulent palace of a place, she realizes she's going to miss Vegas. The show, the camaraderie of the other dancers, the lovely smell of greasepaint and the glittering costumes. The dancing, the gambling and the fabulous unreality of it all. The wheel stops on red. Incredible. Luck is on her side. She still has the magic.

She's just raking the chips in when a text arrives. It's probably Evie again with another crazy party idea. She glances down and sees it's from an unknown number.

> Trying to get away from me? I know you've moved. But you can't hide for too long. I have eyes everywhere.

She holds the pile of chips close to her and scans the room.

"Place your bets," says the croupier.

Savannah hesitates. Who is sending her these messages? And why now? After all this time? Someone is trying to freak her out. But who? Something savage rises into her throat. A tide of outrage. No worthless asshole is going to push her around. Not again. Not like the last time. She types a response.

> Leave me alone. You don't scare me anymore. I know who and what you are.

Then she waits. Nothing. Maybe that did the trick. She gets up to cash in her chips, aware she's moving ever closer to her goal.

By the time she's got the cashier's check in her hand there's still no response. But a small thread of doubt quivers at the back of her mind. She can't be sure who this is because she thought she'd taken care of everything.

Outside, a light evening breeze bathes her in its warmth. It's a lovely night to walk back to Leon's place, but instead she gets the doorman to hail a cab for her. At this point she's not taking any unnecessary chances. She may have the upper hand now, but anyone can turn on a dime. It's happened to her before.

DAISY

When she comes to, it's still dark outside. Too early to get up. The house is like a mausoleum. Cold, quiet and dank. The room smells of stale food and booze. A jab of pain from her blinding headache, and the memory of Wade's stolen album collection sends her reeling back onto the pillow. She's been drinking steadily ever since Saturday's garage sale just to put the entire debacle out of her thoughts. Problem is she's drunk a good portion of her profits away. Now how's she going to get to Vegas?

After chugging a bottle of water and a couple of aspirin, she parts the drapes and looks outside. It's four in the morning, and she needs time to think about her next move. She's desperate to go to Evie's party, but she's come up short. Her house was filled with cheap and worthless junk that raised a little under two hundred bucks plus the guitar money. That's a sad commentary on the value of her worldly possessions, but then she remembers her dear, sweet Ethan who cannot be valued. He's priceless.

But she has to face reality now, and consider her options, which seem really scarce at present.

Evie's already sent another text about the bridal-dress-burning ceremony, which really fired Daisy up, *pardon the pun*. Because she has one heck of a monstrous bridal dress to burn. A tasteless cream satin number with a lacy corset bodice and a flouncy skirt. She remembers feeling like she was decked out in a lampshade, but her mom, who managed to scrape a few bucks together, said that was the only one she could afford. She drags the dress from the back of her closet. It's wrapped in a plastic garment bag. She'll set this prime piece of crap alight. Let it blaze into the night sky like a warning signal for all reluctant brides-to-be. Those who are on the fence about saying *I do*.

Daisy thinks about Evie's freedom karaoke and vows she'll be up there on stage grabbing the microphone and belting out all those girly anthems until her lungs give out. This divorce party couldn't have come at a better time. Marriage is made for sheep and those with no sense of adventure. She'll never make the same mistake again. She's got books to read, places to go and novels to write.

A brief image flits across her mind. She's sitting in a bookstore, wearing a well-cut red cashmere dress and shiny gold earrings, a fancy silk scarf draped around her neck. Eager customers line up, clasping copies of her bestselling novel, and her hand is sore from signing them.

Keeping that picture in mind, she closes her eyes and imagines herself into another body, another mind. Someone unfettered by the constraints of being broke. Someone edgy, creative and willing to take risks. How can she get the money together to go to Vegas?

Try to get a loan from the bank using the house as collateral? They won't go for it. My credit rating is shot.

Sell the house? There's still equity in it, but it's a long-term solution.

Hitch-hike there? Knowing my luck, some serial killer or creepy perv will pick me up.

Go for the cheaper bus option then bunk up with Sav or Zoe? I'll still come up short.

Call Savannah or Zoe and borrow some money. Tell them I'll pay them back once the house is sold.

The prospect makes her cringe. It's so humiliating to admit how much of a loser she is and how her life has amounted to nothing.

She almost jumps out of her skin when her phone rings. It's an unknown number. Is it Wade on a burner phone or *those other guys* she's been trying to avoid? Curiosity gets the better of her and she presses *accept* then waits for someone to speak.

"Hi? Daisy?"

The voice sounds familiar. That soft, persuasive tone. The carefully enunciated syllables. But she's not sure.

"Who is it?"

"After all the times we spent together, you don't know me?"

Is it really him? "Why... why would you be calling me, Blair?"

She's mumbling like a confused kid.

"I missed you guys. A whole lot. You four were so fascinating. The way you always stuck together. You were all so – so – streetwise, so edgy. So sexy."

She chews her lip and digs her nails into her palm. He's still an arrogant prick. Probably gotten worse with age.

He continues. "Guess you know I'm going to be single again, so I thought I'd check out the dating scene. Have a sneak preview of my new life, see who's single and available, and I heard you were all on your own again."

"How did you know that? Have you seen Wade?"

"Maybe I have, maybe I haven't. But jeez, you and Wade go back a helluva long way. And just thinking about those times again brought back a whole lot of memories. Some pretty raunchy if my memory is correct."

THE DIVORCE PARTY

She can hear his heavy breathing and starts chewing the inside of her lip, hoping he's not thinking too far back.

"But hey, I have something far more interesting for you to consider, because I know you've hit some hard times. A business proposition."

"Are you kidding? I'd rather go broke."

"You are broke. Just take a moment to hear me out."

"You want me to sell life insurance for your damn company?"

"Hell no, don't want to alienate my customers." He chuckles.

"Piss off, Blair."

"It's something way more intriguing, and rewarding. I gather Evie's having some kind of party in Vegas, and you're invited along with your two other BFFs."

"Not sure if I'm going."

"Of course you're going. Wild horses wouldn't stop you. I know how you operate, Daisy."

Now she remembers how that breathy, whispering voice of his got on her nerves.

"Okay, spit it out. What do you want from me?"

"I need eyes and ears at Evie's little shindig. Someone to supply details – how much money my wife is squandering, who she's screwing around with, what she's drinking, snorting, smoking or injecting, and what she's spreading on those damn social media accounts of hers. I can't afford any surprises or bad publicity that might interfere with my business or professional reputation, so I'd like to get something on her first. Some late-night fling or little indiscretion. Public drunkenness or indecency. Consumption of illegal drugs. Anything I can get. I need some bargaining chips, if you like, so she doesn't take me for every penny."

Daisy sits back, her heart pumping fast. "You want me to rat out on my friend? Why me?"

"Because I know you're broke. That no-good, loser of a husband, Wade, never deserved you in the first place. And now he's left you high and dry."

"You still didn't tell me how you know about that?"

She can almost hear him grinning. "I'll tell you later but only if you cooperate with me. Now, do you want to go to Vegas? And I mean go in style?"

A pang of guilt stings her, quickly eclipsed by a tidal wave of acrimony. It would be a pleasure to relieve him of some of his money. She finds herself saying yes. *Besides, he'll never know if you're lying,* says another voice inside her head.

He exhales loudly. "Great. Text me your email address, and you'll hear from me first thing in the morning."

The line goes dead and Daisy falls back onto the bed wondering what exactly she's gotten herself into now, and with someone like Blair.

She can almost picture him as he was when they first met all those years ago. The ivory-skinned guy with the deep-blue eyes. That dark wing of hair falling across his face. The long, thin fingers. Perfectly manicured. The full, swollen lips, as if he'd stepped straight from the pages of a vampire novel. At first she'd been drawn to him in the way she'd felt compelled to read and reread her favorite novel, *Dracula*, fascinated by her suspicion that hidden at the core of this perfectly groomed man was a true monster. But he first set his sights on Savannah, most likely attracted by her cool aloofness. Savannah who'd vowed that no man would threaten her independence.

None of them actually knew why Sav had rejected him. All Daisy knew was that he soon turned his attention to the brainiac among them. Zoe, the determined social climber.

ZOE

The door closes on Zoe's final appointment of the day with the parents of a ten-year-old kid whose latest tests indicate possible tumors on the brain. She rests her forehead on her hand and takes a deep breath. It's the toughest part of her job. This negotiation with parents is like a dance, as they try to figure out how much of the truth to reveal to their child. Some parents refuse to divulge anything, preferring their child remain oblivious to the facts. Others favor complete, no-holds-barred disclosure as the best course of action. Usually, Zoe's able to come to a compromise. Iron out an acceptable approach that allows release of some vital information, but withholds the most worrisome aspects of prognosis and treatment.

She's learned that kids are way more resilient than adults give them credit for, but she feels for the parents. It's difficult enough breaking bad news as the impartial doctor, but when it's your own child, the pain must be agonizing.

And that's only one of the many factors that make her question her motherhood quest. She woke up this morning shaking, with one question blazing in her head: *do I really want to be a mother?* It's like walking across a minefield and never knowing if or when the whole thing is going to blow up in your face and, if it doesn't kill you, it'll maim you for life.

Since the evening of Marcus's financial disclosure, she's been considering a life free of messy ties. She has enough emotional trauma to deal with at work, and her college days left her with too many emotional and physical scars. A painful legacy that sometimes makes her heart feel like it's been ripped from her ribcage, squeezed, then shoved back inside. *Damn Blair. Evie is way better off without that bloodsucker.*

And maybe she's not really the mothering type. For sure she's not great wife material. Could be because she chose the wrong husband, but she's always suspected there's something missing when it comes to her emotional makeup. Yes, she can be empathetic at work. But that's learned, professional behavior. If she comes across as too cold or detached, she'll scare the patients away, and that would be financially ruinous in the long run. The lack of a nurturing, loving mother is the best explanation she can come up with. Her dad did his best, but he just wasn't around enough, and he was old school. Didn't hug much, wasn't a great listener, just expected her to get on with her life. He probably would have been way more comfortable with a son. Would've taught him how to throw a football, catch a baseball, crack open his first can of beer, and generally shoot the shit with him.

She blinks her eyes, surprised to feel the dampness of tears. She misses her dad, despite his failings. He kept a roof over her head, fed her. Tried to protect her. Good thing he didn't know what she was up to at college.

She takes a deep breath. *Cut it out. This dwelling on the past. Think about the present.*

But now she has to face the fact that she's never loved

Marcus. Come to think of it, she's never fallen in love. Nobody has ever come near to touching the frozen core at the center of her soul, and that doesn't bode well for a child. The most she's felt for Marcus is the kind of distant familiarity one might feel for a childhood toy or a friend's dribbly old sheepdog. She's always respected his financial success, and the comfortable lifestyle it's allowed her to enjoy. Maybe that's why she's tolerated him all these years, but now he's become a sniveling loser, she feels only contempt for his weaknesses.

She's aware that she's grinding her teeth again, so she packs up her bag. Gets ready to head home and search through her closet for her wedding dress. Evie's idea of a burn-your-wedding-dress party is the most appealing of all the ideas she's sent Zoe's way. On the one hand, the starkly simple Ines Di Santo cream satin sheath was the most beautiful gown she'd ever possessed back in 2010, but on the other, it now represents a dying relationship and loss of independence. It definitely needs to go up in a cloud of smoke.

The leather-lined luxury of her black Audi feels like a haven. Somewhere she can be completely alone to consider how she'll tell Marcus their marriage is over. He's probably not going to accept it without a messy, dramatic showdown, and she doesn't have the stomach for that crap right now. Maybe she'll just leave a note for him. Somewhere hidden. Then once she's on the plane to Vegas, she'll text him and let him know where to find it. She can't be too explicit about her plan to leave, otherwise he's going to cling to her like a troublesome barnacle and she'll never shake him off.

Being away for a while might help him get used to the idea of their separation, and then she'll return to an apartment of her own choosing, which she needs to set up before leaving for the party weekend. Yes, she'll miss the beautiful house and the in-ground pool. The Japanese soaking tub and the gourmet kitchen, but he'll likely have to sell it all anyway to cover his losses. And she has her own income, her own savings. He can have all the rest without involving any blood-sucking lawyers in an expensive drawn-out battle where they'll argue about who'll keep the brass-tapped espresso machine or the black Baroque Versace bath towels. On second thoughts, maybe she'll take a couple of those.

She rounds a corner and the full moon appears. Orange and ominous, it hangs low in the sky. A sense of unease creeps into her mind, as if all her logical planning will somehow fall short. She's always wondered why people don't see situations with the same cold, clear logic she does. Being rational and pragmatic doesn't make her a cold-hearted monster, does it? Marcus will be better off without her in the long run. Won't he? He'll find some soft, pretty, spontaneous woman, like Daisy. Now there's a thought. Maybe she can set them up. Save Daisy's life in the process.

The phone rings. It's Marcus. He sounds breathless.

"Where are you?"

"On the way home. Why?"

"I've made a fantastic dinner for us. Handmade lobster ravioli with white wine sauce. I spent all day at it. Forgot how much I loved cooking."

She sighs. It's a bad sign when he starts cooking. He reserves it for times when he's strayed and is looking for forgiveness. When she gets home, he'll try to feed it to her as if she's a baby, coaxing her with soft Italian words. *Mangia, mangia, mia cara.* Then he'll get all grabby and thrusty, because food is his prelude to lovemaking. Her body goes cold. Now's the time she has to call Daisy and ask for a big favor. It's the only thing she can think of.

THE DIVORCE PARTY

She swallows her repulsion in a gulp. "Sorry, luv, just got caught in some traffic. That sounds great."

"Wine's chilling in the fridge as we speak."

"See you soon." Maybe she can get him so drunk or high he'll fall asleep. Then she can figure out the best way to ditch him.

SAVANNAH

"Friday is definitely a no-go for coverage," says Tia, sweeping up her long braids and piling them into a crown on top of her head. She takes out her phone and starts scrolling. Giggling at the texts as if Savannah isn't actually standing there.

Does she really need that towering hairdo? As if she isn't tall enough already, she thinks.

Savannah had always thought of herself as tall at five feet ten. *But Tia has to be over six feet, and she looks so young*. Not a day over twenty-five. Her beauty so fresh and effortless. Perfect golden skin that doesn't need to be fried under a ruthless Vegas sun to get even a smidge of color in it. This morning Savannah worked for at least an hour with a toolkit of concealer, blush, eye shadow and mascara just to achieve a natural, no-makeup look.

"What about Saturday?"

Tia purses her lips and tries to tear her eyes away from the long lineup of texts and notifications on her phone. *This girl is so in demand.* Savannah wonders what it must be like to live just one day in Tia's busy life. College was the last time she had a close group of friends. But she was always the quiet, reserved one in the friend group. Evie was the wild, spontaneous rebel,

Daisy the pretty-but-ditzy guy magnet, and Zoe the smart, ruthless genius. She, Savannah, the intense introvert, who tagged along behind, methodically driving away the guys who threatened to ruin her newfound independence.

Her relationship with Evie was tense and uneasy right from the start, because Evie always had the shoplifting incident to fall back on. She'd just remind Savannah about it from time to time – enough to manipulate her into doing things like *more shoplifting*. Only it soon became larger items like designer sunglasses and party clothing, all in the hopes of getting in tight with The Golden Guys. What Evie didn't know was that Blair already had his eye on Savannah even without all the designer trappings.

Tia finally pockets her phone and sighs. "Saturday? Yes, I think we can manage coverage." Suspicion flickers in her eyes.

"That's great. I owe you one." But that's a lie. She doesn't want to work on Friday, and now she'll have to come up with one hell of an excuse to get out of the penis piñata event, unless Evie changes the timing. "And for sure I'll stand in for someone on another night if you ever need it. Any time. I mean, except this weekend," she adds with a nervous giggle.

Tia clamps a manicured hand onto her slim hip. "As it happens, I've been meaning to talk to you about something important. We're auditioning a new girl on Friday morning. She'll shadow you during rehearsal, watch the show Friday night, then take over for you on Saturday."

Savannah's heart sinks. She can hear the blood pulsing in her ears. "New girl? Why?"

"We always like to be on the lookout for fresh talent, and this girl was a runner-up in a regional talent contest. We need new blood, just in case."

"In case of what?"

Tia studies a perfect fingernail. "Listen, Sav. I have so much respect for you as a person and an artist. So I want to be perfectly transparent with you..."

Oh no. Savannah's heard this kind of patronizing lead-up before, and it's usually followed by a backhander of some sort. A punch to the jugular, cloaked in flattery.

"So, as I was saying, you have been – I mean, *are* a valuable member of our team..."

She almost slipped up. Already speaking about me in the past tense.

"...but I think we both know you've been struggling a little. I mean your focus is off, which is understandable considering your..."

Savannah's hackles rise. If she was one of those scaly lizards, the frill around her head would be fanned right out. "Considering my what?"

Now she's squawking like a paranoid neurotic, which is not helping her case at all.

Tia shifts her stance, scowling as if she'd like to tell Savannah to get lost.

"Well, you must have had some thoughts about your future, Savannah. I mean we both know your time with our show can't go on forever. And we don't actually hire *mature* dancers anymore."

Savannah winces as she bites her lip. "*Mature.* I'm not even close to forty yet. And I can still do the work. I even have ideas about jazzing up some of the routines. Choreography is definitely something I'd like to explore. Maybe make a lateral move into it."

Tia's eyes narrow. The air becomes icy. "There's only one choreographer for this show, and that happens to be me. I'm tight with the producers, so don't even consider it."

Savannah realizes this discussion is going nowhere, and Tia's already frantically checking her phone again. "Well, I appreciate the chat. And thanks for getting Saturday covered for me. I hope the new girl breaks a leg. I mean, in the theatrical sense of course."

Tia draws herself up to her full towering height. "For sure." She looks past Savannah and waves. Her face lights up with a blinding smile. "Hey, babe," she says, hurrying towards Honey Valentine, one of the hottest new stars in the hotel's headline show.

Savannah slinks away as the two women hug and blow air kisses at each other. Now she's really blown it. She only has a month left, if she's lucky. Maybe less if the new girl works out. Then her only options will be burlesque or pole dancing. No way will she let that happen.

A text comes in. It's Evie again.

> Only two days to go. I've booked a suite at the Aria for Friday night. We'll meet up there at eight.

The Aria is not too far away from Planet Hollywood and her show. *Damn.*

Damn the whole divorce party. It could open up a whole Pandora's box of secrets that no one wants aired. She shivers. That's a scary thought.

On the positive side, the mystery person hasn't contacted her again. But still, she needs to stay on full alert. Needs to make sure no one is following her, so she can get away from Vegas and start a whole new life, way sooner than she anticipated.

DAISY

Daisy is dreaming of a turquoise swimming pool surrounded by giant palm trees. She's lying on a striped canvas lounger in a poolside cabana. A book lies open beside her. Something hot and sexy with a close-up of bulging pecs on the cover. A bottle of bubbly chills in a silver ice bucket and a light breeze tickles her face. Tinkling music plays in the background. It's relaxing at first, then the sound starts to repeat itself. Over and over. Her eyes fly open and her phone alarm is blaring. It's already ten o'clock and she's back to the reality of her vintage IKEA bedroom. A faded gray bedspread is pulled up to her nose, and her phone alarm buzzes on the side table.

    She remembers Blair's promise and checks her email to see if he actually went through with the e-transfer. Scrolling through the usual pile of junk mail she sees a message from the school board flagged with a red *urgent* symbol. She moves it to the trash folder, feeling a brief twinge of guilt. After all, she still has Ethan to think about, even though he's safely away at college enjoying student life and living off a stack of scholarships earned from pure determination and hard work. Tears spring to her eyes when she thinks of her sweet boy, head bent over his open books until three or four in the morning on school nights, while Wade was snoring like a bear in the room next door.

No, she won't bother him with her troubles right now. Doesn't want to put a damper on those heady, fun, first days of college. By the time she sees him again at Thanksgiving, she means to have everything sorted out. Herself and Wade included.

But there's still no e-transfer from Blair.

He's probably reconsidered. Doesn't want to waste his money on her. She lies back and breathes a sigh of relief. How could she even have considered ratting out her friends? All that guilt would have killed her fun. So now she won't even make it to Vegas, but what does it matter? She has far more important things to consider like how soon she can sell the house, how she's going to survive financially, and what she's going to do for the rest of her miserable life.

Her phone rings. An unfamiliar number. Probably a scam. Regardless, she reaches over to the bedside table and clicks the phone open. First there's silence. Then a fuzzy sound like frying bacon.

"Daisy?"

Another familiar voice that she can't quite place.

"Daisy. Long time no talk."

Then it clicks. An echo from college. "Zoe. It is you, isn't it?"

"Yup. All the way from Toronto. I'm driving to work and thought I'd give you a shout."

"I'm flattered. A call from Dr. Zoe Ryan."

"Hey, don't sell yourself short. You teachers are so dedicated. Unsung heroes in my opinion."

Unsung and underpaid, thinks Daisy, her skin prickling at

the patronizing edge in Zoe's voice. And *what's* she driving to work? Some loaded import? A flashy hybrid? Certainly not a rusted-out Dodge with coffee-stained upholstery and two hundred thousand clicks on the clock. Daisy feels like a weight is pressing down on her sternum, crushing the breath from her. She gazes at a dark patch where the ceiling meets the wall, just above the window. Is it possible there's a leak in the roof and the drywall is moldy?

"Are you still there, Daisy?" Zoe repeats.

"Oh – yeah. Sorry. Just got an important message," she lies.

"So, I can't believe we'll be seeing each other in just a couple of days. I mean after all this time, the four of us together again."

Daisy scans the cloudy window. The seals are broken. *Damn.* "Oh, I know, it's amazing."

"Don't sound so thrilled. You okay, Daisy?"

This is her chance. If she can eat some humble pie without choking, she might be able to go to Vegas. She clears her throat. "Thing is, Zoe, I don't know if I'm going."

"You have to." Zoe's voice climbs an octave. "It's not an option."

"Well – it – it's Wade..."

"Did he say you couldn't go? Let me talk to that jerk."

No way would I ever let you do that. Daisy remembers when she started dating him. Zoe was so superior and judgmental. She'd called Wade a lazy stoner. Now Daisy feels her stomach clench. Zoe was right on the money.

"Actually, he's left me."

"Oh my God. How are you managing?"

Daisy could swear that Zoe's tone of voice doesn't quite match the words she's speaking. She can almost hear a little whisper saying *I told you so.* "Actually, it's a relief. But now I'm kind of short of funds, and going to Vegas isn't exactly a priority right now."

THE DIVORCE PARTY

"No *problemo,* girl. You absolutely deserve to go. I'll e-transfer you the money. It'll be my little gift to you, because I'm just dying to catch up on everything you've done with your life."

Daisy flinches. *You just want to wallow in the gory details about how badly I've fucked it all up,* And why does Zoe's cheery BFF act sound so fake? So out of character for the ambitious, driven girl Daisy remembers. "That's so generous. Actually, I was also thinking of looking around for work while I'm there. I need a change of scene."

"Then that's even more of a reason to get your ass on a plane. I won't hear of you staying home. I'll do the transfer right now. You need to book your ticket ASAP."

Daisy feels a tickle of excitement. Like Cinderella. She can go to the ball after all. "No rush, Zoe. And of course, I'll pay you back. That goes without saying." Though she thinks maybe she might not need to. Especially if Zoe isn't asking for it. And besides, she's kept quiet about a few things from way back that could have made life very uncomfortable for Dr. Zoe Ryan. Surely that counts for something.

There's a long silence. Daisy can hear breathing. She hopes maybe Zoe's transferring the money right now. "But I do have a little favor to ask of you in return," Zoe announces, her voice taking on a low, confidential tone.

Daisy grimaces at the phone. Typical Zoe. Two steps ahead of everyone else with her scheming. She always had some kind of scam going on at college. Always into some type of moneymaking enterprise. *Ruthless and determined* are words synonymous with Daisy's memories of young Zoe. "Anything. Go right ahead."

"Okay, my husband, Marcus, is acting like a jerk. See, we've been having a few disagreements lately. Not seeing eye to eye over a few things, and he's a tad insecure right now. If he knows it's a divorce party, he'll be bugging me the whole time. And he's so paranoid, he might just show up there uninvited. So I need you to text me and say how much you're looking forward to our college reunion this weekend. Then he won't be so suspicious."

"Of course. I can do that right now if you like." This is way easier than Daisy thought. Better than spying on her friends and reporting back to Blair, the vampire.

"This evening is better. He'll probably be cooking supper around seven. I'll make sure my phone's on the counter where he can see it. That's when you'll send the text."

"No problem. I'll put a reminder on my phone right now." Zoe doesn't realize how good she's got it with this guy who cares about her and even makes dinner. Wade wouldn't even warm up a hot dog for her. Daisy's heart does a little flip when a text comes in notifying her of an incoming e-transfer for two grand. More than enough to get to Vegas. She goes back to her calendar and enters a reminder to send a text at seven.

"Hey, Zoe, do you have any idea what Evie's up to?" she asks, excited now she's actually going.

The line goes quiet. She can hear Zoe breathing. "Not really. I was hoping you'd know something?"

Daisy's anxious. Wants to get off the phone so she can buy her ticket to Vegas. She's in no mood for gossip. "She seems pretty serious about getting us all together again."

"I thought we'd all made an agreement not to see each other," says Zoe, a hard edge to her voice. "You remember?"

"You know Evie. Never was one for following the rules."

"That's what worries me."

"She's also someone you don't want to cross."

"Dammit. Why does she have to worm her way back into our lives now?"

"Guess we'll find out pretty soon," says Daisy, now she has some impetus to jump out of bed. The sun is out and the clouds have cleared. The mailman has just dropped a handful of letters into her mailbox. She hopes to God they're just flyers and not final demand or disconnection notices. But who cares anyway? She won't be here. It's going to be a good day for packing. "Okay, Zoe. Thanks so much for everything. Love you. I'd better get on and book that ticket."

"And the text at seven?"

"I won't forget."

"By the way," she adds just as Daisy is about to end the call. "Are you happy Evie's splitting up with Blair?"

Something sticks in Daisy's throat. She can't swallow. "What? For sure I am. He's a sleaze. He always thought he was doing us a favor, hanging out with us because he came from money."

"That seems so long ago," says Zoe. "Can't say I remember it clearly."

What is she talking about? Zoe was always parading herself around him, hitching up her minidress, showing her legs. Unfastening the top buttons of her shirt. Trying to get his attention when he was clearly after Savannah. She probably wants to forget that version of Zoe Ryan from twenty years back. But before Daisy can say another thing, Zoe chimes in with a cheery, "See you in a couple of days, sweets."

The line goes dead and another text appears. This time from Blair. He actually came through and sent an e-transfer for three grand. She can't believe he was more generous than Zoe, but then his money comes with strings attached.

But now she has five big ones. She can't remember ever having that much money to herself. She briefly considers refusing it, then reconsiders. Hasn't she earned it? Blair's an asshole who deserves everything he gets. And she deserves some pampering after all her sacrifices for Wade. She'll get a manicure, pedicure and hairdo. Then she'll go shopping. There's no point in packing crappy old clothes. She'll need some fancy new ones now. But maybe she'll wait until she gets to Vegas. There's probably more selection there.

The new start is a reality now, even though she had to compromise her morals to get herself to the starting gate. But who cares? She got what she wanted. Who gives a crap about what she had to do to get it? For sure she doesn't.

ZOE

Zoe gazes up at the towering glass-and-concrete obelisk that looms over Lake Ontario. She checks her phone. This is it. Lakefront Place. *Waterfront living in the heart of the city. Where urban birds fly with night owls. Whoah*! Some copywriter's been plundering their high school poetry journal for this description. Words like *natural, elemental, visionary* are liberally peppered into blurbs accompanying pictures of happy couples strolling down lakeside paths strewn with fallen leaves. A stark Toronto skyline hovers in the background, a nod to the glass towers of commerce that enable these wholesome young thirty-somethings to afford the 1.5 million dollar price tag for twelve hundred square feet of prime, lakefront living. No wonder they're all smiling. A brief memory of Daisy's plight stabs at Zoe's conscience. Was two grand a little on the chintzy side? Maybe she should have upped it to five? She can afford it, she thinks, reflecting on her own little fortune, the majority of it all now safely moved offshore thanks to her forward-thinking lawyer.

"Leave just enough in your Canadian accounts to make his

lawyers happy," said Phyllis. A financial wiz, and lacking conscience, she specialized in showing her mostly female clients how to avoid getting fleeced in messy divorce settlements. "This way he'll still have enough to keep him in coke and weed until he burns his stupid brains out."

She's distracted suddenly by a real estate agent who bursts out from the front doors of the building. He's dark, slender, impeccably groomed like a banker. Sporting chiseled eyebrows and a Hugo Boss suit that hugs his toned physique. He holds out a hand in welcome. "Jaz, short for Jazvinder. Great to finally touch base, Mrs. Ryan."

"Good to meet you, Jaz. Actually it's Dr. Ryan, but you can call me Zoe."

His eyebrows shoot upwards. He's pegged her as a good prospect. "Of course, Dr. Ry – I mean, Zoe." His smile is blinding. His enthusiasm infectious. She pictures them chatting later about the condo, over drinks in some glitzy bar surrounded by other young, affluent, beautiful people. In an instant, the single life becomes everything that Zoe craves. The feeling of unpredictability, the allure of spontaneity. But an image of Marcus snoring on the sofa next to a stack of pizza boxes is enough to prick that magical bubble. She blinks it away. Jaz stares at her, one groomed eyebrow raised.

"Oh – sorry. Tough day."

The smile flashes back across his face. "So, let's go on inside and I'll give you the grand tour." He turns towards the lobby, arms making broad, sweeping motions as he walks. "We're so proud of this development. I can't tell you how many clients are lining up to get a piece of it. I mean, the place hugs the shoreline. And the trails look like something out of cottage country, Muskoka? Parry Sound? Natural, rustic, organic. True country living in the heart of the city."

The glass entrance doors open onto a light-filled atrium

studded with trees. Gleaming tile floors, marble walls and abstract chandeliers hover over gray sectionals, reminding her of the interior of a modern art gallery. Hardly rustic. But she likes what she sees. "Incredible. Everything I've been looking for."

He turns to her. "We have city views, park views, and for the most discriminating clients, *the lake views,* which are naturally pricier. Of course, it's your choice. We can start wherever you want." His direct gaze seems to throw a challenge to her. *Now we find out what you're really worth, Dr. Zoe.*

She straightens her shoulders and meets his eyes which have temporarily morphed from expectant to steely. "Naturally, I'll only consider the lake view units."

He tries to hide an exhalation of relief with a little cough. "Then let's head up to the twenty-fourth floor."

The unit is a symphony of creamy whites and grays, with a view of the lake from every angle. To the right, the blinking lights of the CN Tower add a touch of urban mystique. Two gorgeous bedrooms, one with a room-sized walk-in closet, and two immaculate bathrooms. The kitchen is disappointing. The miniature-sized island and sparse counter space seem out of sync with the huge price tag, but she doesn't intend to do a whole lot of cooking here. Just to sit on that balcony and watch the sun rise and set over the lake is something she wants so badly; she could write a check on the spot to secure it.

"Will they consider throwing in the furniture?"

He wheels around. "Everything is negotiable."

"Good. That may be a deal-maker."

Now he's glancing at her wedding ring and then back at her. "Will your husband be coming to view the place, Zoe?"

She bites her lip. "No. Actually, we're going through a divorce." There, she's said it. There's no going back now, though it's a reality Marcus isn't aware of yet.

His eyes gleam as if that information changes everything. "I see. So how soon do you need possession?"

She thinks for a moment. Glances out of the window and sees a gull swooping and dipping over the water. "Next week, preferably."

His eyebrows shoot upwards again. He's probably already calculating his commission. "Then we'll need to move swiftly on this."

She smiles. "Can we go for a drink somewhere to go over the details?"

He grins back. "As a matter of fact, I know a charming little place just five minutes away from here."

She knew he would.

On the way down, they stop on the fifteenth floor to look at a sparkling outdoor pool surrounded by loungers, next to a rooftop terrace complete with barbecues and dining tables and a state-of-the-art fitness center.

By the time they reach the lobby she's sold. Wild horses and snarling hounds couldn't tear her away from this dream. Marcus and his misery fade away into the past. She'll be reborn into a better version of herself here in this luxurious, pristine paradise.

Later, she walks into her front hallway, a little tipsy from the two dirty martinis she shared with Jaz in a gorgeous little wine bar decked out with vintage Hollywood and Bollywood posters. The deal papers just need her virtual signature and it's a go. She throws down her keys. It's already six forty-five. Daisy will be texting soon. The place smells of cooking. Something spicy and delicious. The sound of singing comes from the kitchen. She enters to find Marcus, clad in his Versace apron, flitting between

THE DIVORCE PARTY

three steaming pots on the stove. She remembers Daisy and places her phone on the counter.

"What's this?" Her stomach curdles.

He whirls around. "Babe. Thank goodness you're here." He holds up a finger. "Just wait."

She holds her breath as he opens the fridge, takes out a bottle of Pol Roger and proceeds to open it. The cork flies out with a loud pop and he pours the fizzy liquid into the two glasses lined up on the counter. "Bubbly time."

She reluctantly takes the glass. "What are we celebrating?"

He's grinning like a happy kid. "Everything's okay. One of my outlier funds rallied. Unbelievable upward trajectory. It made up for close to a half of what I lost from the cryptocurrency debacle in one day."

She feels like a cold hand has just pressed down on her heart. "Great. That's good. Isn't it?"

He puts down his glass and grasps her shoulders. "Don't you see? Everything's back to normal. We're good, the two of us. I'll even go for those fertility treatments. Now I truly understand what having a child means to you, I phoned and made an appointment."

"You did?" Zoe's aware of a thumping in her head from the gin she just consumed only half an hour ago.

"I go on Monday. Aren't you happy for me? For us?"

She's about to force a smile when her phone pings with a text. Daisy's right on cue.

Marcus glances at the phone. "Who's Daisy?"

Relieved she doesn't have to answer Marcus's loaded question, she takes a sip of champagne. "She's an old college friend. A real sweetie. We were best buds in college. It's probably about the weekend."

"Weekend? What about the weekend?"

"I told you the weed was playing tricks with your memory. Remember the invite to a party in Vegas?"

He shakes his head, his gaze troubled.

"Check it out. What does she want?" says Zoe.

"You want me to read your text?"

She nods. "Sure."

He picks up the phone, scans the message, and looks up at her. There's a brief, pregnant pause. She hopes to hell Daisy got it right. He can't suspect anything when she leaves for Vegas. The condo deal will go through. She'll fly back to Toronto and head straight to her lakeside paradise and she'll never have to speak directly to him again, because it'll all be done through her lawyer.

But he grins and her shoulders relax. "I didn't realize it was just a college reunion."

Her heart rate ratchets down ten notches. "What the hell did you think it was?"

"I – I thought you were meeting someone there. A guy. A lover."

"Whatever would give you that idea?"

"I'm just a bit possessive where you're concerned, hun. But you should go. It's good to reconnect with your old friends. And you need some downtime just to chill. When you come back, we'll go to the doctor together."

Then you'll be on your own, buddy. Because I'll be a no-show.

She's amazed at how coolly she's dealing with this situation. "Great. Let's eat."

"Take a seat, my sweetheart," he says, pulling out a dining chair for her, "and get ready to enjoy the best fish curry you've ever tasted."

"Sounds yummy. Just hand me my phone and I'll text Daisy back."

Once Marcus is busy slamming plates onto the counter, Zoe opens her online banking account and e-transfers another three grand to Daisy, making it an even five. Now she'll be getting half of way more money from the settlement, there's absolutely no need to shortchange her dear friend, Daisy.

THE ARRIVAL

Divorce Party Playlist:

I Will Survive: Gloria Gaynor
D-I-V-O-R-C-E: Tammy Wynette
Fifty Ways to Leave Your Lover: Paul Simon
Go Your Own Way: Fleetwood Mac
Dancing With Myself: Billy Idol
Bye, Bye, Bye: NSYNC
Free Bird: Lynyrd Skynyrd
I'm Movin' On: Rascal Flatts
I'm Still Standing: Elton John
Since U Been Gone: Kelly Clarkson
Stronger: Britney Spears
We Are Never Ever Getting Back Together: Taylor Swift

SAVANNAH

Savannah hasn't heard anything yet, but figures Daisy and Zoe must have arrived by now. Maybe they've already checked in at the hotel, or headed to the pool to catch a few rays while they wait for Evie.

Evie. The thought of seeing Evie makes her break out in a cold sweat. Evie was always so jealous of her. Couldn't figure out why Blair had the hots for her the first moment he saw her. She remembers that first frat party where The Party Girls did their wrestling demo in exchange for a steep fee.

"We don't squander our strength and skill on non-paying customers," Evie said, when they were all ready to go. "And we'll be doing a whole lot more of these displays. Take my word for it."

Evie had instructed them all to dress in skimpy bikinis, but she took one look at Savannah in her sleek white, high-cut one-piece and her chin dropped a mile.

"Holy shit. You're almost naked."

Blair was basically salivating as he watched them go through their moves, a carefully choreographed routine of handsprings, somersaults and light wrestling holds. Savannah, with her natural talent for dance, had taken to wrestling more quickly than Daisy who struggled to do a decent cartwheel, but had natural strength that helped her ace the holds. While Zoe, in her form-fitting medic T-shirt, provided witty background commentary.

Later, Evie was dumbfounded when Savannah told her how Blair had come up to her afterwards and begged to take her out.

"His family are loaded. You'd be set for life."

Savannah shrugged. "I turned him down."

"Why?"

"He's not my type, and I prefer being independent. That's all."

"But he's persistent. Doesn't take no for an answer."

"I lied. Told him I'd been diagnosed as clinically frigid."

"And are you?"

"I'll never tell."

Strange that Evie, the girl who considered herself a tough, streetwise badass, actually swallowed the dumbest excuse Savannah could come up with. That's when he'd turned his attention to Zoe. He and Zoe were an item for a while, but months later they split, and Zoe wouldn't talk about it afterwards. Not even with Evie.

Savannah shudders at the thought of him.

But it's four hours till showtime and she feels okay. Hasn't had a threatening text for a while, yet she's still uneasy. Anxious, she glances out of the window. Leon's place looks down on the parking lot of an off-The-Strip tavern that's seen better days. Stained stucco and fake Tudor wood trim do nothing to enhance a shabby exterior reminiscent of stale cake icing.

It's weird, she thinks, that soon she'll meet up with her so-called friends. They might as well be strangers for all they know about each other's lives now, and yet Evie's acting like it's going to be some heart-warming, fun-filled reunion for four old buddies. Savannah didn't ever want them to know she's living here, let alone dancing for a living. She had to come up with the lamest excuse for being late to the party. Said she couldn't get out of work early, so she had to catch a late plane and will join them around nine thirty in Evie's hotel suite for the rescheduled piñata fiasco.

Her head starts pounding. She messed everything up with her dumb choices. Her impulsive decisions. But that could all change if she gets the next few weeks right. She could rewrite her whole life story. Do something real and rewarding. Make a real impact. She recalls how much dance changed her outlook and she's read about inner-city programs where kids get the chance to develop their talents without having to worry about money for fees and equipment. If she does finally open her own dance studio, she vows to dedicate a good portion of her time to finding those marginalized kids and giving them the opportunities that she had to fight for.

She wanders back to the small galley kitchen, picks up sliced cucumber from the chopping board and drapes a clean sheet over Leon's armchair. Lying back, she places a slice of cucumber on each eyelid to combat the puffy, dark bags under her eyes from last night's tossing and turning. After Tia's snide comments, she can't afford to look haggard or they'll kick her out of the show before she can blink.

She drifts off and half an hour later, the apartment door slams shut. Her eyes snap open. and the cucumber slides down her cheek. It's Leon.

He strides into the room. "What the hell? Why are you wearing salad on your face?"

Savannah scratches at her cheeks, pulling off a slice of slimy cucumber. "I wasn't expecting you. What time is it?"

Leon checks his phone. "Four thirty. Why?"

Now she jumps up from her seat. "Damn, I'm going to be late for work."

He reaches out to her. Touches her face. "Keep still." He cradles her chin and picks the cucumber slice from her cheek. "You left a piece right here."

An electric jolt flickers through her body when his fingers touch her face. Standing so close to him, she senses the warmth of his skin. He's such a familiar part of her life, and yet she's never looked at him so closely. Never knew his caramel eyes are actually flecked with gold. His teeth, even and white when he smiles, his skin smooth and satiny except for the long, fine scar above his left eyebrow.

How did he get that? Who hurt him?

This sudden feeling of intimacy and vulnerability is unfamiliar. Something she's avoided for so long. A stabbing feeling that leaves her breathless, makes her body light and wispy. Something that could be blown away with one gust of a desert wind.

"You looked so cute sleeping. I didn't want to disturb you."

"You were watching me?" she says, feeling a downward pressure in her body, then a strange lightness – a fizzing, like when you pop a cork from a champagne bottle. *Give in,* she tells herself. *You can't avoid every opportunity. It's what you want.*

He takes a step closer. "You know, I like having you here."

"Sure. I clean up. And buy real food, not Cheetos and noodles. Who wouldn't like having me around?" *Why is she being so flippant? Just drop the body armor. Show yourself.*

He shakes his head. "You hum when you chew your food. You use mango body lotion. You put cinnamon in your coffee.

And you always check the light switch three times to see it's off."

She can smell his musky cologne as she steps closer. "I like being here."

She touches his arm and traces her finger down the length of it. Their eyes meet. A look of pure understanding passes between them, and then the unthinkable. The cursed phone rings with the quacking duck ringtone she reserves for Tia. *Damn that woman.* All the magic of the moment evaporates. The air conditioner suddenly rattles into action. They stand, arms at their sides, momentarily embarrassed, unsure who should make the first move. The insistent *quack-quack* forces the issue.

Savannah holds the phone up. "I'd better take this."

"Yeah – sure – sorry." Leon backs away. "I'll give you some space?"

She nods and mouths, *"See you after work."* He frowns. Obviously, he's no lip-reader. Tia's strident tones boom into her ear and Savannah blows a kiss his way and curses her for ruining the romantic moment.

DAISY

Daisy basks under a smoldering sun. Exhausted from the flight and all the anxiety of the past week, her body feels like a flower unfurling in the heat. This has been a long time coming and she damn well deserves every moment of it. The glimmering turquoise swimming pool, the swaying palm trees, the waterfall pouring down a sheer rock face (fake rock but it doesn't matter), the curved silver-glass hotel gleaming against an indigo sky, the steady music pulsing in the background, her manicured toes baking in the heat.

She deserves to be here. A little pleasure seeking is long overdue. She takes a slug of her frozen margarita. A couple more of these and her teacher days fade into an alcoholic fog. Soon the liquor spreads like a warm sedative through her bloodstream, and she can finally concentrate on the *now*. The next few days are going to be a blast.

She adjusts her headrest and closes her eyes. It's absolute bliss, this feeling that all you have to worry about is how to suck the most fun out of life. Daisy hasn't really thought of her own needs since she took Wade's hand and allowed him to lead her to the back of the frat house for the first time. He was so eager;

forty seconds was all it took for her to lose her virginity. Wade didn't think of her dreams and desires then, and never acknowledged them afterwards, but she was too blind to see the real person behind that pretty-boy façade. Too caught up with the possibility of enjoying a rosy future with a guy whose family had more money than she could ever dream of.

As she relaxes into drowsiness, her mind drifts back to the past. She thinks of what might have been if she hadn't set her sights on Wade first. What if she'd hooked up with Blair? Hearing from him again was a major surprise. After he sent her the money, she was driven to check out his Facebook page. She pulls it up again on her phone, squinting to see it clearly in the glaring sunlight.

He still reminds her of a vampire, just a paler, older one. In his more up-to-date pictures, his hair gleams too black, like shiny vinyl. His face is pallid, the skin taut as if it's just been freshly botoxed. He's a strange caricature of the good-looking twenty-three-year-old she used to know. This guy looks prematurely aged by stress or hard living. Cosmetic surgery has stretched his face into a sinister and slightly warped mask. It's weird that he never gave her a second look at college, and yet she's the first person he seeks out to do his dirty work. *Why? Is it something he sees in her? A kindred spirit perhaps?*

She scolds herself. *Quit being paranoid.* He obviously preferred fair-haired girls. That's why he went for Savannah first. The classic California blonde. All suntanned legs and sun-streaked hair. But what the hell did she do to turn him off so abruptly?

Two months after their second major wrestling tournament, and a month after their first party act, they'd become the talk of the frat houses. The Party Girls, four sexy, strong, athletic women who didn't take crap from anyone. Who thought nothing of dressing in skimpy bathing suits and rolling across a frat-house floor in sweaty wrestling holds, a circle of paying onlookers cheering them on. Evie was usually so pumped-up by the end of it, she invited guys in the audience to take her on. At first it was just a joke, wrestling with the occasional drunken loser who basically just wanted to run his hands all over a female body, but later things took a turn and got out of hand.

One night she headed outside to cool off after a frat party bout. The sky twinkled with stars and the air smelled of ocean breezes. That's when she heard an odd scream, almost like a yelp, but couldn't be sure if it was a man or woman. The bushes behind the house rustled and footsteps crunched across the gravel. Daisy pulled back behind the ornamental cedar, holding her breath as Blair emerged, holding the side of his neck, his face twisted in a murderous expression. He shoved the front door open, slamming it behind him. A few moments later, Savannah emerged, tall and pale in the moonlight. Daisy stepped into her path.

"What's up with Blair?"

At first Savannah didn't seem to hear Daisy. She blinked her eyes as if trying to focus on her surroundings. "Huh?"

"I heard a scream. Blair looked like he was in pain."

It seemed as if Savannah had suddenly realized where she was. She smiled at Daisy absently. "Oh – yeah. Some kind of insect bit him. Not sure if it was a wasp or something."

Then they'd both drifted back inside, immediately swallowed up in the noise and chatter. By the time they joined the others, Zoe was all over Blair, with her first-aid bag open, tending to Blair's bruised neck. Daisy glanced over Zoe's shoulder, shocked to see that the insect bite was actually a livid plum-sized bruise with definite teeth marks dotted around it. What the hell had Savannah done to him?

Daisy remembers realizing how much she'd underestimated Savannah, interpreting her cool remoteness as shyness when maybe it was something more dangerous.

"Long time no see," says a familiar voice.

Daisy takes off her sunglasses and looks upwards at a slim blonde woman in a white linen wrap, standing over her. She scrambles to her feet. "Zoe – babe. Let me look at you."

She studies her long-lost friend. Her features are more angular, and she can still see the cool, determined college kid underneath, but somehow the platinum-blonde waves don't square with the image of a respected pediatrician. And the brassy tint is at odds with her olive complexion.

She holds Zoe at arm's length. "You look amazing as usual, and you're actually a real doctor now. I can't get my head around it."

Zoe shrugs and giggles self-consciously. "Me too, sometimes."

Daisy leans forward in an intimate gesture. "Thanks for sending the money. You're way too generous."

"It'll be our little secret," says Zoe, settling into the beach chair beside Daisy's. "Don't give it another thought. In the meantime, I need a serious drink."

"I'm onto it," says Daisy, waving at the waiter, a tanned young twentyish kid in a white T-shirt and skimpy shorts.

His eyes shine blue as the pool, and Daisy feels a slight giddiness. He can't be much older than some of her twelfth graders.

"I'll have a mojito. Extra lime," says Zoe. Her wedding and engagement rings flash like rainbow fire. Daisy makes a mental note to ask more questions about her husband, but she'll wait until they're all together so they can enjoy each other's news at the same time.

"Another margarita for me," says Daisy, giving him a wink.

Zoe hands the guy a fifty-dollar bill. "That's for you," she says, beckoning him closer. He grins and leans in towards her. Daisy's mouth drops open as Zoe strains upwards, cups his ear and whispers something to him. He pulls back laughing, exposing even, white teeth. *He's a child and she's a pediatrician. Damn. What's she up to?*

Zoe leans back against the headrest and catches Daisy's eye. "What are you staring at?"

"Did you just proposition that kid?"

Zoe's brows knit. "What do you think I am? A pervert?"

Daisy shrugs. Maybe she misread the situation, but then Zoe was always the one to jump in and take advantage of a situation. Like the time she zoned in on Blair after he moved on from Savannah. Daisy never stood a chance once Zoe impressed him with her med school ambitions and her glowing academic record.

The guy is back in no time with the drinks. As he hands Zoe hers, he winks. Zoe holds the glass up and chugs back half of it. He disappears among the crowds at the poolside. After a minute or so of silence Zoe puts her empty glass down and checks her phone.

"When are we meeting Evie?"

"Around nine thirty. But we can go earlier. She said she'd call when she arrives. The piñata event is happening in her suite."

Zoe rolls her eyes. "Trust Evie to come up with something so tasteless."

Daisy tries not to react. *Zoe's still doing her hoity-toity act.* "I think it's kind of funny. I for one will be the first one to smack that paper dick."

"You off men?"

Daisy's head feels light. The heat and the liquor are working too fast. She needs to eat. "We'll have that conversation later over drinks."

Zoe pulls herself out of the chair. "Well, I'm gonna take a walk. I need to clear my head and make a few important calls. Then I'll take a long, luxurious bath."

Daisy's bubble of hope suddenly pops like an overinflated balloon. Why is Zoe leaving her so soon? "You're going for a walk in this heat?"

Zoe seems distracted. She's scanning the bodies around the pool. Is she bored already? "Maybe just a little wander. Pick up a smoothie or something."

Daisy perks up. "I could come with you."

She swears Zoe's mouth flinches. "No – no. You look so – so settled. We'll hook up later when Evie's here."

It feels like someone's poured cold water over her head. "Okay. Sure," is all she can manage.

Zoe looks down at her with the patronizing look that always pissed Daisy off. "Hey, I forgot to say how stunning you look. You haven't changed."

"Really?" says Daisy.

"I mean it. You're sooo lucky. Catch you later, hun."

And Zoe is gone in an instant, her expensive linen wrap fluttering around her toned calves. Daisy sits back, hurt and indignant. She was always the meek little sidekick, desperate for any crumb of attention from her arrogant and self-absorbed friends. And now Zoe's just passed up on spending an afternoon with her, for a swift hookup with a college boy.

Then she remembers the money in the safe, back in the room. The thick wad of bills in her wallet, the positive balance in her checking account. In her entire life she's never had this much money to splurge on herself. Maybe it's time for a little more extravagance. She catches the eye of a young female waiter.

"Where's the nearest shopping mall?"

The girl is stylish with a diamond piercing in her nose. "Depends what you're looking for."

"Clothes. Hair salons. That type of thing."

The girl sucks her lower lip and looks Daisy over. "Well, there's the Forum shops in Caesars Palace, but that's high-end designer stuff. Versace, Gucci and all that. Minimum thousand bucks for a purse."

Daisy shakes her head. "Won't do. Where else?"

"There's the Miracle Mile Shops at Planet Hollywood. Prices are reasonable and it's a fun place not too far away on the other side of the Strip. You can walk it. You'll be there in five minutes."

Daisy gathers up her towel. Now that Zoe's dumped her and left her with a whole lot of spare time, she'll have no problem spending a good chunk of money on a full facial and makeup, hairdo and some nicer clothes than the junk she packed in a hurry. She'll show them who can still turn heads. She doesn't need to pay for the attention of some wet-eared pool boy.

No siree. Her sights are aimed way, way higher.

ZOE

Zoe checks her phone again. Nothing from Marcus. Maybe he hasn't come across her note yet.

She placed it on his bedside table propped against the touch lamp, minutes before leaving for the airport. Now she admonishes herself for being so careless. Marcus has the attention span of a second-grader when he's high. Barely aware of his surroundings, he often flops onto the bed fully-clothed. One flip of the duvet and that envelope will flutter to the floor and probably end up gathering dust under their king-sized bed.

Nothing is going her way. The flight was bumpy, her nerves in tatters by the time she landed in this godforsaken city that feels like the interior of a raging furnace. She has zero interest in meeting the so-called friends she left behind so many years ago and she's banished that version of herself to the trash can of the past, along with all the other garbage memories of her early days.

She hurries through the crowds of bikini-clad bodies, away from the poolside chaos. Why was Daisy acting so weird just now? Watching her every move. *God*, it was definitely more than a bit creepy to feel Daisy's eyes glued on her the whole time they were sitting there.

She remembers Daisy as the cutest, most vivacious and bubbly member of their tight-knit group, but she always had the worst luck when it came to men. She still has the big, trusting eyes that lured all the guys to her initially, but then they'd back off just as quickly. Zoe never understood why. With that pale dewy skin and incredible blue-black hair, she looked like Snow White in the flesh. Is it even natural? And if she's as broke as she claims, how can she afford the regular color appointments? Even a millimeter of gray roots screams out from hair that dark. And Zoe knows about the cost of keeping up appearances. Her bottle-blonde hair sucks up more money than she could ever have imagined, but all that will change once she's on her own again and goes back to her natural chestnut color.

Now the heat is so intense her lips are parched. She pushes the glass doors open and falls into the air-conditioned interior where she can think clearly. The white band of skin on Daisy's ring finger shows how quick she was to rip off her wedding ring. Not surprising from what Zoe remembers of Wade. A sweet but ineffectual guy who thought his angelic face and curly blond locks were his passport to rock star fame. Too bad he lost himself in drug-induced dreams of stardom, rather than doing the hard work needed to make it big in the music business. And then there was the whole uproar around grad when Wade's parents disinherited him after learning he'd gotten Daisy pregnant and was going to marry her. Nobody knew exactly how that went down, and Daisy wouldn't say a word about it afterwards.

Looks like Daisy's damage is more emotional. Zoe detected a hint of anxiety and paranoia behind that sweet, agreeable exterior. And she basically accused Zoe of going off for a quick fling behind the change huts with that adolescent pool boy.

What the hell does she take *Dr.* Zoe Ryan for? A cradle-robber? She'll feel like crap when he delivers the pineapple smoothie and antipasto plate Zoe arranged as a surprise. She'd wasted half an hour listening to Daisy's gurgling stomach but had no appetite herself, and certainly had no intention of watching Daisy eat. Instead, she needed some alone time to figure a few things out. Like when she should transfer the down payment for the condo, and how best to respond to Marcus when he realizes they're through.

She pads through the marble-floored pool lobby, welcoming the air-conditioned comfort and thinking that Daisy must have had some hard knocks in her life to always assume the worst of everyone. But there was always something so vulnerable about her that made her a natural victim. Evie spotted it when they first met. That's why she always treated Daisy like her little puppy. Kept her close, gave her some leeway but yanked the leash tightly if she got out of line. And Daisy never forgot who was in charge.

She stops dead at the casino door as a sudden realization hits her. *Here they all are again, dropping everything to answer Evie's call.* Sixteen years later, now she's a successful, well-respected doctor, she's still letting Evie call the shots.

That thought is enough to send her stomping through the hotel looking for the front doors that let onto the Strip. Of course, as in every Vegas hotel, you have to pass through the clinking circus of slot machines to find the exit. Maybe she'll have a little flutter later at the craps or roulette table, but maybe not. Throwing money away is not something she takes delight in. She knows how hard she's worked to acquire wealth and how devastating life is without it.

Finally, the front doors are visible. Carefully hidden so you could be lost for days in the labyrinth of the casino. Outside, a belt of heat slaps her in the face. How can anyone survive here in the summer? It's so hot you could scramble eggs on the sidewalk.

A continuous parade of taxis drives up, drops off passengers and luggage, then drives on to pick up the next group of tourists. She looks around. Where else but Vegas can you find a fake Eiffel Tower and an imitation Statue of Liberty as well as a stucco replica of a Venetian palazzo complete with faux canals, and gondoliers from places like Wyoming or Ohio? It's all so vulgar when you compare it to the real thing. These poor suckers arriving by the carful have probably never walked along the Seine River, stood at the top of the Eiffel Tower or crossed the Rialto Bridge in Venice. Suddenly she feels a restlessness, a sense that coming here was the worst idea possible. She's still carrying the baggage of the past – all the worry that's holding her back.

Just then, her phone *pings* with a message. It's Evie. When the hell is she going to show her face?

> On a secret mission in Old Vegas to find just the right décor for the suite. You wouldn't believe the tacky costume and curio shops here. Meet me in the penthouse suite at 9.30pm.

That's almost six hours away. What on earth are they going to do until then? And besides, she's determined to arrive late, just to show Evie she's not calling the shots anymore. Savannah will be late too, but then that's to be expected. Evie always found it difficult to manipulate Savannah. But all this subterfuge is typical Evie. She thrives on drama. Sneaking around like a secret agent on some undercover mission. Some people never change.

The heat outside is so unbearable, Zoe ducks back into the hotel. A nearby bar advertises frozen slushy drinks. She sits at the counter, orders a mega mango peach drink and cools her hands on the frosted glass. Thinks back to college.

The first Christmas holidays the four of them stayed behind in La Jolla while everyone else went home to enjoy warm, snuggly family time around lavishly decorated Christmas trees.

They'd been hanging out in Daisy's room trying to figure out The Party Girls' official rules. So far they'd only come up with party hard, never snitch on a friend no matter what and avoid commitment.

She was lounging on the beat-up sofa painting her nails, Savannah sat cross-legged on the floor, eating a bowl of macaroni, while Daisy and Evie sprawled on the bed sharing a bag of Doritos. Evie came up with the great idea of competing to see who had the most extreme Christmas from hell story.

Savannah went first. "Last Christmas I spent the entire holiday watching my mom bawl her eyes out, while she drank herself into a stupor and rambled on about Christmases spent with my dad. Then she passed out with a lit cigarette in her hand and set her bed on fire. I had to call 911 and they hosed the bed down. I'm never going back. I've made the break. She can burn the house down for all I care."

"Good on you," said Evie. "She'll suck the damn life out of you if you give her the chance. Drag you down into her misery. I know all about that."

Zoe paused her painting. "My dad is working nights the entire holiday. Says he needs the overtime money to help with my college fees."

"Don't you feel the least bit guilty that he's working his fingers to the bone and you're not going to be there to at least do some shopping or cook a couple of meals for him?" said Savannah.

"I could say the same for you, Sav," said Zoe. "Couldn't you be there to support your poor, lonely alkie of a mother? Don't lay the guilt trip on me. My dad actually prefers working than spending time with me. Besides, he's got his buddies and his bowling league."

"My mom's doing a whole week of mud wrestling. No way I want to be part of that spectacle," said Evie, rolling across the bed and pinning Daisy's head in a scissor hold.

"Fuck you, Evie. I just put my eyelashes on," screamed Daisy, squirming to get away.

"I taught you how to break the hold just last week," said Evie. "Try harder."

"Okay, you asked for it," said Daisy with a groan as she flipped her legs around and kicked Evie square in the gut. Evie let go of Daisy's neck and collapsed into herself with a guttural gasp, her arms wrapped around her belly, while Daisy rolled astride her and pinned her down. Sav and Zoe watched in horrified silence as Evie groaned and writhed. Daisy's face went sheet white. She rolled off the bed into a standing position. "You told me to try harder. That's what I did."

Evie held herself and moaned for a long moment, then suddenly burst out into peals of laughter. Everyone's shoulders slumped with relief.

"Had you guys going there, didn't I?" She sat up, a wide grin plastered across her sweaty reddened face, but when she went to stand up, Savannah noticed the hint of a grimace. Daisy had actually hurt her. Evie, their unofficial tough-ass leader, had received a shit-kicking at the hands of someone she considered less skilled than her. Evie wouldn't forget this, even though she *acted like it was nothing at the time. Things between Evie and Daisy became strained after that, only getting worse with the whole Wade debacle.*

The sound of a text shakes her from her daydream. *Damn. It's Marcus.* Sweat drips down the back of her neck. The stink of gas from the departing cabs makes her nauseous. She forces herself to read it.

> The hell you're leaving me. I'll be on the first plane to Vegas tomorrow. Our love is too precious to throw away.

Damn. Damn. Why did she leave the letter in such a prominent place? And does he know where she's staying? *Yes.* She used their joint credit card without thinking. Maybe she can go back to the check-in desk and get them to move the deposit charge to her own personal card. Suddenly she's in dire need of another drink. Maybe she'll spend the entire weekend drunk.

She types a response.

> Don't bother coming here. It's over. Call my lawyer.

Now she has to call Phyllis again. At this rate she'll be holed up in her room the whole weekend conducting business. Another text comes through.

> You are one cold-hearted BITCH.

She won't dignify that insult with a response. She'll go to the lobby, change her billing info, get a long, cool drink at the bar and talk to Phyllis. She'll know what to do. She glances along the snaking thoroughfare of the Strip, now backed up with cars and buses and the occasional brave cyclist. The glittering hotels shimmer and waver like hallucinations in the heat. How is she going to get through this crappy weekend without going crazy, and what exactly does Evie have in store for them?

SAVANNAH

Savannah stands at the crosswalk and taps her feet, waiting for the *walk* signal. This isn't the usual way she comes to work but there's nothing normal about today. Her stomach is in turmoil.

She allows herself to run over the events of the previous hour. The mind-bending discovery that Leon has feelings for her. She couldn't have misread the signs. The way he looked at her as if he really *sees her*. She's never met a man so tender and gentle. Maybe he's been crazy about her since the first time she sat at his bar and ordered peach schnapps and soda. Also, she loves that he's never come on too strong. That kind of sensitivity is rare. It's like he understands instinctively that she's been hurt before, even if she's never spelled it out to him.

She was relieved when he told her he's actually thirty-one and not twenty-seven as she'd thought. Still a little younger than she'd like, but not enough of a gap that she feels like a cradle-robber. He'd wanted to walk her over to the theater but she insisted she'd be okay as long as she took the busy way to work. At first, he wouldn't take no for an answer, but when a call came in for an extra side job, he took back the offer.

"Gotta pay my college fees next week, so I need all the cash I can get. These little gigs come in handy."

Now the prospect of spending the entire evening away from him with a bunch of women who might as well be strangers seems terrifying. And the thought of reliving those screwed-up years of college makes her feel physically sick. She's not that person anymore. Why can't Evie accept that and just move on with her life? Make a fresh start now that she's escaped the clutches of a man like Blair.

She remembers Evie's text. *I'm counting on you, and you know why.*

For what? Does she have something new to tell them? Or has she found something else out? Something that she's tried to run from all these years.

The white *walk* light flashes and she's carried along with the swarm of tourists crossing the street, away from the dancing fountains of the Bellagio and towards the bustling shops, restaurants and nightlife of Planet Hollywood. Normally she gets to the theater through a side door situated in an alley that runs by the side of the hotel. But bad people lurk in alleys, and she doesn't want to take unnecessary risks, especially now she's found a new reason to be hopeful about her life.

The glass doors swish open onto the shiny black floors of the Miracle Mile Shops. Her theater is situated in the center of the mall, by the town square with its chlorinated fountains, fake cobblestones and painted-on sky. The place is bustling. Tourists driven inside by the blistering heat find respite inside the air-conditioned corridors lined with stores and restaurants. She passes by a lingerie store and suddenly feels the urge to slip in and buy something cute for later. Sorting through the rows of frothy little numbers, she decides on a black-and-nude-lace body suit trimmed with peach bows, then throws in a couple of lacy thongs in sea green and lilac. She hopes her face isn't flushed as she hands the sales clerk her credit card and opts for the plain brown bag instead of the shiny black-and-pink one.

"For the environment," she explains, trying not to blink too hard. Truth is, taking that brightly colored bag into the dressing room would invite a barrage of unwanted questions from the other dancers, and she's never been the chatty type that bares all her secrets to just anyone.

Evie and the others always regarded her as a bit of a mystery, pressing her to open up about her loneliness. But she'd just clam up and shoot them a look that dared them to keep asking. Evie usually gave up and moved on to Daisy, who was an easier target. That way, Savannah earned a kind of mystique, which she's not about to let go of tonight. She won't give anything away except some basic, mostly fabricated information about herself.

Unless she's forced to...

"We'll throw in some sexy body spray as a bonus," chirps the sales clerk. Savannah blinks back to the bright reality of the store. What was she thinking of? Telling all? No way. She turns to leave as a dark-haired woman in an indigo T-shirt and shorts stops by a rack of velour loungewear nearby.

Instinctively, Savannah falls back behind a tall rack of silk robes. The woman moves on to a display case of lacy lingerie, handling the flimsy pieces as if she's never seen such pretty clothing in a long time. Savannah takes in the pale skin and deep-blue eyes. *It has to be Daisy and God, she hasn't changed a bit.* Still stunning in her Disney princess way.

For a moment she's tempted to step forward and surprise her, but her body freezes. Daisy's bound to ask what she's doing here. She'll insist they chum along together and go for cocktails and Savannah won't be able to get to work. Daisy always had severe FOMO. Never wanted to be left out of any social event. But even if she slips out without Daisy seeing her, what's to stop her taking in a show at the conveniently close theater nearby, where Savannah will be strutting her stuff in about an hour? Daisy has hours to spare before Evie's party starts. Now she'll have to worry about her finding out about the dancing gig and blabbing to the others about how the ambitious scientist is now a Vegas showgirl.

Now she'll have to wear extra-thick stage makeup and be on the lookout for Daisy in the audience. That kind of preoccupation is bound to interfere with her concentration and cause her to mess up one of the routines. *Damn.* This entire weekend is going to be a gong show. She wishes she could just hole up in Leon's apartment and spend the next couple of days getting to know him better, but he has to work. The weekend's his busiest time.

Daisy moves on to a pink gingham bra and pantie set trimmed with lace. She's trying the wholesome girl-next-door look. She was always a chameleon. Changing her look to suit the guy or the situation. How can she forget the evening Daisy basically stole Wade from under Evie's nose? Evie never forgave her for that, and maybe she'll bring it up tonight. Who knows and *who cares?*

Finally, she tears herself away and turns to slip out of the store, but not before glancing back at Daisy who's frowning and tapping something frantically into her phone.

She's just about to leave when her phone *pings* with a new message. Is it Evie, changing the arrangements yet again? Or Leon asking what time he'll see her tonight? She checks her phone and her heart almost stops. There's just one cryptic line.

> Are you having fun yet? Just wait until later. C.

She pulls back against the doorway, heartbeat echoing in her skull. Checks back at Daisy now studying her phone.

Is Daisy sending these messages? How can that be possible? Maybe she was texting someone else at the same time. Was it just a coincidence?

For certain it can't be C.

Because C or Cal is dead. Has been for a long time.

DAISY

Daisy stashes her phone into her pocket. *Damn the real estate agent* trying to lowball her with a lousy offer for the house. She told him to hold out for offers over the asking price. She can wait it out, now she's got some money and plans to make a fresh start here. All she can see ahead is a rosy future. And it begins right here at Planet Hollywood, in the Miracle Mile Shops.

She needs a total change of attitude. No more guilt and paranoia. She has to start taking a few risks. Be more assertive. When the pool guy stepped up with that incredible antipasto plate and the iced smoothie, she nearly tripped over her lounger, amazed at Zoe's generosity. Life is now about taking what's owed to her. Wade tried to crush all that with his self-centeredness and total lack of drive.

But now that she's seen the gorgeous Tuscan grandeur of the Bellagio and its dancing fountains, taken in the curved glass-and-steel façade of the Aria, the massive leaning towers of CityCenter and the Vdara, she feels like she's in a dreamworld. And for the first time in her life, she can buy whatever she wants. She's done without for so long. Survived by clipping coupons, paying the minimum credit card payment with overdraft funds, and putting her own dreams aside so Wade can realize his. Things are going to change, big time. She'll suck every moment of excitement from the weekend, and she's got a few hours to kill until 9.30, according to Evie's last message.

Heaven knows where Zoe went after the pool. She was so restless and fidgety. Couldn't seem to settle, and was way too preoccupied to chat about anything. Is that how the whole weekend is going to be? Everyone immersed in their own secret agendas, too caught up with their own problems to let loose and have fun? Well, Daisy's done with looking back. Wade still hasn't contacted her so he's as good as gone from her life.

To get things started, she buys a pink lace bra and panties set and three silky thongs. Feeling a rush of euphoria, she steps out into the hallway. It's so Hollywood glam. Glossy, black-tiled floors, black granite walls shot with fuchsia pink – lined with boutiques and restaurants. Quaint patios and real fountains. All buzzing with activity. A world away from the blank cream walls of the classroom. She could live here. She'd even get used to the street hawkers passing out call-girl and escort ads. She's missed out on all the laughter, fun and people. Hordes of them all united in the search for pleasure and entertainment. And plenty of guys. Cute, smiling and available.

She stops at a nearby salon – *Society Hair and Makeup*, takes a deep breath and steps inside. Five minutes later she's installed in a seat in front of a long mirror as master stylist Alain sifts through her choppy layers.

"Someone's done a real knife and fork job on you, luv," he says in a strong British accent. "Shame really. You've got great hair. Lots of body and a natural wave. And that face. Angelic."

"Can you do something?"

"Do something? I'm a hair artist. I don't just cut hair, I transform it. I can make those waves dance. See, I work with your hair, not against it. Do you trust me?"

She checks out his reflection. At the shaved sides of his head and the three tight braids stretched across the top of his scalp. At the cascade of roses and parrots tattooed on his arms. The metal rod piercing his septum.

"Do I trust you? I guess so."

"Then you're a bloody bad judge of character," he says, grinning and revealing a row of gold fillings. Seeing them triggers an unpleasant memory. Wade had some shady friends. Junkies who would've mugged Alain and extracted those teeth just to buy more crank. She shudders. What if Wade has actually gone off with those guys again? He never really kicked his college drug habit. Kept it under wraps when Ethan was a baby, then started dabbling in some small trafficking operations when the money was low and he was desperate. *Damn him.* He ruined her life. She should've gone all out for Blair or Cal instead, but Cal decided to turn against her.

Alain taps her shoulder. "You're frowning, luv. Quickest way to get wrinkles. Just close your eyes and relax. Forget all your worries, or as my old gran used to say, *'Pack up your troubles in your old kit bag and smile, smile, smile!'*"

Fifty-five minutes later. After she's watched Alain's arms fly around like windmill blades with scissors attached, he turns her chair towards the mirror for the great reveal. She gasps in awe. He's transformed her stringy black hair into a shiny, bouncy chin-length bob complete with bangs that frame her face, enhancing the drama of her milky skin.

Alain pats and primps the hair. "It's stunning. Very Art Deco. Very Gatsby."

"That's my favorite novel." She can barely breathe, let alone get the words out. Now she really is Daisy Buchanan, but who is her Jay Gatsby? Definitely not Wade.

"So, Ayesha will do your makeup. Something smoky and glam. Then you need to go shopping. *Old Navy* just won't cut it." He plucks the shoulders of her plain blue T-shirt. "Don't worry. I'll tell you where to go."

Ayesha is a magician with the makeup brushes, so Daisy feels like an Egyptian queen when she leaves the beauty salon. She keeps glancing into mirrors to check out her sultry, smoky eyes as she heads off to the stores Alain recommended. She hasn't owned any fancy clothes since her wedding. Plain sweatshirts and stretchy black pants have been her go-to outfit for years.

The sales clerks are all over her in the first store, handing over armfuls of slinky dresses, flimsy camisoles, floaty pants and fancy shoes that make her look five inches taller. She drops a thousand bucks and stumbles out from the store, heart racing at her extravagance. She could definitely get used to this type of lifestyle. She clutches the bags and floats through the mall, the crowds blurring around her until someone catches her shoulder, knocking the wind out of her.

She turns to the sound of a familiar voice. A tall man with dyed black hair and tight, pallid skin stands, gawping at her. "Daisy?"

"Blair?"

She's not sure whether to smile or cry. Time can be so cruel. He's utterly changed.

He rests a hand on her shoulder and smiles, a blinding white, porcelain-tipped smile. "Fancy a drink? We have a few things to talk over."

"Uh... okay," she says, suddenly conscious of the fistful of bags she's holding on to, the swag that his money has paid for.

"Great," he says, steering her in the direction of the darkened lobby cocktail bar. "It's so good to see you."

ZOE

Zoe hides in a shady corner of the Liquid Pool Lounge sipping a frozen smoothie. Passion fruit and guava blended with a heavy shot of tequila, and tasting so smooth she's quickly into her second drink. Soon all her worries about Marcus dissolve away into a warm, fuzzy haze, and the buzz of alcohol motivates her to scroll through interior décor websites to find the perfect look for her new lakeside condo.

She could take inspiration from the hotel and go for clean lines, cream tones and vivid splashes of turquoise and yellow. Or she could stay understated and neutral with gray, silver, and cream with dark wood finishes. She's just considering the idea of installing a Brazilian wood bar, when a cute fortyish guy in a black polo shirt emblazoned with a dolphin logo cuts across her line of vision. He stops at the bar. The bartender raises a hand in greeting and fills two giant glasses with ice, then tops them up with plain water. The dolphin guy takes them and gives a thumbs-up. As he turns to go, he catches Zoe's eye. His tanned face switches quickly into a smile as he approaches her. Up close, his blue eyes are intelligent, ringed with white, most likely from wearing sunglasses or swimming goggles, and his hair is a tangle of damp, dark ringlets.

Zoe decides at that exact moment she feels a certain connection with him. It could be the alcohol skewing her judgment, intensifying her senses, but this is Vegas. People act impulsively here. They seize the moment.

She returns his smile. "Do you work with dolphins?"

He grins. "Guess the logo is a dead giveaway."

"It sure caught my attention," she says, thinking maybe his broad swimmer's shoulders and stacked pecs are pretty easy on the eyes as well.

He puts down the drinks and reaches out a hand. "Dr. Zack Costa, marine biologist. I'm here for a convention on the conservation of larger aquatic species. Dolphins are my specialty."

"So cool. I'd love to see one up close."

He taps his foot on the ground. "Might be tough to set that up in the middle of Vegas, but hey, I can sure as hell tell you a lot about them."

"It sounds intriguing. You know, I actually did an in-depth study of marine mammals in my sophomore year."

"Are you a scientist?"

She shakes her head and sips the last inch of smoothie. "I'm a doctor. A pediatrician."

He whistles through well-shaped lips and reaches a hand out. "Wow. Impressive. Pleased to meet you, Dr...?"

"Zoe. Zoe Ryan."

"Dr. Zack and Dr. Zoe. Sounds like a great handle for a TV show."

He holds on to her hand, and her gaze. She hasn't felt that warm, squishy feeling in years. "We'd deal with kids and animals."

"Now that's an original concept." He laughs, revealing even, white teeth. "How long are you staying here?"

"Maybe until Monday."

"Why don't you come and look at some of our exhibits tomorrow? I'll fill you in on our projects."

She's about to ask him what he's doing tonight but remembers Evie and the party. "That would be great. What time?"

"Sessions start at nine. There's a break at twelve. But you probably won't be up anywhere near that time after a Vegas Friday night."

She tilts her head. Why is she slipping into this coy, girly mode? She's a respected doctor. She straightens her shoulders. "You could be right, but I'll make a point of taking a walk over as soon as I get my head straight with a coffee."

"We're in the section that overlooks the T-Mobile Arena. Massive glass walls and lots of greenery." He stands for a few moments longer watching her. "I know it sounds cheesy, but I feel like I've met you somewhere before."

"I get that a lot. It's a doctor thing."

He takes a deep breath, and picks up the water glasses. "Gotta get back to base camp. See you tomorrow, Dr. Zoe."

"For sure, Dr. Zack."

He nods and strides away. Zoe can't wipe the grin from her face. She has a date for tomorrow with someone who actually excites her. Someone with a working brain in their head. Someone that won't look baffled when she tries to discuss scientific discoveries, or the complexities of a puzzling diagnosis. That feeling of anticipation will be enough to carry her through Evie's childish games tonight.

She glances at her phone. It's just past seven. She needs to eat before she gets too wasted and makes a fool of herself propositioning more eligible guys. And Daisy's probably wondering where she is. She sends a text.

> Are you in your room?

There's no response so she checks out the menu and orders a seafood taco to go. Might as well have a good, long soak in the tub before getting ready. Two minutes later Daisy responds.

> I'm out. At an amazing show. It'll be over at eight thirty. I ran into an old friend.

> Who?

> Just someone from home. Gotta go. I'm getting dirty looks.

Zoe's a bit stunned that Daisy went off and didn't mention anything about going to a show. Maybe she'd have liked to go as well, but then she wouldn't have met Dr. Zack and besides, she's the one who ran out on Daisy and left her sitting by the pool alone.

It's probably one of those lame ventriloquist or Motown tribute shows. Not something Zoe would've been interested in anyway. Daisy is so easily pleased. Not surprising after spending almost twenty years with Wade. She wonders how many crappy bars Daisy schlepped around, watching him from the sidelines, sipping on warm beer while Wade did his frontman thing. And then later, when she couldn't get to the gigs, sitting at home with a screaming baby, wondering if Wade was making the moves on some starstruck teen girl looking to get a leg up into the business.

Zoe thinks about all the gala dinners she's attended. All the opera, ballet and theater opening nights. On the red carpet at TIFF, mingling with the stars. All strictly black tie and evening gown events. Being with Marcus was good for climbing up the social ladder, even if he could barely converse about anything but stock prices and mutual funds.

Feeling an unfamiliar surge of empathy, Zoe quickly types a message:

> Have fun. See you around nine.

> Will do. Not far away. Just at Planet Hollywood.

Daisy's two-facedness always bothered her. Most of the time she acted like butter wouldn't melt in her mouth, but all through college, she was dealing drugs on the side. Small-time stuff but she was definitely the one who got Wade involved. First, smoking weed, then lines of coke at parties, and slipping him some E at concerts. Zoe remembers Wade as a mommy's boy in need of protection. And yet Daisy is still acting the innocent, probably claiming Wade ruined her life when maybe she was most likely the one who corrupted him. There's a side to Daisy that Zoe suspects they never saw. Right now, it's a gut feeling, but it's also one of the reasons she never wanted to stay in touch with any of her college buddies, especially Daisy.

She shudders. More importantly, what does Evie want to tell them? *Why has she brought them all together?*

"One seafood taco coming up." The bartender's voice cuts into her thoughts.

"Oh – er – thanks." She takes the plastic basket with the paper-covered taco inside. A warm bath beckons as she hurries out from the bar and across the pool deck towards the hotel and the elevators. Once inside the air-conditioned back lobby, she feels a sudden relief. Of course, it was the heat and alcohol that made her panic. The elevator door opens and she steps inside, reassuring herself that everything will be okay this weekend.

That their secret is safe and Zoe can get back to her fabulous new condo and restart her life.

But then a fresh burst of resentment grips her. Why the hell did they all come running to spend the weekend with Evie? Why are they still under her spell?

Suddenly the divorce party seems like just another one of Evie's sick jokes. Why reunite three ex-friends who have so many good reasons to stay away from each other?

The elevator door swishes open onto the empty corridor. The silence is almost electric. Zoe checks both ways to see that no one is around. She feels sick about the upcoming night and wonders exactly what Evie has in store for them, and she vows that, if she makes it to the morning, she'll spend the rest of the weekend with Dr. Zack, the marine biologist, talking about dolphin habitat and migration patterns.

At least there's something safe and comforting in the certainty of animal science, unlike the fickleness and unpredictability of the human psyche.

SAVANNAH

Savannah collapses into her chair and checks out her reflection in the dressing-room mirror. She's ridiculous. Makeup slathered on so thick she looks like a sad clown, her pathetic attempt to disguise herself in case Daisy showed up to her performance. Muddy mascara tears stream down her cheeks, forming sulky lines at the corner of her lips. Too bad the plan backfired and the spotlight landed on her.

The other girls file in, throwing bewildered looks her way before they lift off heavy headdresses, remove candelabra earrings and kick off their shoes. No one says a thing. Savannah knows they'll leave it to Tia.

A sudden flurry of footsteps tells her she won't have to wait long for the fallout. Tia arrives at her side, eyes blazing, hands clamped on her hips.

"What the hell were you doing out there? You almost tripped Regine up. You know how much distance to keep between yourself and the next girl. And your head was down the whole time, when you know our number one rule is to *face your audience with a radiant smile*. Instead, you were trying to hide behind the scenery which, incidentally, you blundered through like a rampaging elephant. You sure the cops aren't after you?"

Savannah stays silent. It's all true. She knocked down a potted palm when she tried to slip behind it, then tripped over the base of the plaster pedestal when she tried to put it together again. That sent her hurtling into a glittering candelabra which, fortunately was lit with electric candles, otherwise she would have literally set the house on fire. On a positive note, the audience thought it was all part of the act. She'd never heard so much laughing and cheering in all the time she'd worked there. She bows her head. "Can I speak to you in private?"

"I guess so. Just wipe that junk off your face first." Tia turns to go, then swivels on one heel. "And that's another thing. Go easy on the makeup. This is a glamor show. But then you already knew that."

She flounces off, leaving a trail of lavender and sage perfume in her wake. Regine pats Savannah on the shoulder. "No hard feelings, Sav. You're just having a bad night."

Savannah looks up. "Thanks, babe. Bad isn't exactly the word I'd choose. How about disastrous?"

"Hey, I thought it was cute. The audience loved it. Maybe we should add some slapstick to our show. Lighten up and stop being so tight-assed about everything."

"I don't think Tia's up to any new choreography ideas right now. Especially from me."

"Maybe some other time then. Go have a drink and spend some quality time with that cute guy you've been seeing."

"How do you know about him?"

"Saw some tall hunk of a guy walk you to the stage door the other night. Must say, you got good taste."

"He's the best thing in my life right now."

"Hold on to him, girl, or someone's gonna steal him right from under your nose."

Savannah stands up and hugs her. "Thanks, babe. But I'd better see Tia first."

"Don't let that wannabe princess boss you around. I knew her when she was dancing topless at the Flamingo burlesque show. She thinks she's above all of us now. Maybe you'd better remind her about that."

"Cheers, Regine. You're a good friend."

She high-fives her and sits down to wipe the last of the makeup off.

On the way to Tia's office the phone *pings* with another message. *Damn, it's Daisy.*

> Was that really you, Sav? You were amazing. And so funny. Didn't know you were a comedian as well as a dancer. Waiting to see you at stage door.

So that glamorous babe in the audience was Daisy. Even in the glare of the footlights, Savannah couldn't mistake the glossy black hair and the porcelain skin.

God, she can't go on pretending she doesn't work here in Vegas, so she might as well come clean and tell the truth. This game is way too stressful. But something nags at her. The last message from her stalker coinciding with Daisy texting in the lingerie store. What's Daisy really up to? Did she already know Savannah was working at the theater and showed up to let her know it's not a secret anymore? And what has Daisy really been up to since she left college?

She's not looking forward to seeing her in person. She was always one to take rejection personally. A vindictive streak ran like a jagged fault line under that perfectly sweet and innocent exterior.

She remembers Daisy's little drug sideline, and how swiftly she dealt with the late-payers, planting drugs where they'd be found in routine drug checks. She got more than a few kids kicked out of college. But then they were all desperate at that time. Savannah with her chronic shoplifting and Zoe with her sugar daddy compulsion.

And then there was Daisy's dogged and deliberate pursual of Wade, who was Evie's friend first. Daisy craved attention. A stand-out, pretty girl who just couldn't resist the urge to bat her eyelashes and wiggle her shapely behind until the guys came running. Cal was her first target, but he wasn't into her. Afterwards she set her sights on Wade.

At the time, Daisy had a thing for Shakira. Loved the way she danced. Even begged Savannah to teach her Shakira's signature champeta-style belly dance, but Daisy's body was stiff and awkward. Nothing worked. She'd just watch Savannah roll her hips in the sexy, fluid motion that came natural to her, then storm out of the room, tears pouring down her face.

But Daisy pulled out all the stops the night of Wade's concert. Styled her long dark hair in tousled waves, wore a tiny, handkerchief-sized top that barely covered her boobs, and a pair of skin-tight jeans topped with a gold chain belt. She'd even sprinkled glitter powder over all her exposed midriff, shoulders and cleavage. Too bad Evie decided to go casual – plain denim shirt and jeans. No match for Daisy's glitzy nymphet look.

Daisy sparkled in that room. Wade couldn't keep his eyes off her. She even pulled off some decent hip-wiggling in the process. Savannah and Zoe watched from the sidelines as Daisy wrapped her web of magic around him, shutting out Evie who'd thought Daisy, her loyal sidekick, would never, ever double-cross her.

But maybe after all that's happened to her since then, she's changed. Grown up, matured, become more empathetic.

Maybe they all have.

Savannah chews her lower lip. Can you really reinvent yourself? Or is it impossible to leave behind the person you used to be? Is it still there, at the core of your being? Immovable and unchangeable.

She types a response.

> See you outside in fifteen. I'll explain everything.

Daisy responds immediately.

> Can't wait to hear about it. See you soon.

She ducks into Tia's office. Tia's sitting cross-legged in her leather swivel chair holding her chin in her hands. She has a scared, defeated look on her face. As if she's had bad news.

"You wanted to talk to me?"

It takes a moment for Tia to register Savannah standing at the door. She finally looks up, her eyes moist with tears, her hair disheveled. She waves a hand dismissively.

"Forget it. Everyone's entitled to a bad night. Just go home and rest, Sav."

Savannah steps forward. "Are you okay?"

She shrugs. "Ever get lost in a relationship that turns out to be just a charade?"

"I haven't had much luck when it comes to love. Guess I'm too gullible. Always believe the best of people, guys included."

Tia scrapes shiny ringlets back from her forehead. "Well, that's me for sure. I'm a sucker for any guy that tells me I'm beautiful. You probably think I'm entitled – superficial, and you'd be dead right. I just don't like to admit it."

Savannah feels a stab of guilt. "You have a lot riding on you, Tia. A whole lot of pressure and you need some kind of outlet. Hey – a girl gotta have some fun." She places a comforting hand on Tia's shoulder. To her surprise Tia bursts into tears. Her body shakes with heart-rending sobs.

"You don't know the half of it, Sav."

Savannah takes her phone and taps out a message to Daisy.

> Something important came up with my boss. I'll see you in Evie's suite at 9.30.

The response is immediate.

> Sure. Whatever. See u then.

It's brief, curt and sounds definitely pissed off. Now they're off to a rocky start and the party hasn't even started. But this is Savannah's livelihood. She could score major points with Tia if she plays this right. She puts her phone in her pocket and pulls a chair up beside Tia. "Tell me about it. Maybe I can help."

Tia's shoulders sag with relief, while her eyes shine with gratitude.

When Savannah finally steps out into the bright lights of the Strip, it's almost 9.15. The crowds are gathered around the dancing fountains of the Bellagio, swaying to the velvet tones of Frank Sinatra. If only she was heading out to meet Leon at some candlelit restaurant. They'd sit in an intimate balcony overlooking the artificial lake. Afterwards they'd hold each other close on a dance floor, not needing to say a thing, just feeling the electric connection between them. That's how Savannah communicates her passion best. Moving her body.

The fountains shoot upwards in a final grand cascade, then retreat back into the surface of the lake. She has one good reason to feel happy about tonight. Tia finally admitted that the Rat Pack number does need some jazzing up and she's willing to work with Savannah on some comedic choreography. That's actually a major triumph, and means she might have a longer career here in Vegas than she thought.

But for now, she has to get through this weekend, and she's already running late for the party. Cabs fly by but they're all taken. If she walks, she'll be far behind schedule. So she'll have to walk to the lobby entrance where cabs come in and out every few seconds. It's around the side of the building, which means she'll be away from the busy flow of tourists for a few moments. She takes a deep breath. Crowds mill around her, swarming up the steps to the hotel, trooping up and down the Strip in search of excitement.

Is anyone watching her? Daisy's long gone and probably getting ready to make an appearance in the party suite. All Savannah has to do is get to the Aria. She did a quick makeup job in the dressing room and had the forethought to leave a dress there as well. It's just a little black shift dress with white silk trim, but it shows off her long legs. Anyway, she's past caring about appearances. She doesn't feel the need to impress Evie or any of the others now.

She turns away from the steps and makes her way to the corner at the far side of the hotel when a face materializes into the periphery of her vision. A familiar face, or is her mind playing tricks on her? A tall guy wearing dark glasses (at night, which is weird) stands motionless at the opposite corner of the side street. A slow grin slides across his face and her heart thuds into her throat. *Is that Blair, or some other weirdo?* Her mind ratchets through all the possibilities. *Why on earth would he be here? Is he here to blackmail her? Threaten to tell the whole truth about what happened to Cal?*

She doesn't wait to see if this person is really watching her. Instead, she ducks her head down and runs, full speed towards the white lights of the lobby entrance.

Breath coming in gasps, she dares to look behind her. Is that him silhouetted against the bright streetlights? She blinks and almost runs into the metal bars surrounding the taxi bay.

"Everything okay, miss?" says the bellman, a stocky, powerful-looking guy with a smiling face. She could hug him, but holds back.

"I need a cab. Quick."

"Pleasure, ma'am. Just step this way."

He guides her to a waiting car, holds the door open and she falls into the stuffy interior. She hands him a twenty-dollar bill.

"Thanks." She can barely speak as he tips his cap and the cab takes off towards the corner. She sits back in the seat and peeks around the corner of the window. The guy isn't there. Was it real? Seeing *him* again? Or was it just her overactive imagination?

"The Aria," she says, checking the driver's reflection in the rear-view mirror. He's looking at her like she's lost it.

But the way things are going this weekend, she won't be surprised if she does.

DAISY

Daisy lies back on the bed and squeezes her eyes shut. Were the past three hours even real? She touches her heart and finds it's racing the way it always did on Saturday nights when she was twenty and she, Evie, Zoe and Savannah got decked out in front of Evie's mirror with the glam Hollywood lights around it.

They'd chew Juicy Fruit gum, link arms and head down to the local coffee shop or maybe the bar, if Evie scored them fake IDs. Daisy remembers looking up at the sky and the stars and the electric-blue shimmering street of lights that held the promise of heart-pounding romance that she'd always dreamed about. Dreams cultivated by her gran who was crazy about old Hollywood musicals.

On nights she babysat young Daisy, she'd get out the old vinyls and play "On the Street Where You Live" from *My Fair Lady*, or her absolute favorite, Rossano Brazzi singing "Some Enchanted Evening" from *South Pacific*. Daisy made her play that song over and over, twirling around the living room, draped in her gran's silk scarves.

So, later in life, when a cute guy smiled at her from the other side of the room, her whole body came alive. That's how she fell for Wade the night his band was playing at a dingy local nightclub.

He stood at the front of the stage, all wild, blond curls, pouting lips and skinny-hipped jeans, looked straight into her eyes, and sang his heart out to her.

Evie was beside herself with envy. She and Wade had been an item right from the start – close friends, though Evie was hoping for something more. She'd encouraged him to get a band together, even helped them score a few gigs around town. And oh, how she nattered on forever about his potential.

"He could be a new-millennium Robert Plant. With the right encouragement he could go places. Look at him. He's gorgeous, and he has such a magnetic stage presence."

Daisy remembers every detail of that gig. Evie trying to push her aside while they watched from the front row of the mosh pit. How she pouted her lips, swayed her hips and undid the top four buttons of her denim shirt to show off her cleavage. But Wade never spared a glance for her. He was too busy fixating on Daisy who'd decided her Shakira look was the one to capture his attention.

And yet, Evie's had the last laugh on her, because Wade's dream of rock stardom never materialized and he became a balding, disillusioned slob. How could she know he'd get hooked after just one hit of coke? It was all downhill after they were married. Starting when his parents stopped his allowance and cut him out of the family. She can thank his so-called friends for that. *Damn that snitch, Cal.*

She sits up abruptly. The last thing she wants to do tonight is dwell on the past. After all, this is supposed to be a weekend of new beginnings for Evie, and now for her.

That's why she felt a sense of hope and possibility when she ran into Blair earlier tonight, sitting so close to him she could smell the spicy, floral scent of his cologne. Once she got over the initial shock of his stiff, botoxed face she found herself wondering why she'd never been interested in him at college.

He acted like the perfect gentleman. Didn't come on strong, asked a whole lot about Wade and seemed genuinely interested in her stories about Ethan. On her part, she clucked and *awed* at the pictures of his teenage daughter. He didn't say too much about Evie, except that he was counting on Daisy to keep him posted about the party.

"I can't risk my career or my family name. Not now my daughter's doing so well. She's headed for an Ivy League school. Wants to go into international law or business. And you know Evie. She's unstable. Impulsive. It's actually been a nightmare living with her all these years."

"Know what you mean," said Daisy. "Evie always liked to call the shots. Didn't like anyone to cross her."

Blair threw back his drink. "Exactly. That's why I'm counting on you."

Daisy tapped her fingers on the table. Took a deep breath. "So where's Wade?"

"All in good time," he said, checking his phone. "Deliver some good intel and I'll tell you what I know."

He'd left with a chaste kiss on her cheek and a playful wink. "Daisy, Daisy. Still fresh as a flower. You were always the cutest of the four. Too bad we didn't hook up."

Daisy stood, watching him disappear into the crowd, her cheeks burning. And she'd always thought he was such a jerk.

THE DIVORCE PARTY

But this was a gentler version of the Blair she'd known. Maybe it was really possible that people grew and changed for the better.

In need of distraction, she'd made her way to the nearby theater and bought a ticket to the *Vintage Vegas Revue*. What a shock it was to learn that Savannah, the girl who'd studied hard to get crazy-high averages in all the sciences, who'd set out to conquer the world of scientific research, was now a Vegas show dancer. At college she'd always cultivated a cool and haughty persona. As if she was in a different league to everyone else. So what happened to that dazzling academic career?

Daisy has to admit that, onstage, Savannah was a natural. Lithe and glamorous. Strutting across the stage in champagne-colored sequins, her blonde hair swept up in a glitter-sprinkled chignon, and dressed with a plume of flamingo-pink feathers. A classic Vegas showgirl. So graceful, yet unexpectedly funny.

But it was so weird the way she blew Daisy off after she'd waited twenty minutes at the stage door. Maybe she was embarrassed that her cover was blown. Was she ever going to tell them about her real job?

She took up valuable time Daisy could have used to get ready, and now it's nine fifteen and she's still not dressed.

She jumps up from the bed. No matter what happens tonight, she's going to have an awesome time. She checks out the two dresses she bought. Both strong possibilities for the festivities. The sales clerk advised her to go with jewel tones. She decides on the deep indigo silk, and slides it on. A plunging sweetheart neckline enhances her cleavage, while a sheer sequined overskirt barely covers the thigh-skimming slip underneath. Silver strappy sandals and a sapphire pendant completes the look. She stands back to check out her reflection.

Her eyes fill, but she blinks back the tears. Can't risk messing up the makeup job. She snaps a selfie and considers sending a revenge pic to Wade. But he's never answered any of her other texts, so what's the point? She won't allow him to spoil her evening. No way.

She texts Zoe who's in the room next to hers.

> Almost ready. You?

A long interval before Zoe responds.

> Almost. You alone?

> Yup. Where's the friend?

> Seeing him tomorrow, maybe.

> Knock on my door when you're leaving.

> Ten minutes?

> OK.

She places her phone in the new beaded evening bag, just as another call comes in. It's an unfamiliar number. Probably one of those scammers warning her about a security breach on her Visa card. She laughs. They're welcome to all the details. There's about eight bucks left on her credit limit. Good luck to them. She answers. A deep male voice responds. Abrupt and straight to the point.

"Wade Walsh?"

She takes a deep breath.

"Don't know anyone with that name. You've got the wrong number." She chokes on the last few words.

"You sure? He gave us this number. You telling us he was lying?" The voice is downright hostile now.

Daisy doesn't like the sound of this. No wonder Wade's gone off the grid. "I told you; I don't know anyone named Wade Walsh."

"Better be telling the truth, sweetheart. We got your number."

"Thank you and goodbye." She clicks the phone off, feeling a swell of nausea that threatens to send her running to the bathroom. Why the hell would Wade give her number to strangers? Taking a deep breath, she swallows hard. Can't mess up her new face. Why does he always have to ruin everything?

Damn. What kind of trouble has he got himself into now? And why is it she feels like she has three thumbs? Was it one of his junkie friends looking for easy money? Hopefully it's not something worse like a gambling or drug debt. Maybe it's just someone calling about a gig. That has to be it. Finally, she throws her phone into her purse and falls back onto the easy chair.

She glances over at the minibar. Up until now she's resisted helping herself to it, because she knows the hotel charges ridiculous prices for those tiny bottles, but she can't stop herself from grabbing a bottle of vodka, screwing off the cap and downing the whole thing in one gulp.

Fire rushes through her belly as she throws the bottle into the garbage, and smooths her dress down. Now she's ready for whatever the evening throws at her, but she has to keep an eye on Evie.

Blair is expecting a report tomorrow and she can't screw this up. For some strange reason she wants to impress this guy who she'd always thought was a creep.

And maybe even a little scary considering his part in the Cal situation.

ZOE

When Daisy's text comes in, Zoe's just reading through the last paragraph of a fascinating article on how a newly-discovered dolphin fossil has finally provided a link between marine dolphins and the river variety. Scientists discovered that a renegade pod of dolphins made the move to inland rivers to escape the overcrowded oceans, approximately six million years ago. This could definitely be a hot topic to talk over with Zack tomorrow. It's incredible how her brain has suddenly clicked into academic gear after meeting him. So much so, she's spent the past hour combing the net to find out all she can about the latest scientific advances related to dolphins.

She takes a while longer to respond to Daisy.

It's been a long while since she's felt so energized, so invested in the sheer exercise of research and discovery, even if it is just scrolling through Google, which can hardly be deemed scholarly. Maybe these past ten years she's just been going through the motions. Attending the obligatory annual medical conferences to keep up with the latest pediatric trends, but keynote addresses bore her, not to mention the endless, dreary workshops where her head inevitably becomes a wobbly basketball balanced on a bendable neck.

She's always been a better hands-on learner. Loving the chemical stink of the lab, the gurgling flasks, the intense focus on pinpoint accuracy of measurements. Why she ever made the move to medicine sometimes escapes her, but Marcus was extremely persuasive when he pointed out the financial benefits of medical specialization, particularly pediatrics.

"You need to cater to this new breed of helicopter parents, Zoe. They'll move heaven and earth to protect their precious offspring."

She can't blame him entirely though. Her career has been rewarding financially and professionally, but that urge for new challenges has been nibbling away at her resolve to be the best pediatrician out there. And she's not really worried about leaving her patients. She knows they're in great hands while she's away. Perhaps it's time for a sabbatical. Time to get her teeth into some pioneering research.

But now she only has ten minutes to make herself presentable. She snaps her laptop shut and jumps into action. Thank God she already blow-dried her hair, though she spots dry, split ends from the relentless Vegas heat.

It's been a while since Marcus made contact. Either he's spending the night at an airport hotel so he can catch the first flight to Vegas in the morning, or he's given up and gone to shoot pool with his Bay Street buddies. Not that she cares anyway. Their relationship should have ended years ago. If he shows up, she'll stand firm and tell him it's over.

She checks out the dresses laid across the bed. The first, a clingy, champagne-colored sheath, with nude mesh insets and loaded with sequins; a Marcus dress. He always loved her in bling, even though she insisted she wasn't a glittery type of person. The other dress is a simple one-shoulder dress in emerald green with a ruffled hem and deep side slit. That's more her style. Classy and understated. She slips it on and curses at the side zipper – always a pain in the butt when it nips the soft underarm flesh. Usually, Marcus helps her with all that. After struggling for a few minutes, she gets it fastened and smooths down the skirt. A simple pearl on a slim, gold chain finishes the outfit and she's ready to go.

It's 9.28 and a text comes in from Evie. Christ, is she already waiting for them? She hardly dares read it.

> Running behind schedule. Wait for me in the suite. Enjoy drinks and appetizers!

Zoe sits back down on the bed. *Am I really going to go through with this night?* Cold reality hits her as a host of memories floods into her head. She closes her eyes. Why is she grinding her teeth again? The answer is clear. She'd never planned on seeing these women again. They're crazy. Unhinged. Evie, swaggering around like a well-oiled UFC fighter, ready to step over anyone that stood in her way of snagging one of The Golden Guys. Daisy, the butter-wouldn't-melt-in-her-mouth drug-dealer with a scissor-hold that could crush a leg. And Savannah, the enigma, who could body slam someone twice her weight and steal a watch from under a sales clerk's nose.

Zoe had never wanted to be part of their stupid wrestling club, and only agreed to be the medic because she wanted to get close to Blair and Cal. Now she wishes she'd never met any of them, because the sad truth is, you can't bury your past. Those demons always find a way to work themselves back into your life and destroy everything you've tried to build. *Damn Blair and his deception.* And Cal. Poor Cal. Who would have thought the guy who had everything would meet such a terrible end? And why was she wrapped up in it, when it was nothing to do with her?

Guilt by association. That was her crime. She should have followed her gut and spoken up instead of becoming part of a terrible pact that now threatens to come back and ruin her. *What the hell is Evie up to?*

But it's too late to even contemplate backing out. That time is way past now. But there have to be safeguards. Some kind of damage limitation or else events could spiral out of control like they did at that godforsaken grad party sixteen years ago.

For a start everyone must agree to check in their phones at the door. There can't be any covert, compromising pictures taken. No social media surprises. Zoe's career depends on a squeaky-clean reputation.

She tosses back a glass of water. Stands up and faces the mirror. Tells herself, *You can do this, Dr. Ryan. You're an intelligent, respectable woman who made a few impulsive choices in your past. Since then, you've more than atoned for them. Pull yourself together and you'll come out of this ordeal, reputation intact.*

After refreshing her lipstick, she clicks her evening purse shut, making sure she has both room keys. Giving the room a last check around, she leaves the bedside light on, then lets herself out of the room. A bellboy is standing outside Daisy's room with a huge arrangement of flowers. Zoe hurries along the hallway to find Daisy, glamorous in indigo chiffon, face flushed, accepting the gift.

"Got a secret admirer?" says Zoe, craning her neck to try and read the card. But Daisy whisks it away and disappears into her room. The bellboy stands there, awkward, hands dug into his pockets. Zoe rummages in her purse and pulls out a five-dollar bill.

"Thanks," she says as he tips his hat and speed-walks off down the corridor.

"C'mon, princess," she calls in to Daisy. "Evie's going to be late, so let's go get a head start on drinking her booze."

Daisy appears at the door again. Composed now. Her flushed cheeks making her even prettier.

Zoe whistles. "You look knockout, Daisy."

Daisy smiles that shy smile that hasn't changed in sixteen years. "I haven't dressed up since Evie's wedding, so maybe it's fitting that the next time I dress up is at her divorce."

"As long as the next one isn't at her funeral."

Daisy knits her brow. "That's bad luck, Zoe. Take it back."

"Just kidding. C'mon. Let's get this party started."

"I'm so excited," says Daisy, pulling her door shut and linking an arm into Zoe's. "C'mon, Dr. Zoe. Let's go have a blast."

Zoe feels the first fluttering of anxiety in her gut as Daisy drags her along with a surprisingly tight grip.

How can she trust these women after what they did?

THE PARTY

Divorce party cocktails:

The Deadbeet Time Robber
The Screw-my-ex-driver
The Half and Half Knot
The Adios Motherf...er
The Love on the Rocks
The Rum Baby Rum
The Liar, Liar, Pants on Fire
Alimontini
Love Gone Sour

SAVANNAH

Savannah approaches Evie's suite, wondering why there's a muscle-bound guy in a dark suit standing outside the door. She hesitates. Maybe she'll just abandon the idea of going to this ridiculous party. Run back to Leon's place and wait up for him. Finish what they started the other night. But the doorman steps forward to greet her just as she's about to turn around.

"Looking for Evie's event?" He talks as if his teeth are gritted together, which makes for an ultra-aggressive tone.

"Uh... yes."

The deadpan face lights up in an unexpected smile and he throws the door open. "Welcome to the party. I'm Tom, Ms. Cummings' personal assistant. She requests that you make yourself comfortable inside. Eat, drink, relax. She'll be here shortly."

Personal assistant? Why does Evie have a PA who looks more like a personal bodyguard. And what's with the Ms. Cummings name? But then she remembers that's Blair's name. Evie was so keen to change her name from plain old Evie O'Sullivan to the more glam-sounding Evie Cummings. Strange she hasn't dropped her married name yet.

She steps into a marble-floored lobby lit by a chandelier dripping iridescent crystals. A waiter appears at the end of the short hallway, immaculate in white shirt and black tie, holding a tray of champagne. She takes one, cradling it like a lifeline, and sweeps past him into a massive room whose floor-to-ceiling windows showcase the neon skyline of Las Vegas.

It's breathtaking and so familiar. That disembodied feeling as if she's suspended in the air, hovering above the kaleidoscope of flashing lights. Ever since she arrived in Vegas all those years ago, it's been like living in a fantasy world. An illusory place. A faux version of real life without the day-to-day monotony. And that's served her well. She'd had enough of grim reality back in Evanston.

Blindsided by the stunning view, it takes her a moment to turn and notice the back walls of the penthouse, covered in a dizzying collage of photographs. Diagonal lines of pictures radiate outwards like the spokes of a wheel, from a portrait of Evie at the center and a huge sign that reads, The Party Girls. On closer inspection she discovers a multitude of poses featuring herself, Daisy, Zoe and Evie in wrestling gear, party gear, lounging on beds, couches, beaches, and parks – sometimes together, sometimes alone, and sometimes with Evie. Pictures that Savannah doesn't even remember being taken, of moments she can't quite recall experiencing. Moments of joy and laughter, solitary reflection, and wild recklessness. Portraits so up-close and intimate, she can't help feeling goosebumps prickle her arms, especially when she gets to the pictures that feature Blair, Wade and Cal. Her blood freezes at the sight of Cal's face. What was Evie thinking when she put this together?

"What the actual fuck," says a familiar voice behind her. She whirls around and there's Daisy, gorgeous in indigo blue. Zoe stands behind her, cool and classy as ever, in a green silk dress.

"It's a fricking shrine," says Daisy, hand plastered over her mouth. "I mean, over the top doesn't even cover it."

Zoe's eyes widen as she scans the display. "Don't know about you guys, but this gives me the chills. I couldn't rustle up more than two or three pictures of the four of us. Guess I didn't exactly make picture-taking a priority in college."

"I don't think any of us did," says Savannah, holding her arms out. She might as well play the game and pretend she didn't already run into Daisy. Now she just has to hope Daisy won't blab too quickly about seeing Savannah's show. "Hey, guys. Long time no see."

"Group hug," says Daisy, snuggling close.

Zoe puts an arm around Savannah's shoulder and air kisses her cheek. "This feels so weird being together again after all this time. You guys look fantastic."

"Look at you, Zoe. You made it. You're a real, genuine pediatric specialist. I'm in awe," says Savannah, glancing at Zoe's expensive strappy sandals. They must be Jimmy Choos. Zoe always did hanker after the luxury items.

She looks over at the picture display to see if there are any of them at the golf club where Zoe worked. The place they often hung out in the good old days when they were all still friends. Sure enough there's one right at eye level, of Zoe with her arms draped around the shoulders of a silver-haired guy in a turquoise golf shirt, a chunky gold chain around his neck. That guy, Marvin, owned a massive commercial real estate company, and Zoe was always hovering around him. Taking gifts and handouts, no doubt. That was the only way to feed her craving for the good life. She gives Zoe a sideways glance to see how she's reacting to these candid shots, and already Zoe's frowning as she studies them.

"Not sure I want to be reminded of that time in my life," she says, tossing back her champagne and moving on. "In fact, I'd love to get my hands on the originals."

Savannah squints and spots a picture of Blair, Evie's soon-to-be ex, chugging back beers with Zoe. That must have been around the time that Zoe and Blair became an item. The relationship began in a hurry, much to Evie's annoyance, after Savannah turned Blair down, then it ended just as quickly a few months later. No one knows why they broke up, but Zoe probably doesn't realize how lucky she is to have escaped a life with him. Only Savannah knows what he's capable of.

She blinks, realizing Zoe has turned away from the photos and is now talking to her. "So, you look amazing, Sav. What are you up to these days?"

Savannah catches Daisy's raised eyebrows from the corner of her vision. "Oh – I'm in the entertainment business. On the admin side."

"Sounds intriguing – but you were so into science. And you were a shoe-in for that PhD fellowship..." The waiter arrives with a fresh tray of champagne. She pauses and swipes a glass. "What changed?"

"I worked in toxicology for a while. Hated it."

"Ooh, so you know all about poison," says Daisy, draining her glass. "I sure could have used your expertise these last few years."

"Me too," says Zoe. "Although Marcus is well on his way to poisoning his own system. He wouldn't need any help."

"Really?" says Daisy. "He's that bad?"

Zoe laughs. "I'm exaggerating. He's sober enough to run a highly profitable investment company."

"Awesome," says Daisy, swiping another glass of champagne. "Can't say the same for Wade."

"Better take things easy," says Savannah. "We have the whole evening ahead of us."

Daisy laughs and shakes her head. "I'm going all out. No holding back."

Zoe sips her drink. "Speaking of letting it all out, are you going to tell us why you just up and disappeared off the radar, Sav? We all promised to be there for each other, after – after..."

Savannah's gut twists. Why won't Zoe let up? But she knew they'd have a whole lot of questions. Why wouldn't they? She was a fool to have accepted the invitation. But she needs to reassure herself she's safe. That they don't know *everything*. She swallows. "I just had to get away. I had no choice."

Zoe's brows knit. "And that's it. That's all you're going to tell us?"

Savannah tears herself away. "For now."

Zoe squares her shoulders. "Well, aren't you the mystery woman."

Daisy grins from ear to ear. "So I have to tell you, this invitation came at just the right time for me."

Savannah had forgotten just how pretty Daisy is. She hasn't aged a bit. And she's still so bubbly, trying to make the best of every situation.

"Same here," says Zoe. "Things have been a little tense at home."

"Ooh, give us all the dirt, please," says Daisy.

"Later, when we're all together," says Zoe, turning back to the photo display as if she's at a gallery. She sighs. "I mean artistically some of these pictures are really good, but they feel just a tad invasive. As if Evie was trying to annoy us or something."

"Well, they just plain old creep me out," says Daisy, "so I'm going to turn my back on them and concentrate on having fun. I need to chill – take the edge off. It's already been a busy day."

Savannah raises her glass, determined to put on a brave face. "C'mon, let's make a toast to old times and good friends."

They clink glasses. Daisy drinks and wipes a hand across her mouth. "Can't get enough of this stuff. It beats the five-dollar crap I usually drink."

Zoe's nose wrinkles. "You can still buy wine for five dollars?"

"For sure. I actually found a drinkable white for five bucks a bottle."

Savannah chuckles. "I guess drinkable is the operative word there."

"Hey, if you're desperate you'll overlook any taste deficiencies."

Zoe finishes her second drink in one swallow, reminding Savannah that she could always drink them under the table. After wrestling tournaments, they'd unwind at some low-life bar, and when the three of them were hanging over the toilet, puking, Zoe was still propping up the bar, downing more shooters. "So, when does this twisted sideshow get on the road?" she says.

Zoe never liked to be in the dark about anything. Always had to be the first to know, and that made for a whole lot of rivalry between her and Evie. When Blair and Zoe hooked up Evie was livid.

"You know Evie," says Savannah, "always had to be fashionably late."

Daisy saunters over to a table where another waiter is laying out a massive charcuterie platter loaded with meats, olives and cheeses. "Mmm, this looks delish," she says, filling her plate.

Savannah's stomach grumbles as she arranges a selection of meats and cheeses on top of a slice of focaccia. She hasn't eaten since about four when Leon made her an omelet, and she's danced an entire show in between. If she doesn't eat she'll pass out, and the champagne is already blurring the edges of her vision.

Zoe throws herself onto the leather sectional sofa. "How do you two manage to fill your faces with food and stay slim? If I don't stick to kale, cucumber and chicken breast, I'll break the scales."

"I still dance to keep fit," says Savannah, glancing at Daisy. "Just for fun, of course."

Daisy winks and bites down on a prosciutto sandwich. "Well, I spent almost twenty years eating leftovers, so my kid could be happy and healthy, and so my lazy-ass husband could grow a paunch while I worked my butt off. I guess you could say I have a speedy metabolism."

"Speaking of Wade, what's up with him?" says Zoe.

Daisy puts down her sandwich. Her eyes fill with tears. "We're done." She coughs and makes a strange, gulping noise. "He finally left me. Checked out last week. But I'm fine. Perfectly fine. In fact, never better. Tell you the truth – I'm glad to be rid of him."

"I hate to bring this up but I always wondered why he never asked his parents for help," says Zoe, picking at the Greek olives. "I mean, wasn't his father in the plastics business? Surely they'd want to make sure their grandson was safe and well cared for?"

Daisy slams down her plate, eyes blazing. "I can't even speak the names of those disgusting people. Cutting off their own flesh and blood. They wouldn't listen to Wade. And they refused to even meet me. I've never forgiven them for what they did. To him. To us. To their grandson."

"Any idea why they were so against it?" says Zoe.

"Yes. I think I do," Daisy hisses. "But let's just drop it. I don't want to talk about it."

Savannah wishes Zoe would stop with all these questions. It's like she's picking at a scab and she can't stop until she draws blood. Can't she see that Daisy's close to tears? It's obvious to anyone with a shred of sensitivity that this whole discussion is triggering painful memories for Daisy, but then Zoe always was low on empathy. That's why it blows Savannah's mind that she actually became a pediatrician. What kind of bedside manner does she really have with her young, vulnerable patients? But then it's entirely possible she can fake anything for the right amount of money.

Suddenly the food sticks in her throat. She'd forgotten how toxic these women are. The Party Girls were not nice people, herself included. They did bad things to survive, to get what they wanted and to make sure they kept it. Have any of them really changed? She puts down the plate and sighs. This whole party thing is so fucked up it's giving her a migraine. She takes her phone out, impatient to get something going. The waiting around and rising anticipation is excruciating.

"Why don't I text Evie? See what her ETA is."

Daisy snaps out of her mood. "Let's wait. It's just nice here with the three of us. Isn't it?"

"We can catch up a bit before she comes and takes over," says Zoe. "Because then we won't get a word in edgewise."

Daisy brightens up. "Let's do a little reminiscing about the good times."

Strange, Savannah can't remember too many good times. The only time she felt good was when she was dancing.

Zoe picks at the stuffed olives and saunters over to the photos again. "Okay. Let's start at the beginning. Freshmen year. This picture of us roasting marshmallows over a fire in the park."

Daisy squints at the rustic setting. "I don't remember any of this. Evie for sure wasn't the campfire type."

Savannah searches her memory and can't find any reference point on which to hang this image. "You're right. Evie always said she hated having smoky hair and clothes."

Zoe scrutinizes the picture closely. "And I wouldn't have been seen dead wearing an O-Town T-shirt."

"Oh my God," says Daisy, scrunching up her eyes to focus on Zoe's clothes, then fixing on a picture of herself in a skimpy sweater over faded jeans. "I did *not* go for the bare midriff look."

Zoe shrugs. "Looks like they're photoshopped. But that would take an incredible amount of time to put together."

"I agree. They don't even look real," says Savannah, moving closer.

"Well of course they are," says a voice from behind. It's familiar but altered by a slightly affected accent. "You guys simply forgot about the great times we had."

They all wheel around like dogs called to heel. Guilty of snooping where they're not supposed to. Savannah's pulse quickens. Throbbing like an insistent drumbeat as Evie emerges from the shadows of the lobby and they all gasp in unison at the sight of her.

DAISY

Daisy is the first to recover and rush towards Evie – or the woman who resembles the old Evie, and wrap her in a bear hug. When she pulls back, she can barely keep her eyes on the face that contains all the elements of the old Evie's features, only stretched out, puffed up or elongated into a strangely skewed arrangement.

"Daisy, you're such a babe," says Evie through swollen lips, inflated with so much collagen, her top lip almost grazes her nose. "How do you manage to stay so young?"

Daisy tries to smile, despite the sick ache in her gut. Tries not to fixate on the two apple-shaped swellings under Evie's eyes. Evidence of recent cheek implants. And her strong, aristocratic nose looks like it's been attacked by the surgeon's scalpel more than once, leaving a puny, narrow bridge with a fragile, reddened tip.

She shrugs and averts her eyes for a moment. "Good old soap and water – and a touch of Oil of Olay. Can't afford much else."

She glances back and wonders if that's a tear squeezing out from the corner of Evie's elongated eyes. There isn't a wrinkle to be seen on her face, but the overall effect is shiny and taut like the skin on a drum. There's a few hundred grand of work on this face, but the result is a bizarre mess. *A grotesque mask.* What has she done to herself and why? The thought makes her dizzy.

Evie's immobile face suddenly cracks into a smile, or rather two deep grooves appear around her mouth area, revealing blinding porcelain-capped teeth.

"Well, it is sooooo good to see you, babe." She tosses her mane of tumbling, dark waves aside, then moves on to Savannah and Zoe, who quickly try to rearrange their expressions of frozen horror as they hug and blow awkward air kisses on each side of that ghastly face. They're freaked out too.

Evie's body, on the other hand, is a more successful triumph of cosmetic surgery; tight, rounded buttocks under a clingy white minidress, a tiny waist and flat-as-a-board midriff. Firm, pert boobs, a gleaming cleavage, brown sinewy arms and gleaming blemish-free legs. She's a living Barbie doll, with a mangled face that's been overworked by the surgeon's scalpel. It's going to take a whole lot of getting used to this new version of Evie.

Once all the hugging is over, Evie holds out her arms and surveys the room. "So, what do you think of the picture display, guys? Isn't it an incredible trip down memory lane?"

The pause that follows is too long. Daisy checks out Savannah and Zoe, whose mouths are still gaping open in disbelief. As if they've been punched in the gut and haven't recovered enough to take a breath. Daisy swallows and slides back into a familiar role as Evie's loyal cheerleader. It's the least she can do, considering the terrible ruin of her face.

"Awesome, Evie. In fact, we were just discussing how generous it was for you to put this together. Weren't we?"

She looks hopefully at the others, raising her eyebrows until

Zoe jolts into sudden action. As if someone's jabbed her with a cattle prod.

"What? Oh – yeah. I mean, between the three of us, we don't even have a handful of pictures from college and here you are with a display that captures every nuance – every special moment of our college days."

Somehow Zoe's wry tone and overly lavish praise makes the pictures seem even more bizarre. Savannah jumps in to save the situation, her words spilling over each other in confusion.

"She means you must have valued – I mean, really treasured those years to have wanted to record them so thoroughly – I mean so extensively, so artistically – I mean – oh, shit, I think I'm getting drunk."

Evie, who's been eying them with a steely glare, breaks out the dazzling smile again. "I hear you, Sav. Let's crack open another bottle and get this show on the road." She snaps her fingers and the waiter rushes over, tray in hand. "We need more bubbly and tell Tom to fetch the piñata in fifteen."

Once the cork pops on the next bottle, and a DJ arrives to start up some background music, Daisy feels the tension draining from her shoulders. They sip the champagne and cruise along the photo display.

As they move along the wall, Daisy's memory becomes blurred. Maybe these are real moments, though she can't remember balancing at the top of the slide at a kids' playground looking utterly stoned, or sitting on the bench overlooking the ocean, a huge spliff stuck between her lips. That's when things become seriously weird. Following the stoner portrait, there's an entire column of photos devoted to her and Wade. Wade sucking on a purple glass bong that she's holding, Wade taking a handful of brightly colored pills from a bag she's offering him, Wade shoving the handful of pills into his mouth, Wade standing on the lawn, stoned, arms held up to the sky, the sun illuminating his golden hair, while she skulks in the background, smirking. It looks bad. Really bad. As if she was his private pusher. Always ready with a steady supply of weed, ecstasy, molly. Next to the druggie pictures are scenes of Wade running along the beach with Evie on his shoulders. Evie and Wade doing shooters at the golf club. Evie and Wade eating giant cookies at a bakery. Evie sitting at Wade's feet while he plays a guitar. So many wholesome, sentimental moments.

Daisy's gut twists. "I didn't realize you'd spent so much time with Wade before – before…"

Evie tilts her head and shakes a finger, her eyes stern. "Daisy – Daisy – you forgot. Wade and I were friends for a long time. And we were *so close*. Remember? I took *you* to his concert. At The Bean? That's when you two hooked up. He didn't give me a second look after that."

Another pregnant silence follows. Daisy can't summon up any response, her heart has slid into her throat, blocking her windpipe. Even Zoe and Savannah are tongue-tied. Then Evie throws back her head and howls with laughter.

"Just kidding. Look at the three of you. Can't you take a joke? No hard feelings, Daisy. Especially considering the way things turned out with you two."

"What do you mean *how things turned out?*" Daisy backs away, her head swimming. She trips on the sofa leg but manages to right herself. Her face burns. "How do you know about Wade and me?"

"News travels fast, babe. Especially when it concerns old friends."

"But I haven't told anyone about Wade and me. Only Zoe." She darts a look over at Zoe. "Did you tell Evie?"

Zoe frowns and shakes her head. "This is the first time I've talked to Evie. I don't gossip. No time for it with my job and all.

But it's a good thing, isn't it? I mean, you were just telling us how much of a liability he was. Weren't you?"

Savannah lays a comforting arm on Daisy's shoulder. "And now you're free to make a fresh start. Think about yourself and your own needs for once. Do the things you've always wanted to."

Evie beams at her, or is she gloating? "Exactly. Listen to what they're saying. This could be a great opportunity for you now Wade's out of the way."

"I still don't know how you could have found out, Evie. Unless... unless..."

"Unless what? Unless I called him? Unless Blair told me? How can you accuse me of going behind your back?"

Evie's hard-edged voice always reduced Daisy to a quaking, spineless mess. And even though Evie's smiling, her eyes are cold and cruel.

Daisy's shoulders tense up, but she forces herself to breathe more deeply. "I guess – I guess I'm overreacting. I mean – it's just that my life's been so hard for so long. Like I've been sleeping through it. Not really living it."

She bows her head and then the waterworks come. She might have known that alcohol would bring out the maudlin side of her. She's always been a sad drunk. Now a torrent of long-repressed tears starts flowing. Her entire body shakes with the memory of all her sacrifices. The missed opportunities, and unlucky breaks. Of the once youthful Wade reduced to a balding, couch-bound slob. A beautiful promise never kept.

Evie's wiry arms close around her, like the metal jaws of a trap, pressing Daisy's face into her bony shoulders. "There, there, babe. Don't ruin your makeup for a loser."

"You're right." She sniffles, gulping down the sobs. "I just paid good money for this facial."

That's when Evie bends really close to her ear and, through

swollen lips, hisses, "Blair told me where Wade is. He's back home. His father just died and he's with his mom."

Daisy rips herself away, her eyes searching Evie's inscrutable mask of a face. "Say what?"

"Hey – take it easy. He's grieving."

Now the edges of reality are blurring. Did Evie really say what she thought she said? Grieving? Wade always hated his father. And according to him, so did his mom. Is he back there, working on her? Trying to get back into the will after he's divorced Daisy? But her vision is blurry, her head fuzzy. It must be all the champagne. And Savannah and Zoe are staring at her with a look of morbid fascination painted all over their faces. The kind of look reserved for car crashes or public vomiting. She'd better pull herself together. Calm down so she can really think hard about what to do.

Evie snaps her fingers. "Enough blubbering. Bring in the piñatas, Tom. Let's have some fun."

Daisy's face flushes crimson when the bodyguard walks in holding not one but two giant penis piñatas, both constructed in lurid shades of blue, red and pink. One with a large B for Blair on the tip, the other bearing a large W for Wade. He leans them against the wall.

"Why did you do this?" She can't take her eyes from the Wade piñata.

The bodyguard returns with a giant baseball bat and a massive rubber mallet which he sets down on the floor.

Daisy looks from one to the other, wondering which weapon would inflict the most damage, and how hard she would have to swing it to wipe that smug smile from Evie's spiteful, ruined face and knock her out cold.

Silence her for good.

ZOE

While Tom the hulk is rigging up the piñatas on a low metal rail that looks specifically designed for kids' birthday parties, they crack open another bottle of bubbly.

Zoe's feeling all kinds of wild emotions, brought on by the never-ending river of champagne. That initial horror at Evie's appearance has given way to a low vibe of anger at the hack of a cosmetic surgeon who butchered Evie's uniquely attractive face and transformed her into a frozen-faced Muppet.

She's met those guys at medical conferences, with their chunky Rolex watches, fake tans and springy hair implants. So many quacks among them. And Evie must have picked a real winner, considering her botched-up rhinoplasty. Some of those guys should be made to pay mega-compensation for the messes they make, but most victims are too ashamed and humiliated to risk any kind of lawsuit. To do so would be to admit there's something weird or pathological about going under the knife so many times until the damage is irreversible.

Zoe's come across cases like that even in teens. Kids with such bad body dysmorphia, they're addicted to cosmetic surgery, and their parents who prefer to live in stubborn denial, pretending nothing is unusual about their eighteen-year-old daughter begging for a boob job or liposuction or a buttock enhancement that could go terribly wrong.

"Speaking of marriages, what's happening with yours?" says Evie.

Zoe snaps out of her daydream and realizes Evie's talking to her. Now she's finished with Daisy, who's standing at the window, still as a statue, looking out at the bright lights of the Strip. It's as if Evie's moving on to her next target. But Zoe won't give Evie the satisfaction of knowing her marriage with Marcus is on the rocks. That she's actually failed at something.

"Oh – just the usual highs and lows. Pressures of work and all that."

"But I thought you said..." Daisy blurts out, stopping as soon as Zoe flashes a warning look at her.

Evie's eyes widen, as if she senses some juicy tidbit of information is being deliberately withheld. "Didn't you marry a *much* older man?"

Ugh. Evie knows exactly how to go for the jugular. Probe the sensitive places. "He's a few years older than me. Doesn't act it though."

"Is that why you didn't have kids?" says Evie, one side of her swollen mouth twisting into a smile. "Maybe he's too set in his ways? Or could it be just down to aging sperm?"

Zoe grits her teeth, determined not to let Evie get to her. "Sometimes you put these things on hold *when you've built a successful career*. And besides, it's not too late for me to reconsider. There are so many options *I can afford*."

Zoe smiles back, knowing the career jab will cut right to Evie's frozen heart. She was always envious of Zoe's intellect and determination. They face each other in a silent standoff.

"Hey, why are we wasting time on negative talk?" says

Savannah. "Here we are together after so many years apart. Shouldn't we be celebrating that at least?"

"Exactly," says Daisy, turning and snapping out of her funk. "We were the wild and crazy foursome from the wrong side of the tracks."

Savannah raises her glass. "Four misfits whose parents never made it to parent-teacher meetings."

Evie clinks Savannah's glass. "Yeah, my mom would probably have punched the teacher's lights out if she'd said anything bad about me, or at least got her into a half-nelson on the classroom floor. Besides, she was always working, so I can't be too hard on her."

"My mom swore she'd never set foot in a high school again after she was expelled in tenth grade for toking up in the girls' bathroom. Anyway, she was too afraid to miss a house party or draft night at the Mustang Club," says Daisy.

Savannah sighs. "My mom went once in seventh grade, but her booze breath was so bad I never reminded her again, and she never asked me."

"Same with my dad. He never asked, so I didn't tell. It's a good thing they stayed away," says Zoe. "Considering how well we all did to make it to college on our own merits."

"And don't forget our little sidelines that helped to supplement the scholarships," says Evie. "I'd say we were all quite enterprising young women."

"Sidelines?" says Savannah, frowning. "What are you talking about?"

"We've already reminded ourselves about Daisy's little drug-dealing empire, but take a look at this," says Evie, directing them to a series of snapshots near the windows. They lean in closer to see the series of grainy pictures taken inside a department store that clearly show the young Savannah taking sweaters from a rack, ripping off the labels and stuffing them under her shirt so she looks pregnant. Savannah's face drains of color. "Is this – is this...?"

"It's a joke," shrieks Evie. "I thought it would be a hoot to see your reaction. Priceless! But you were so talented, I swear you could've jacked a diamond ring from under a jeweler's nose if you'd wanted."

"I'm not proud of that," says Savannah, tearing the pictures down from the wall and ripping them apart.

"You can't turn your back on who you are – or were," says Evie.

"Especially if you keep reminding us," says Savannah, clearly shaken.

"I mean, we don't really change, do we?" says Evie. "We might think we do, but I like to believe our true nature is etched in stone by the time we're eighteen. All we do is add more window dressing to cover up our real selves."

Savannah turns away, her head bowed. Zoe feels uneasy. Why is Evie doing this? But then Evie always had to let them know she held some kind of trump card over them. She's still the same manipulative, mean-spirited bitch. Her worst fears are confirmed when Evie directs them to the next arrangement of pictures.

"I mean, that's why you married an older man, Zoe. You were always more comfortable with the *mature* types."

Evie points to a series of pictures showing the young Zoe with silver-haired, affluent-looking men – sitting on their laps, arm in arm with her head on their shoulders, clinking champagne glasses over a fancy dinner.

"I think that picture was taken at your charity drive to raise money for your imaginary gran's cancer treatment. That was a real brainwave of yours."

"I'd forgotten about all that," says Zoe, feeling suddenly nauseous. She'd stifled these shameful details of her past. Why had she been such a sneaky little grifter? Truth was, she'd been so desperate for money to supplement her scholarship awards, nothing was out of bounds. Eventually, she'd tried hard to escape that legacy and her fear of running into someone she'd conned was one of the main reasons she'd moved to Canada.

"Hey, buck up," says Daisy. "You never got caught."

"Guess that's a good thing," says Evie. "Con artist isn't exactly a great addition to your professional résumé."

Livid, Zoe turns away. This is just another reason why she'll never want to see these old *friends* again after this weekend. They belong to a more desperate time. They don't know her as she is now. Respectable and respected. How could she have been so stupid to come here? She sobers up suddenly. This old baggage is not welcome. And what other crap does Evie have up her sleeve?

"Hey, lighten up, everyone," says Evie, clapping her hands. "At least we can be proud of our wrestling team. I've made you all framed portraits of our final championship presentation. You'll find them in the goodie bags I've prepared."

Definitely not going up on my bedroom wall, Zoe thinks as she glances over at the others who look just as ticked-off as she feels. It's all a blatant display of power on Evie's part. Maybe even a signal not to mess up her stupid party or else...

"C'mon guys," Evie yells, disturbing Zoe's thoughts. "We're here to have fun. To celebrate a new chapter in my life."

She beckons them towards a table covered with darts and paint bombs. On the wall above, a series of doctored photos and caricatures of Blair are arranged, with circular target lines printed over them. Zoe's shocked at how much Blair has changed. Looks like he's been going to the same cosmetic surgeon. Husband and wife developed the same habit, experienced the same body dysmorphia.

"So this little game is called *Let's mess up the cheating*

husband," says Evie. "Choose your weapon and we'll release some anti-male stress."

Soon a hail of darts and paint bombs pelt Blair's static faces. Evie and Daisy start by lobbing the paint bombs hard at Blair's nose, shrieking at the explosions of color, but Savannah becomes very quiet. Sporting a steely, fearsome expression, she fondles the darts – evil, sharply pointed missiles. Then she picks one up and winds her arm back, squinting to take aim as she launches it right between Blair's eyes. One after the other, her missiles hit dead-on like bullets hitting a bullseye. She throws them with mechanical precision, like a lethal robot.

Zoe stares in awe. *What's up with that?*

"You look like you want to annihilate him," she says. "Like you really mean it."

Savannah blinks as if she's waking from a trance. "What? Did I...? Huh?"

Evie squints over at her. Her mouth twists in a slow grin. "Maybe she does. There's a lot we don't know about our girl, Savannah."

Zoe laughs. "Hidden depths there, Sav. What exactly were you running from when you left us all after grad?"

SAVANNAH

Savannah freezes. She's stunned, grasping the neck of the cold, steel dart. Three faces stare open-mouthed at her. Something came over her when she grasped the first one. A sudden blaze of rage. The urge to hit out. To gouge soft flesh with the needle-sharp tip. She's only felt that urge one other time in her life, but it scares her. She drops the dart back on the table. She's not that terrified twenty-something girl anymore. But just as the silence becomes unbearable, the cute DJ who reminds her of a young Denzel Washington, cranks up the music.

Evie snaps into action, flips her curtain of hair to one side, claps her hands above her head and wiggles her toned buttocks. "C'mon, ladies. We're getting way too serious. Let's get down. Let's light up that dance floor. Feel the rhythm."

"Earth to Savannah," she hears Daisy yell, and then some unseen hand dims the lights, and a line of vibrant neon pink snaps on around the open space in the center of the room. Above them a disco ball begins to rotate, sending white flakes of light spinning across the floor.

Even Daisy snaps out of her dark mood, throws her head back and sashays onto the dance floor, prowling like a cat around the other two. Evie throws her arms up in the air and struts onto the dance floor as if she's a model on a catwalk. For a moment the shadows soften her twisted mask of a face. The lights caress her toned body and she looks beautiful again.

Savannah lets the music trickle like soothing balm, calming her frayed nerves. Soon the bad feelings slip away and she starts to dance, twirling and swaying as if there's no one else in the world except her and the music. Daisy sidles up, her blue eyes gleaming in the bright disco lights. "You're such an awesome dancer. It's like the music takes you over."

"For me, dancing is like breathing. And – hey – thanks for not saying anything about the show."

"No worries. I have too much other crap on my mind right now."

Savannah leans in closer. "You think Wade's trying to distance himself from you so he can get back into his mom's good books?"

Daisy puts a finger to her mouth as if to silence Savannah. "I don't *think it*. I *know* he is."

"What the...? You're kidding. Why would he desert you, the mother of his only son?"

Daisy looks like she's been slapped in the face. "What do you know about my son?"

"Only what I heard from the others, and what you've said about him," says Savannah, taken aback. *What's wrong with Daisy? She's acting so paranoid.*

"I don't want to talk about him right now," she says before flouncing off the dance floor, leaving Savannah staring open-mouthed at her retreating back.

Before she can even begin to process Daisy's brush-off, Evie screeches above the music, "Time for the piñatas. Let's break some balls."

Savannah stumbles backwards as Tom pushes the piñata

stand to the center of the dance floor. The music changes to something low, pounding and primitive. Evie, her face contorted by a look of pure hatred, picks up the mallet and swings it with all the force of her muscular arms. She smacks the Blair piñata, narrowly missing Tom's head. He ducks away just in time, then scuttles away into the safety of the hallway.

With each stroke Evie screams and yells with all the guttural force reserved for childbirth. "Liar. Cheating bastard. I'm gonna get a knife and stick him like a bull, then watch all the blood drain out until he's good and dead."

Woah. That is more than a little extreme. Savannah feels uneasy. Evie's crossed a line, talking about death and blood. Does she really mean it? But with one more swing, the piñata explodes, releasing a cascade of penis-shaped sugar candies onto the floor. Evie bends over, hands clasping her knees and gasping for air. The mallet rolls across the floor. Savannah grabs it, before anyone else does any damage with it. Evie straightens up, grinning. Everyone watches her, barely daring to breathe.

"Sorry about that. Guess I got carried away. I'd never go after Blair. But good riddance to that sorry piece of dirt, I say. More bubbly, Tom, and make sure Daisy has her weapon."

Evie pushes a dazed and drunken-looking Daisy towards the other piñata. Savannah feels uneasy. As if cold water is trickling across her shoulders. Daisy looks out of it. Not in full control of herself.

"C'mon, Daisy. Let it all out!" screams Evie.

DAISY

Daisy feels like an Amazon. She hasn't felt this riled for years. She could fight wolves with her bare hands the way her heart is pounding. And she's had it with lying men. It's clear to her now, after all these years, that Wade is just a spineless loser. Why couldn't she see it before? She's been a blind fool for so long, clinging onto the hope that good things were just around the corner. That he'd somehow burst onto the music scene and really make it. She's traded her dreams for a half-life with a lazy, spoiled man who's left her high and dry so he can make up with Mommy, now that his father – the brute who cut her out from the family all those years ago – is gone.

It's time she quit being a doormat and made a stand. Leave all these negative and toxic people behind and find a real, mature man with ambition and drive. Or maybe she'll turn celibate. She's read about women who feel relieved not to worry about sex or relationships. In fact, they say it's truly liberating.

So when she takes the baseball bat in both hands, she feels currents of strength rippling through her shoulders. She lifts the heavy bat into the air, swings it in a circle and smashes it down on the Wade piñata.

"W is for Wade the weasel who sucked the life out of me. W is for weapon. If I ever see you again, I'm gonna take this baseball bat and smash your stupid skull open." Then she takes a run at the giant penis and slams the piñata so hard it dislodges from the hanger and crashes to the floor. She stands over it and brings down the baseball bat over and over, bashing and smashing it into tiny pieces, her arms moving like pistons.

Evie stands close, applauding. "That's the spirit, Daisy. Get in touch with your inner warrior. Set her free."

"Holy shit! You're fearsome," says Savannah, still sporting a sheen of sweat on her face from her little darts episode."

"Look out, Wade," says Zoe, shaking her head.

Daisy's body is still quivering with energy. All the lethargy of the last ten years has flown away, and she feels like Superwoman. Freed from her shackles. Now she needs booze and plenty of it. Her evening has only just begun.

Evie clicks her fingers. "Bring on the cocktails."

Soon the waiter appears with a tray of martini glasses. Evie produces a lighter from her cleavage. "I call this one *Liar, Liar, Pants on Fire.*" One click of the lighter and flames burst from the drinks. "Down in one," squeals Evie and they all gather round and chug down the flaming drinks. Daisy's not even sure if she's singed her eyebrows but she doesn't care at this point. The liquor goes down so smoothly.

After a couple more – a fruity tasting *Alimontini*, and a mint-filled *Rum Baby Rum*, Daisy starts to feel wobbly. The disco lights make her head spin, so she can't feel her fingers. Her knees suddenly buckle under her, and she has a sudden urge to drop to the floor, when Tom the hulk appears from nowhere and scoops her up into his arms. Daisy looks up at him. He's tanned and smells good, like spicy flowers and luxury soap. His muscular arms cradle her as if she's a baby. She feels the need to kiss him, so she wraps her arms around his neck, weaves her fingers into his hair and brings his face down towards hers. Meets his soft lips and kisses him like a fiend.

Evie starts up a chant. "Go for it, Daisy. Go for a real man."

Daisy feels her phone vibrate. *Is it Wade?* She places a finger on Tom's lips and goes to check her screen. *Damn, it's Blair.* She can't let Evie see he's calling her, so she throws it back into her purse. *He can wait,* she thinks as she moves her face towards Tom's waiting lips.

ZOE

Zoe throws back the *Rum Baby Rum* cocktail. Where did Evie find these cute creations? And the names are so apropos. She imagines serving them at a chic housewarming party in her brand-new condo to... which guests? Does she even have anyone to invite? Of course, Jaz will come and maybe he'll have a couple of friends and then there's always Alice, the pharmacist at one of her consulting hospitals. Come to think of it, she doesn't have that many close friends.

Work has taken up most of her time and when she does socialize it's with Marcus's mostly older crowd. Now she'll be forced to make a whole new set of friends at thirty-seven. But she can do it. She did it before at college.

She takes an *Alimontini* and sips it. Hell, she hasn't lost her touch. She could always drink these losers under the table. Case in point, Daisy, who looks like she's totally blasted. And so early in the evening? At least the booze has shut her up, or maybe it's Tom the Incredible Hulk who's now occupying her flapping mouth. *Thank Christ.* On the other hand, Savannah's a quiet drunk, no doubt trying to forget about her extreme outburst when she morphed into a scary knife-throwing ninja. That girl has hidden depths.

What exactly is she running from? It's strange that she and Blair were actually the last ones to see Cal after *the incident* and no one ever thought to ask if anything out of the ordinary happened before they left him. Zoe had never liked Cal, who always seemed so overconfident to the point of arrogance. A second-string quarterback, he sported bleached blond streaks and salon-tanned skin. Wore shirts that displayed bulging pecs and biceps. Girls would come onto him all the time, and yet she never saw him out with a girl just having a drink or chatting. Never saw him hug or kiss a girl. At parties she'd often catch him staring at Savannah, with an intense, brooding expression on his chiseled face, but Savannah didn't seem to notice, or if she did, she never followed up on it.

A cute waiter brushes by her carrying a tray of red jello shots.

"Time for dessert," screams Evie. "I call these *Love Gone Sour*."

Zoe takes two, feels the gooey, sour sweetness slip down her throat, and suddenly her mind blanks out all the worrying thoughts and everything is okay again and she makes her way back onto the dance floor. Soon they're all dancing around, holding the penis candies between their lips like sugar cigarettes. The mallet and baseball bat disappear, the moments of violence are forgotten and the party's on again.

Zoe drains another glass of champagne. She could drink until her brain is numb. Gone are the filters that regulate her day-to-day behavior. Good riddance to the respectable Dr. Zoe Ryan façade and that sterling reputation she's built her practice on.

The music changes and Usher starts up with 'OMG'. Zoe closes her eyes, tosses back her hair, and gyrates around the dance floor, reveling in her newfound freedom. Savannah follows her into the pinky-snowflake light and suddenly they're twenty again. Hormones surging through every part of her body as she grinds her hips and shimmies her shoulders against Savannah who moves like a dynamo, her limbs doing impossible moves as if her bones are made of rubber.

Zoe's flying now, aware of every inch of her body. Every nerve ending tingles. God, if the dolphin expert walked in, she could jump him right here on the dance floor in front of everybody. Ride him like he rides those beautiful dolphins. Caress his silky skin and just give in to every pleasure she's ever denied herself in the name of maintaining her status.

Sometime after the fourth tray of jello shots is passed around, the penthouse door opens, letting in a small group of unfamiliar guests. Zoe tries to focus her eyes and ignore the blurred border around her line of vision, but she's sure one of them is Dr. Zack, the dolphin expert, and all those other people are wearing the same dolphin T-shirt. *Must be other delegates from the convention. How did they know about the party? But who cares? My wish just came true. So embrace it and don't wait until tomorrow,* she thinks, as she swims through the other bodies on the dance floor and throws her arms around his shoulders. "Zakky. So great to see you."

His face lights up. "Fancy meeting you here, Doctor," he gushes as she takes both his hands and pulls him onto the dance floor.

"You need to catch up with me," she whispers, as the waitress passes by with another tray of shots. He takes two, downs them, licks his lips and tosses back another.

Then they're dancing together, or rather moving together. She feels like she's swimming through a warm ocean.

What do they call it? Twerking?

She's heard that term somewhere. Maybe from one of her patients.

Her patients? She's a doctor, for Christ's sake.

But another small and twisted voice says, it feels sooo good when he slides his body behind hers and puts his arms around her waist, grinding his hips into her ass.

Where did he learn to move like this?

Another couple of shots and his hands slide down to her buttocks. *Woah, they're on the dance floor. In full view of everyone.* But she glances around and everyone's into their own private scene and no one's paying any attention to them. *Let go, let go. You want this,* the voice tells her, and she turns around and jumps upwards, wrapping her legs around his waist, kissing him with a ferocity she's never experienced before.

"Let's find somewhere more private," she whispers.

"You're sure?"

She nods and he hobbles across the dance floor, carrying her towards a doorway that leads into a red-curtained bedroom with a circular mirror on the ceiling and suddenly he's all over her, pulling off her dress and she's ripping his shirt off so hard the buttons snap, until they're naked, their bodies fitting perfectly together on the velvet-covered bed.

SAVANNAH

Where the hell am I? is Savannah's first thought when she wakes up, rubs her eyes and tries to focus. Curtains are drawn. She's in a dark, unfamiliar room. Also, *who the hell took my clothes off and dressed me in a long T-shirt?* Her hand flies to the lower half of her body. *Thank God my panties are still on.*

But her head pounds as if someone's beating a pair of drumsticks on her scalp. Why did she drink so much? Why allow herself to be swept into another one of Evie's crazy escapades? For so many years she's lived a cautious, private life. Under the radar. Why stop now?

She moves her eyes sideways, trying to ignore the sudden stab of pain screeching behind her eyelids. A full bottle of water sits on the side table, next to a pack of Tylenol. Small mercies. Someone's looking after her. Easing up onto her elbow, she unscrews the top of the water bottle and guzzles down at least half in one go. Next, she pops two painkillers and falls back onto the pillow to wait for the fog to clear and the pounding to stop.

A text comes in. *Damn.* She's not ready for Evie yet. Not after last night. As she reaches for her phone, she scans the room. Most likely she's in one of the other bedrooms in Evie's suite. Thankfully not the room she watched Zoe hump her way into with that slippery-looking guy in the black T-shirt.

She looks at the phone display. It's Leon. *Damn, damn, damn.* She wasted a perfect opportunity last night. A chance to start up where they left off last. Recapture that warm, floaty moment when her insides melted and they were about to fall into each other's arms. Instead, she's made a complete fool of herself.

She reads his message.

> Missed you last night.

A little sad-face emoji follows.

> Missed you too. Drank too much. Sick headache. Crashed at Evie's suite.

> Aww. Try ice-cold coconut water and a three-egg omelet with home fries. Don't forget the extra-hot sauce.

> Yech – maybe I'll puke.

> No chance. Guaranteed cure.

> See you tonight?

> Working late. Extra side job.

> See you much later.

> Hugs and kisses.

> Save them for later 😊 🩶

She feels better already. The warm, bubbly feeling spreads from her head to her toes, just as the door swings open and Evie comes in looking perky and way too energetic in a skimpy gold bikini that shows off every curve and muscle of her sculpted body. A broad-brimmed straw hat throws her face into shadow.

Last night was a real shocker, when Evie first walked in. Savannah wanted to cry out and hug her. Comfort her for the loss of her humanity, because Evie, once a living, breathing powerhouse, has become a semi-human plastic person, carved up by a bunch of predatory surgeons. It's not like Savannah hasn't considered treatment herself. An aging face spells the end for show dancers like her. But she'd rather grow old gracefully than turn out like the retired dancers who often return to sit in the front row sporting trout lips, ancient doll faces and ruined knees, sighing at the life they lost.

"Let's get moving, Sav. Breakfast poolside, then we'll soak up some rays."

She snaps back to the present. To Evie tapping her manicured foot on the floor.

"I don't have my swimming stuff."

Evie tosses a flimsy white two-piece to her. "I've never worn this, and you can put the hotel robe over it. You'll look knockout."

"White goes see-through when it's wet."

"Live on the edge, Sav. Maybe it won't."

"Sound logic – hey, what about Daisy and Zoe?"

"Still sleeping. I'll leave a note. They probably need to sleep late."

At the poolside restaurant, it's another cloudless day and the temperature's already in the nineties, but under the canopy it's breezy and comfortable. Savannah picks up her second coconut water and takes a sip before digging into her spinach feta omelet. Leon was right. The coconut water was a magic hangover cure. Evie picks away at a bowl of cantaloupe and honeydew. Savannah's only seen her swallow two pieces so far.

Evie watches Savannah spread grape jelly on her sourdough toast. "You must still be dancing to eat like that."

Savannah gulps, almost choking on a clump of spinach. "Sure. In my spare time."

Evie tilts her head and studies Savannah's face. "Tell me about your life, Sav."

The blunt question takes Savannah off guard. She looks away and tries to busy herself cutting up a stray mushroom. "I'm in the entertainment field. Management. You know – taking care of temperamental creative types. I'm based on the West Coast."

Evie's face is obscured by a large pair of shades, but her eyebrows rise above the rims. "That's it? That's all you're going to give me?"

"What about you? What's your plan going forward?"

Evie sits back and twirls her fork. "Haven't decided yet. Maybe when the money's settled, I might get a little place in Manhattan. Near the park. Soak up a little culture. Browse the museums. Check out the opera, theater, ballet. I've always wanted to take ballet classes. Just never found the time to pick it up again with my kid and all that."

Savannah feels a surge of pity mixed with guilt. "Look, Evie. I know it can't have been easy being married to Blair, but... but..."

Evie's swollen lips turn downwards. If only her eyes were visible, but all Sav can see is her own tiny reflection in the dark lenses.

"How do you know it wasn't easy? You don't even know why we're breaking up. Or is there something you wanted to tell me?"

Sensing the hint of venom in Evie's tone, she puts her fork down, her appetite diminished. She can't say anything. Not yet.

Evie has to come clean first. Let them know why she brought them all here, because Evie always has an ulterior motive.

"No – nothing. It's just the way you bashed that piñata. Seems like you're super angry at him."

Evie spears another piece of melon and pops it in her mouth. "You bet I have anger issues. But hey – changing the subject – why did you just up and disappear three weeks before my wedding?"

The air suddenly chills, and Savannah is aware of every extraneous noise around her. "I don't want to talk about it."

Evie's frowns under the shade of the hat. "Losing Cal was a real blow to Blair."

Savannah can hear her own heartbeat. An ocean rushing in her ears.

"We were all shocked," she answers.

Before they can start up another conversation, Daisy and Zoe burst through the glass doors, as if they're on a life-or-death mission. Savannah pushes her plate away and spears a raspberry from the fruit platter. Evie turns to look.

"What the hell's gotten into those two?"

Zoe's first to reach them. She hovers – a dark, looming presence – blocking their sunlight. She holds out her phone.

"Explain this bullshit, Evie?"

Savannah leans forward, squinting at the screen. A video of Zoe, butt naked, writhing on top of that nerdy guy from last night as if she's playing Twister. Evie's hand flies to her mouth as if she's trying to stifle a giggle.

DAISY

Daisy's never seen Zoe so angry. The cool, self-possessed young woman she remembers from college morphed into a sex-crazed dynamo when she leapt up onto a guy she barely knew and wrapped her legs around his waist, devouring him with her lips like a lovestruck teenager. No wonder his hands were all over her. Grabbing her ass and grinding his groin against her as if they were dry-humping in public. Daisy, drunk out of her mind and nestling on Tom's lap, had a brief moment of shocked sobriety.

Now today, Zoe looks like she's ready to erupt. She hovers over Evie, her hands balled into tight fists, as if she's going to take a handful of her hair and rip her out of that wicker chair. Behind her, Daisy pats her back. They can't make a scene here in this happy tourist mecca. "Take it easy. There has to be an explanation."

Zoe turns and shoves her so hard, she stumbles against the neighboring table. Daisy whispers an apology to the startled young newlyweds holding hands over their mango crêpes.

"Explanation? All I know is that some anonymous asshole

THE DIVORCE PARTY

texted this video to me this morning." Zoe throws back her shoulders, eyes flashing a warning.

She thrusts her phone towards Evie. Savannah leans over to watch. Daisy already watched this movie first thing this morning when Zoe stuck the phone in front of her sleepy eyes to see a video of Zoe, naked and rolling across a circular bed entwined with the equally naked guy from last night. Evie hands it back, her face expressionless. Savannah covers her mouth with her hand.

Zoe's voice hovers on a knife-edge of hysteria. "How do I know whoever shot this isn't going to slap it onto social media? It could go viral. Then it's just a matter of time before my patients see it and call my practice and that's the end of Dr. Zoe, respected pediatrician. Parents won't let their precious children near a kinky nympho exhibitionist."

Daisy's heart drops. Everything Zoe's saying is true. She's literally screwed if this video gets out. But Evie's up on her feet. "Calm down, Zoe. Take a seat. Have a coffee and let's figure this out together."

Zoe stamps her foot. "You don't get it, Evie. You don't know what's at stake here. My hard-earned reputation. My career. Everything I've ever worked for. Down the toilet, just because of one drunken night."

Savannah takes Zoe's hand and speaks in a calm, consolatory tone. "Sit down, Zoe. We're here for you. Let's work this out."

Thank goodness for Sav, Daisy thinks, letting out a deep breath. She's starved and her head is still fragile from last night's party, not to mention she's had to put up with Zoe ranting about the video from the very first moment she blinked her eyes open.

She takes a seat at the table and Evie calls the waiter over. Come to think of it, she wouldn't be surprised if Evie wasn't behind this sordid business with Zoe. She remembers Evie's vicious gossip about Wade going back home. They've rekindled their old friendship. Has he been telling her things about their marriage? About their son? All she knows is, she'd better keep a close eye on her from now on, and if Blair wants inside info, she'll be sure to pass it on to him.

The coffee arrives and Daisy gulps it down, thankful for the handful of painkillers that have demolished her blinding headache. Seems Tom, unlike Zoe's opportunist partner, was the perfect gentleman as well as an amazing kisser. Though she was far gone last night, she woke up fully clothed and alone in one of the suite's three bedrooms. And when she finally crawled out of bed, Tom was nowhere to be seen. Most likely, he put her to bed and tucked her in. What a sweetheart.

"Did you tell that guy you're a doctor?" asks Evie.

Zoe lets out a huge sigh. "I met him at the poolside bar yesterday. He's a doctor too, a marine biologist, so I told him about my work. We talked about dolphins, for God's sake. Why?"

Evie scrutinizes a piece of watermelon before picking a single seed from it. "Well, maybe he thinks he can squeeze some money out of you in return for keeping the video under wraps. Has he sent you any other message?"

"No." Zoe shakes her head. "But why me?"

Savannah puts her hand over Zoe's. "Why anybody, Zoe. This is a crazy place. Anything goes here. Brings out the worst in people."

Evie's head swivels around. "Sounds like you know the place well."

"Of course she does. She works here," Daisy blurts without thinking. Her hand flies to her mouth. She's really done it now. Let Savannah's secret out. What kind of friend is she? "Sorry, Sav. Guess the hangover killed a few brain cells."

Evie's not about to let this go. "So why did you tell me you worked on the West Coast?"

Savannah flushes deep crimson below her tan. "I do – I mean – I did. I worked in San Diego. The management company sent me here for a special project."

"Special project?" Daisy says, before she bites her tongue. *Why can't she keep her mouth shut?* But Savannah's eyebrows have risen and her eyes are drilling into Daisy's as if she wants to gag her.

Now Zoe's knocking her fist on the table to get their attention. "Excuse me, but what happened to the friends-helping-friends talk? I need to do some major damage control but I don't know where the hell to start."

Evie turns slowly towards Zoe as if she's an irritating fly buzzing around her fruit bowl. Daisy decides not to offer any suggestions. She's blabbed enough already.

"Right," says Evie. "I can start by sending Tom to find that guy you were with. The one with the dolphin logo on his T-shirt. Shouldn't be too difficult if he's at a convention. Of course, there is a chance he isn't the one who did it. There were others at the party. Most of them wearing that same T-shirt. So they're all together somewhere. We can search them out. And Tom can be very persuasive when he wants to be."

"You can say that again," says Daisy, just as Savannah elbows her arm.

Zoe rubs her eyes and exhales. "I know where he is. Let me talk to him first. Tom can check out the waiters and all the others."

Savannah places both elbows on the table and leans towards Zoe. "In the meantime, you should close down all your social media accounts. That way it's more difficult for anyone to reach your circle of friends and spread something damaging."

"Good thinking, Sav," says Evie. "So now, why don't you both sit back and enjoy some breakfast."

Zoe takes a slug of coffee, then gets up. "I'm gonna order room service. I need to go back to my room and do all the social media stuff. It takes a while to sort that shit out."

"Okay, babe. I'll go and find Tom right now. Get that ball rolling." Evie passes a napkin over her swollen lips and stands up. "Daisy, I'll join you and Sav poolside later."

Daisy nods and pours herself a large glass of water as Evie and Zoe thread their way through the crowds, and the waiter stops by with the menu. Suddenly she's starving.

"I'll take eggs Benedict with a side of avocado and some home fries – oh – and wholewheat toast."

He hurries away and she looks up, suddenly aware of Savannah's eyes fixed intently on her. "How can you have such an appetite after all that's just happened? And after you almost puked out every secret I trusted you with?"

Daisy doesn't want anyone laying a guilt trip on her. She's borne enough of it for the last twenty years. "Back off, Sav. We're adults now, not kids. And I have no idea why you're so ashamed of living here and being a dancer. You're amazing – so talented. You should be proud of what you do."

Savannah closes her eyes and presses her lips together as if she's trying not to spill something important. "All I want is a peaceful life. I don't really want *this* – *this*... I don't want to reminisce about the past. In fact, I thought we'd agreed never to see each other again, and I was okay with that, but here we are, back together and I'm not sure why. I have a bad feeling about it. So I'm going to leave it at that. Enjoy your eggs Benedict. See you later."

Savannah gets up and stomps away before Daisy can protest. What the hell is wrong with all these so-called friends of hers who keep walking out on her? They're just killjoys who don't know how good they have it. They've clearly never had to live hand-to-mouth like she has. Well, let them be miserable, because she's having the best time she's ever had in years, and now she's going to relish her delicious breakfast, take a little stroll around the pool in her new pink bikini, and wait for Blair to give her a call.

Fifteen minutes later, the waitress takes Daisy's empty plate and Daisy blithely bills the breakfast to Evie's suite. The main pool is hopping now. A heady scent of coconut lingers in the air, but every lounger is taken up by sunbathers slathered in lotion. Kids splash in the shallow end. The older ones dive-bomb their parents as they pull bottles of chilled beer from poolside buckets of ice. This is way too frantic for Daisy, so she heads towards the adults-only pool. More her speed.

She walks up a narrow walkway bordered by a tall hedge, and turns a corner into a smaller pool area that boasts a see-through infinity hot tub at the far end. Music pumps out from a sound system behind her, topless bathers dance in the water. But she has to take off her sunglasses to see the couple at the center of the largest group. Evie, whose perfectly-sculpted breasts are pressed tightly against Tom's gleaming pecs as she shimmies up close to him. She feels a twinge of envy. Did Evie pay him to schmooze with her last night? Is he some kind of paid escort? And Evie sure doesn't look like the friend who's trying to help Zoe. Why the hell doesn't she have him out scouring the place for the mysterious cameraman?

She pulls back into the shelter of the tall hedge and takes a deep breath. Evie hasn't seen her. Doesn't suspect anything. She thinks hard. Blair asked her to report back on Evie. Maybe she can get a bit of leverage out of this new development and find a way to keep Evie in line should she need it. She's already got something on Savannah, who made her swear not to say another thing about being a showgirl living in Vegas. And now Zoe has this porn video hanging over her head that could destroy her career. Daisy feels a sudden sense of power over them all. For once she could be the one in control.

Her new motto is to live for the moment. *Seize the day.* She's used *The Dead Poets Society* plenty of times in her high school classes to understand that *carpe diem* is exactly the mantra she's adopting now.

She reaches for her phone and waits until Evie's in a tight clinch-up with Tom then snaps a few pictures first, followed by a video just for insurance. Now she plans to buy herself the sexiest beach cover-up she can find and head over to where Blair's staying to show it off.

ZOE

Zoe makes her way towards the main convention area and finds the sign for the Marine Biologists' Convention. Of course, she tells herself, there isn't going to be a Dr. Zack when she asks at the entrance. The guy from last night is probably some local opportunist with a T-shirt bought from a local aquarium who prowls the bars in search of single women looking for a temporary fling.

But she's stunned when the lean young man at the registration desk nods his head and directs her to the open door of a conference room where a session is in full swing. So Dr. Zack actually does exist. Her stomach lurches. What the hell is she going to say to him? And how will she face him after last night when Dr. Zoe morphed into an insatiable sex fiend? Her memory is foggy, but she's sure she made the first move. She blushes at the thought. *God,* she's a thirty-seven-year-old professional, not a sex-crazed kid. She's Dr. Zoe Ryan, distinguished pediatrician, guest speaker at The World Pediatric Conference in Bangkok, author of numerous scholarly papers on iron deficiency anemia in toddlers, so what was she doing, twerking like some hormonal tweenie on a Vegas dance floor?

The room is dark, but she tries to focus on the video showing on the big screen. Scientists in wetsuits dive down into the sparkling ocean and swim alongside pools of racing dolphins. Then Zack appears in living color onscreen. He's pulling himself out of the water, and onto the deck of a research vessel, his dark curls wet and gleaming, his slim body encased in a jet-black wetsuit. *Oh God.* Her body tingles as she imagines herself sliding into a pool with him right now for an underwater repeat of last night. *Pull yourself together,* she tells herself. *This is not why you're here.*

The presentation ends to loud applause. Lights go on and there's Zack, standing at the podium. He spies her and smiles. She gives a small wave in return and he hurries over to her, his tanned face split into a wide smile. He strides over and hugs her, whispering in her ear, "You were incredible last night, Dr. Zoe. A lioness. I've never met anyone quite like you."

Her insides turn to mush as brief images come back to her. His lean muscles, the coconut scent of his skin, those soft lips. "You were pretty amazing too," she says in a husky tone. "But there's a problem."

He holds her hands and pulls back, a hurt expression on his face. "What could possibly be wrong about two consenting adults making love and enjoying every moment of it?"

She disengages her hand and pulls out her phone. "This."

His eyes scan the video for a few seconds, then he hits pause. "What the hell?"

She shoves it back into her pocket. "I was going to ask you the same thing. I thought you'd taken it."

He shakes his head. "Why would you even think that? In fact, how could I have physically managed that? We didn't let go of each other the whole time. It's not like I had the chance to pull my camera out of my pocket and start shooting."

Of course he's telling the truth. "But it seemed such a coincidence you showing up at the party. In fact, how did you happen to know about it?"

He strokes the side of his face and thinks. "After I talked to you at the poolside bar yesterday, some guy approached me and invited me to a party in the penthouse. Told me to bring along a few of our delegates, said they needed a good mix of guests. We usually have a good time at these things. Free drinks and food. The student delegates love it because they're working to get through college. I don't usually join in. I prefer to stay in my room and study, but last night I was in the mood for a little fun. Didn't take much to persuade me."

Zoe feels a sense of uneasiness. Of nagging suspicion. "What did this guy look like?"

"Big, burly guy. Square shoulders. Black brush-cut. Looked like a linebacker."

Of course. Sounds exactly like Evie's right-hand man, Tom. Though that doesn't prove anything. Just that Evie engineered Zack's attendance at the party. Has she been watching Zoe, or was it just a coincidence?

"If this gets out onto social media it could ruin my reputation and screw up my entire medical practice." Wings of panic flutter inside her gut. She's going to puke.

He places strong, warm hands on her shoulders, steadying her. "It wouldn't be too great for me either. We have to fix this. I have an idea. Wait here."

Lightheaded and dizzy, she leans against a potted palm tree. Her stomach gurgles. She should have eaten breakfast. Zack returns with a petite, brown-haired girl in khaki T-shirt and shorts. "This is Anya. Anya – Zoe."

Zoe nods, though she's not at all interested in meeting new friends right at this moment.

"Anya is a hacker, and a whiz when it comes to the internet. I think she can help us."

"How?" asks Zoe, hoping little Anya won't have to view the torrid video.

"There's a bunch of things you can do," Anya chirps as if she's an old hand at salvaging sullied reputations. "But first, is it actually online yet?"

Zoe shakes her head. "Not when I looked half an hour ago."

"So we need to keep a lookout for it appearing online on YouTube, TikTok, your social media feeds."

"I've closed them down."

"That's good, but we'll still run a check."

"Then what?"

"Then we can do something called Search Engine Suppression. We create a network of neutral videos and basically swarm Google, Yahoo and some of the others, so that the original video disappears in a sea of harmless, touristy pieces."

"See, I told you she was good," says Zack, grinning.

Zoe's shoulders slump. "It sounds good, but it also seems like a whole lot of work. And you're busy right now."

"We can spare Anya for the morning. Take her along to your room and work on this together. In the meantime, I'll ask some of the other guys that were at the party if they noticed anything out of the ordinary going on."

Zoe could cry. Why is he being so nice to her? "This is amazing. I can't thank you enough."

"Maybe we can talk about that later." He smiles, and Zoe feels warm and lightheaded again. This guy is hotter than anyone she's ever met. "Better get going now in case you're already the hot ticket on YouTube."

She hurries away, following Anya, and feeling a sense of relief now she's seen him, but at the back of her mind is that nagging question: if it wasn't Zack that took the video, who was it? Which person at that party wants to ruin her reputation and put her career in jeopardy? She knows who the most likely suspect is, but that seems way too obvious.

Surely Evie wouldn't be so blatant? Maybe it's time for a little stealth and cunning to sort this out. And Daisy owes her. Possibly she could be useful now. Maybe a little spying is in order.

SAVANNAH

Savannah sits in the back seat of the cab chewing her nails. So much for a relaxing day at the pool. All she wants to do is get back to Leon's place and shower. She'd have walked if it hadn't been so scorching outside, and fighting through throngs of sweaty tourists isn't going to help the throbbing around her temples.

She checks her phone. No more creepy messages, thank God. But then it's weird that they've stopped since the party began. Quiet is not always good. Maybe they're plotting – figuring out some nasty surprise like Zoe received this morning?

The cab pulls up outside Leon's apartment block, and she thinks about the shadowy figure at the end of the side street, when she was running to the taxi stand. Could this person be watching her even now? Is Evie trying to exact some kind of twisted revenge plan on all of them and she's using Tom, her right-hand man, to help her? But why? What motive could she have? They were all involved in the incident with Cal. They all agreed to keep quiet. But does she know something more about what happened afterwards?

"I'm feeling a little paranoid today," she says to him. "Could you just walk to the front door with me? Jealous ex-boyfriend – never know when he's going to show up."

The skinny young driver who introduces himself as an architecture student, springs out of the car and holds the door open for her. As she gets out, she thinks to herself how unsettling it is that the past just stays with you and won't let go. Living with uncertainty and fear for any length of time, scars you. And even if you run away, you're always looking over your shoulder, wondering who's waiting in the shadows ready to jump out and scare the shit out of you.

She gives the driver an extra-large tip and pushes in through the glass doors. An icy blast of air-conditioner chills her all over. One evening down, one more to go. *Damn this stupid Chippendales show tonight.*

And then, according to Evie, there's still going to be a freedom karaoke and some dress-burning ritual, but heaven knows where that's going to happen. She needs a good, long sleep to get herself together. Why did she even agree to join this stupid weekend party? It's already caused major problems for Zoe, and who knows what else could happen tonight, especially with Evie in charge of things.

Her phone *pings* with a message. It's Daisy.

> Sorry about giving away your secret. Promise I won't say anything else. Are we still friends?

A sad-faced emoji with a single tear under its eye follows the childish message. Typical Daisy. She hasn't managed to grow up and yet she's mother to a college freshman. How on earth did she manage that?

The elevator doors swish open and she walks inside still thinking about Daisy. She remembers her as a needy person who craved attention. Often from other people's boyfriends. Like Wade who was Evie's friend first. She pitted herself against Evie to prove she was able to beat her at something, and Wade was so caught up with her after that evening, he had no time for anyone else.

One time Savannah had gone to get a tournament schedule from Daisy's dorm room. She stopped when she heard a low, whining sound. Edging forward, she peeked around the partly open door and saw Wade on his knees by the bed. Daisy was wrapping up little baggies of coke, oblivious to Wade whining and begging her to let him have a hit. Savannah left feeling sick to her stomach. She'd warned Daisy to ease off on the drugs but Daisy shrugged her off, telling her to quit being so preachy and besides, she could give them up whenever she wanted. But maybe, Savannah thinks, Wade couldn't.

The elevator lurches to a halt and Savannah steps into the hallway just as Leon's door opens. He immediately breaks out into a broad grin. He looks laid-back and casual in tan shorts and a white linen shirt that skims his muscular shoulders.

"Thought you were spending the weekend with the girls."

"God, I needed a break. Last night was crazy. Too much champagne and now I'm bushed. Think I need to nap and recharge."

He sighs and touches her cheek. Her body trembles. Why does he have to leave now?

"You can't stay a while?"

He smiles, his whole face lighting up. "Have to be somewhere in five minutes. I wish I could stick around."

"What's so important that you're in such a hurry?"

"A job that will pay the rest of my fees owing for next year."

Savannah's eyes narrow. "Is it escort work? Romancing a widowed billionaire?"

He takes both of her shoulders and lightly shakes her. "Absolutely no happy ending involved in tonight's job, I assure you. It's all above board."

"Okay. If you must."

"I must," he says, bending down and softly kissing her cheek. A waft of blueberry and vanilla turns her insides to liquid.

She waves as he heads off to the elevator and a text comes in from Evie.

> Chippendales at eight. Don't be late. Zoe's all sorted. We dealt with the video.

Ugh. Another excruciating night away from Leon. The only bright spot is that it will all be over soon and she can get back to her old life, at least for a while.

Another text arrives as she's letting herself into the kitchen, which is startlingly clean. Maybe Leon's been converted to a regular cleaning routine. Maybe they could really live together. She glances at the message.

> You like the young stuff? Too bad. I'd go under the knife just for you. Carve my face up if it made me look younger.

She throws the phone down like it's diseased. Who is doing this? Why can't they leave her alone? Then she remembers Evie's face. Carved up by cosmetic surgeons. A gross caricature of the woman she once was. Had someone pressured her to do this, and is that someone her husband, Blair?

Savannah leans her hands on the windowsill and looks down into the tavern parking lot.

A knot of guys file in through the doors of the tavern, already half drunk. On instinct she pulls the curtains shut. Her mind is scrambled. Is it Evie or Blair sending those messages?

Does that mean Blair is actually here, and he knows exactly where she lives?

Is he watching her right now?

And what will he do when he finds her?

DAISY

Daisy tries Blair's number again. It goes straight to voicemail. *Damn. When he finally checks his phone, there'll be seven missed calls from me as well as ten text messages. That reeks of desperation.* But Daisy has a thing about people not answering their phones right away, or sending responses to her texts. She's always quick to answer everything, grateful for communication of any kind. Why don't other people think like her?

She's wasted so much time waiting for people to get back to her. All those years she spent pitching that stupid romance novel to a long list of literary agents. Three whole years of waiting, checking her emails two or three times a day in the hope that someone would leap in with an offer of representation followed by a feverish bidding war between two or three top publishers. In the end, she hasn't a thing to show for it except a couple of dog-eared manuscripts fading in a drawer and a folder of politely impersonal rejection letters. *Guess you have to experience real romance to write about it,* she thinks and her life has been no fairy tale so far. But all that's about to change. She'll damn well make sure it does.

She limps towards the steps leading to Planet Hollywood where Blair is staying.

Her clothes cling to her body, her underarms are sweaty. Why the hell did she decide to walk from her hotel in the mid-afternoon heat? When she'd looked down the Strip, the Planet Hollywood towers seemed only a short distance away, but like all of Vegas, it's just an illusion. In reality it was a long-assed trek in ferocious heat.

No wonder the streets are empty and everyone's crowding under outdoor canopies chugging down arm-length frozen margaritas, and huddling under sprinklers that spit out a continuous haze of cool vapor. She stopped along the way and doused herself a few times, so now she probably looks like a drowned dog.

Inside the Miracle Mile mall, the cold air hits her with an icy blast worthy of a winter storm in Chicago. Now she's shaking from the cold and her clothes are plastered to her skin. This can't be healthy. She needs a hot drink and something substantial to eat. Definitely a sit-down to rest her ruined feet. There's a sandwich shop ahead that serves hot food and has cozy carpets on the floor, so she makes a beeline for it before the early evening crowds start lining up.

Ten minutes later she's the proud owner of a super-sized chicken, chipotle and avocado sub with a steaming bowl of cheddar-broccoli soup on the side. She's just scraping the last spoonful from the bowl when her phone rings. She answers.

"Hey?"

"Hey you, Daisy."

There's no mistaking Blair's husky growl. Daisy shudders, remembering his pallid, stretched face. And now she's seen Evie's cosmetic surgery cocktail, she can only imagine the two of them together look like a pair of ghouls. No wonder they want

THE DIVORCE PARTY

to split up. But then she remembers Blair actually sought her out, helped her to get here, and besides, he's loaded.

She tries to sound cheery. "So what's up, Blair?"

"I'm the one who should be asking you that, Daisy. I paid you good money, and I expect a return on my investment. You think this is a free ride?"

There's an edge to his voice that tells her he means business.

"Didn't you see all those texts I sent you?"

She can hear him fumbling with his phone.

"Oops, sorry. I missed them all. My ringer was turned off. I see them now. Good for you, Daisy. I like your persistence."

"I don't hold back. Not anymore. New resolution. And I have something for you. A video. From the pool this morning. I'll send it to you right away."

"Fantastic. I knew you'd come through for me. You were always such a loyal friend."

"Just a moment." She scrambles to open her phone, her fingers greasy from the sandwich. *Shit. I'm all thumbs. And now the screen is freezing up. Why didn't I spend a few more bucks on a newer phone?*

"I'm waiting, Daisy. And I don't see any videos coming my way."

Her head feels light and wobbly, but she forces herself to hold it together. Why is she acting flustered? He's being so nice to her now. She feels a new sense of confidence as the video appears.

"Take it easy, Blair. Videos take time."

She clicks the send button and waits. Even amidst all the hustle and bustle of the busy sandwich shop, she hears the sharp intake of his breath. He's seen the video.

"Good work, Daisy. Perfect. You caught that lying, two-timing bitch in the act."

The tone of his voice is ominous, bitter. Vengeful? But she stays quiet.

"Sorry to be so blunt, but you don't understand what it's been like to live with that woman all these years. She's sly and manipulative. You of all people should know how controlling she is."

"What do you mean?"

He laughs a dry little laugh. "Evie always talked about your Party Girls clique. How she had you all under her thumb. You in particular. She said you would have walked off the edge of a cliff if she'd told you to."

"That's not true. We were friends. Good, loyal friends." But deep down, Daisy knows he's right.

"Have you ever heard of toxic people, Daisy? Well, Evie's poison and I want rid of her and I'm not going to let her take half of my hard-earned money along with her. She messed up our daughter, who's finally away at school and probably drinking up a storm because of her."

Daisy's mouth is dry, her thoughts racing. "Well, if all that you're saying is true, then I've just helped you take my toxic friend down."

"Just one thing to remember, sweetheart – I'll be rid of her for good once the divorce goes through, but she's not done with you guys. I can tell you that for sure."

"What's she planning?"

"That I don't actually know, but cheer up, Daisy. I have a question for you. Why did you ever let that loser, Wade, con you into marrying him?"

She pushes her plate away. "Guess I was blinded by the whole rock star thing."

He sighs. "You know I would've given Evie up for you."

"Why didn't you say that all those years ago?" She feels a

dull ache that starts in her chest and works its way up to her throat.

"I was young and stupid then. Guessed I missed my chance but hey, it's a new day. New future. Want to come up to my room and then take a swim?"

Her heart starts to pound. She laughs. This is just the kind of spontaneity she's looking for. No need for explanations or plans. Just act on impulse. No prevaricating. "For sure. But you have to promise you won't do anything with that video until this party weekend's over."

He laughs. "For sure, Daisy, my pretty flower. But I still need more hard evidence. I hope you'll keep it coming."

"As long as you tell me what Wade's doing at his mom's place."

"So Evie must have told you. Come up for a swim and I'll tell you all about Wade. I have a whole cabana reserved for us, and a chilled bottle of Chardonnay with your name on it."

Her heart leaps. "See you in five."

Now she has to rush to the swimsuit store, and grab the skimpiest bikini she can find. She decides to leave half of the sandwich. Doesn't want to show up with a bloated gut. Not when Blair's waiting for her.

ZOE

Zoe checks herself out in the full-length mirror. She looks taller and slimmer than usual. Probably one of those skinny mirrors. Typical Vegas. Trying to trick her into thinking she's a younger, edgier, more glamorous version of herself. That way she'll be riding on a constant high and way more likely to drink and gamble.

This is a place with no clocks, where time is irrelevant and all you have to think about is pleasure seeking. Pigging out at buffets on mountains of breaded shrimp, deep-fried chicken wings and glutinous pasta, drinking yourself silly on foot-long, sugar-packed cocktails and frittering away enough money to keep you guilt-ridden for the rest of the year. It's also the most vulgar place Zoe's ever visited. Tacky and gaudy with its fake Eiffel Tower and Statue of Liberty. She thinks ruefully of the two weeks she spent this winter at the eco-paradise in the Turks and Caicos Islands. White, sandy beaches, pristine waters and home-grown garden-to-table meals. Plenty of local seafood prepared by Michelin-star chefs. At least Marcus has good taste when it comes to holidays.

Thinking about him makes her feel unsettled. This whole

video fiasco has clouded her feelings towards Zack. She's embarrassed that she came on so fast with him. Normally she's always on her guard, but she was attracted to him from the moment she saw him. And the lovemaking was so hot. The best she's ever experienced in her life. But maybe it's better for everyone concerned to treat the whole incident as the humiliating one-night stand she never had in her twenties. She's behaved like an impulsive teenager rather than Dr. Zoe Ryan, respected pediatrician and research scientist. And once Zack set her up with Anya, he seemed in an awful rush to get back to his sessions. No doubt they're infinitely less troubling than a sex-crazed, married woman. But even though Evie's insisted they apparently found the culprit – a part-time waiter hired for the party who thought he could make a few bucks by blackmailing Zoe with his sleazy home video – Zoe still feels uneasy. There are too many ways the footage can still be leaked out.

Earlier Evie and Tom appeared at the door of her room, brandishing the kid's phone. Tom rubbed his fists as if he'd recently cracked them across someone's jaw. With Anya's help they cleared the video from the cloud and erased every trace of it, then Tom stepped on the phone a few times and smashed it into oblivion. But Zoe knows that video could still be lurking somewhere in the cloud, that vast network of digital hiding places, just ready to make an appearance at the most inopportune time. And she's sure Evie still has access to it.

After this shock to her status quo, there's something familiar and comforting about the thought of home and Marcus and his expensive colognes and high-end suits. He's a great cook, and what wouldn't she give for a dip in their lovely infinity pool right now, since she's spent the past couple of days feeling alternately sweaty and frozen. Also, the sex with Zack was fantastic but not something she wants to upend her life over. In fact, the thought of getting used to a new guy's habits and routines is just too tiresome to contemplate. How could she tolerate someone with sweaty feet or bad dental hygiene? Though Zack did smell good – like coconut and sunshine.

Dammit, why can't she get him out of her head and just be a good, loyal wife?

Maybe it's taken all this time being away from Marcus to discover how much she appreciates him. How badly she wants to slip back into the cocoon of her daily routine, insulated by her comfy cushion of money. She'll snap a selfie in this figure-hugging black dress and send it to him later with a few heart emojis attached. Tell him she's changed her mind. Maybe that will placate him.

Strange, the thought of going back home has made her even more determined to enjoy herself to the fullest tonight, but she'll behave herself this time. Which reminds her – she meant to recruit Daisy to do a little digging around Evie just in case she has something else up her sleeve. Evie is definitely not to be trusted.

Picking up her silver metallic Gucci evening bag (a tenth anniversary gift from Marcus), she smacks her lips together to evenly spread her Christian Louboutin lipstick and struts over to the door to the comforting click of her Manolo Blahnik silver-and-black satin pumps.

Daisy doesn't answer for a while, but a scuffling sound comes from inside the room and possibly the low murmur of a man's voice. Could it be Tom? After last night's episode, which Zoe still hasn't erased from her mind, she has a fleeting memory of Daisy curled up on the big guy's lap with her lips locked on his. She knocks again. Daisy comes to the door, radiant in a tiny white dress trimmed with blue piping that matches her eyes. Her face is flushed but her dark hair looks utterly charming styled in that cute bob. In contrast, Zoe feels suddenly way too *put together*.

"You look amazing, Daisy. You ready to go?"

Daisy glances behind her. "Can you just give me a minute?"

Zoe nods as Daisy ducks back into her room. The low murmur of voices float under the door. Zoe's tempted to make some kind of excuse to push her way in to see what's going on. Instead, she leans against the door using the slightest pressure so that it opens a crack to give her a view along the short hallway and into the room where Daisy is talking to a guy. He's standing in front of the window looking out onto the Strip. He turns and Zoe's heart does a flip. Could that be Blair? Older, but still with that floppy, dark hair and the pallid skin now stretched tightly over the defined bones of his face, making him appear more vampirish than ever. She'd know him anywhere.

But why is he here in Vegas, and in Daisy's room?

Her heart skips a beat as Daisy turns the corner and heads towards the open door. She moves quickly into the empty hallway as Daisy comes out, wide-eyed and childlike. "Just had to get my lipstick." Her eyes flicker sideways in a lie.

"C'mon, Daisy," says Zoe in her best persuasive voice. "You sure that's all you went back for?"

"Of course. Why do you ask?" says Daisy, fussing with the fastener on her purse.

"Just thought I heard voices in there."

Daisy shrugs. "I forgot to turn off the TV. I was watching *Say Yes to the Dress.*"

"Let's get a move on," says Zoe, shocked at Daisy's detailed lie. How can she be trusted? And what else is she hiding? Does Evie know about this little arrangement?

Suddenly she feels a deep sense of unease about the long night ahead of her.

SAVANNAH

The floor trembles from the pounding music and Savannah hasn't even reached the main showroom. She's running late. Too afraid to walk to the Rio because of her mystery stalker, she'd called a cab, forgetting it was Saturday night. She had to wait over an hour for it to show up.

Evie's got a whole evening planned for them. She texted an itinerary, that starts at the Chippendales' show at the Rio, followed by a private supper in a luxury nightclub, with SPECIAL entertainment and *freedom karaoke*, followed by the bridal dress burning at a mystery location. Savannah doesn't like the sound of the final event. Or the thought of being led blindly to some godforsaken place she never agreed to go to.

Besides, she's had time to think about the creepy texts. Her mind keeps swinging back to Evie. Could she be sending them as some kind of twisted way to find out more about the Cal incident? Is she really capable of something so vicious? Has she found out something more about the actual circumstances of Savannah's escape after grad? What she had to resort to, to get away? Savannah thought she'd covered her tracks. Made sure any loose ends were tied up and no suspicion would fall on her.

In an instant, her heart leaps into her throat as someone barrels into her from behind. Pinpricks of light splinter into blinding flashes and she wheels around with such force her elbow meets someone's jaw. It's Daisy, staggering backwards cupping her jawbone.

"Savannah? What the hell? You almost broke my teeth and I don't have a dental plan."

"You rushed me from behind. I panicked." She reaches a hand out. Touches Daisy's shoulder with her fingertips. "I'm so, so sorry."

Daisy shrinks away. "Holy shit. That was like – extreme paranoia. What's going on with you? I never pegged you as a violent person."

Savannah shrugs. "It's nothing. Just a self-protection reflex. You get like that after you've lived here a long time on your own."

Daisy keeps stealing weird sideways glances at her. "You're not some undercover cop, are you? Or in witness protection? I mean, no one's asked you to your face yet, but we're all wondering why you left town so quickly. One moment you were there, and we were planning a bachelorette night, then next minute you were gone. No warning, no explanation, no message. We were worried sick."

"I did get back in touch."

"Yes, after two years of us wondering if you were lying dead in some ditch. And with no address. Evie finally tracked you down through Facebook. We didn't even know if you were still in the country."

Savannah exhales, her entire body deflating. If only she could just tell someone. Let go of all the guilt that's hounded her all these years. "I had no choice."

Daisy seems to have forgotten about the undercut to her jaw. She places a comforting hand on Savannah's arm. "You know you can talk to me, and I won't breathe a word to anyone."

"Huh? Like you didn't blab to everyone that I was living here? Have you told them I'm a show dancer yet?"

"No. I promise I haven't. You can trust me, Sav. Tell me what you're running from."

Savannah opens her mouth hoping the words will just slide out without actually mouthing them, but there's only silence followed by the shrill sound of Evie's voice from the doorway.

"Show starts in two minutes, ladies. Get your asses over here. These hot bods won't wait."

Daisy squeezes her arm. "Later? Promise?"

Savannah nods. Mute. But she has no intention of unloading her secrets to anyone. She gives Daisy a little shove. "C'mon. Let's go enjoy all those gleaming pecs."

Midway through the show, the audience morphs into a seething mass of crazy women, screeching for more stripping, hip-thrusting, and frantic crotch grabbing. Savannah curls into herself as Evie, Zoe and Daisy let loose, yelling along with the crowd as the dancers perform a country and western number, complete with rippling six-packs peeking from under skinny denim boleros, leather chaps over tiny stars-and-stripes briefs, and a row of toned asses wiggling under the spotlights. The naughty cowboys spill off the stage into the audience, searching the rows of women for the most eager ones to come up on stage and join in.

Daisy screams, "Pick me, pick me!" Evie shimmies her swelling cleavage, and Zoe wiggles her slim hips. Savannah shrinks into her seat, wishing it would swallow her up. Thankfully the nearest cowboy lunges over a line of women and grabs Daisy's hand, completely bypassing Evie whose eyes direct daggers at Daisy's back. Savannah's seen that look before, when Wade picked Daisy out from an entire row of fans.

Daisy is unfazed – totally oblivious to Evie's open hostility, as she skitters onstage pulled by her cowboy escort. The three chosen women are seated on saddles, straddling them awkwardly in tight minidresses. Daisy, already flying high from the three double gin and tonics she just inhaled, whoops and hollers like a Wild Western cowgirl as her chiseled Chippendale partner gyrates his groin against her back.

Zoe leans across to Savannah. "Yech, she'll need a shower after he's rubbed his sweaty thighs all over her."

Savannah shrugs. "Don't think she cares at this point."

"Well, I wouldn't have minded a piece of that," says Evie, hissing with rancor. "But then Daisy always was a little slut. Stealing other people's guys whenever she got the chance."

"Too right," says Zoe, her face flushed pink from the dry martinis she knocked back in record time. "She was with someone in her hotel room today."

Evie's eyes gleam under the lights. "Who? Spill."

Zoe chews her lip and shakes her head. "Couldn't tell you, I didn't see him clearly. Probably someone she picked up at the pool."

"Figures," says Evie. "She already made moves on Tom. Sure hasn't wasted any time since Wade left her."

Savannah glances towards the stage where the cowboys are whooping up a storm and pretending to rope their female fillies. She grits her teeth and tries to smile, wondering when this gong show of a night is going to end.

DAISY

Daisy's flying high by the time the show's over. She went all out tonight and hasn't held back. After all these years of fading into the background like a sad wallflower, her cowboy cameo moment onstage with all those hunky Western dudes was the pinnacle of excitement. She still has it.

The magnetism.

The look that puts her ahead of all the others – Savannah, Zoe and Evie, of course. That goes without saying. The charisma that made the dancing cowboy pick her above everyone else. She's forgotten how much of a rush that can be. Too bad when she came back to her seat afterwards, Evie's chin was so low it almost scraped the floor. Evie can't stand being passed over. Especially not in favor of Daisy. And Savannah and Zoe were giving her weird looks. Suddenly she feels she's just slipped back in time, back to being Daisy the pretty, put-upon airhead.

"The show was awesome," she squeals. "I can't believe you all look so sour."

"Maybe I'm too old for this," says Zoe, wiping a smudge from her designer purse.

Daisy points out a group of silver-haired ladies, clustered around a gleaming mahogany-chested Chippendale dancer clad only in tiny briefs and a bow tie. A photographer snaps a group portrait. "For your information, there are sixty-five-year-olds here getting deeper into it than you guys. They know a good time when they see it."

"Okay, point taken," says Evie, sighing. "Let's push on to the next venue. I've hired a limousine to take us to the Marquee Nightclub at the Cosmopolitan. We're having nibbles and some very special entertainment."

Soon they're coasting down the Strip in a white stretch limo and Daisy feels like a movie star, but why the hell are the others so subdued? Zoe is obviously used to the *finer* things in life. Probably feels the limo is vulgar and ostentatious. Evie's still pissed about not being picked to go onstage, and Savannah – well, Savannah is just a mystery. Some hidden undercurrent is driving her, or maybe she's harboring secrets that might just shock them all.

"C'mon, guys," she says, trying her best to inject a little sparkle into the flat mood, "we're supposed to be celebrating Evie's freedom. Her new start. Let's show some enthusiasm, for God's sake. Who's game for some sunroof screaming?" She cranks up the music. Some electronic rave-type stuff with a head-pounding bassline that shakes the sides of the limo.

Zoe's face twists into a weird grimace masquerading as a smile. "Okay – you're right, Daisy. C'mon. You and me."

Zoe and Daisy stand up and poke their heads out into the hot evening air. The crowds fly by in a blur of tanned faces and tropical clothing and the lights are a continuous neon blur. Daisy raises her arms, turns her face up to the stars and screams,

"Par-tay, par-tay!" Zoe joins in with a backup "Woo-hoo!" and next thing she knows Evie's cracked open a new bottle of bubbly and they're toasting the night with plastic glasses of champagne.

By the time they've done two runs up and down the Strip, all four of them have forgotten their gripes and troubles and crammed themselves into the sunroof opening. Now they're well into their second bottle of champagne, and waving their champagne glasses for all the world to see.

When they reach the Cosmopolitan, they're giddy, breathless, drunk and the best of friends again. At school, the highs and lows of their crazy foursome kept Daisy in a permanent state of stress. Tidal waves of utter bitchiness, loathing and evil gossip, followed by tranquil periods of absolute devotion, when they'd walk together into a wrestling tournament, arms linked like the tightest team ever.

Now the foursome make their way to the elevators and the twenty-fourth floor. Soon they're passing beyond the velvet rope and entering a series of cavernous clubrooms, packed to the brim with dancers and party animals. Evie leads them through the crowds until they come to a small, private area separated from the noise by a velvet curtain. Inside, the room is dark and lined with plush couches. They kick off their shoes and settle on the sectionals and two waiters appear, carrying a large silver ice bucket on a stand, filled with more bottles of champagne. Daisy makes a mental note of the number of bottles. No expense has been spared. Blair would definitely be interested in this extravagance. And when the platters of spicy shrimp, oriental rolls, pâté and caviar are laid out on the shiny black table, Daisy snaps a few pictures.

"For my Instagram," she explains.

Zoe already has a hand up. "No pictures please. Not tonight."

"Just the food and bubbly," Daisy explains as she shows the picture to Zoe, who nods and sits back.

"So where's the entertainment?" says Savannah.

Evie gives a wicked grin. "Should be showing up any time soon. Get ready for a blast."

Savannah excuses herself. "Gotta take a bathroom break. All that champagne. Be back in a jiffy."

Once Savannah's left, someone pushes aside a curtain and four hot guys dressed in skimpy briefs, white collars and bow ties stream in, holding serving cloths over their arms.

"Voila, your own personal servers. Take your pick and enjoy, ladies," says Evie, who grabs the arm of the second guy, a tall gold-skinned athlete, and pulls him astride her lap. Her hands are all over him, feeling those tight buns and the swelling muscles of his thighs. Not to be outdone, Daisy takes the hand of the long-haired blond Adonis and lets him whirl her around in a circle until she falls, giggling, onto his lap. Zoe dances awkwardly with the third guy, a tanned dancer-type with a choirboy face who looks way too young to be doing this job, so she keeps a respectable distance away, while the curly-haired fourth guy joins in with them as he waits for Savannah to return.

Evie's groping at her "waiter's" tight buttocks when Savannah swishes in through the curtain, takes one look at Evie and friend, and stops dead, her eyes wide with shock.

"What the hell is going on, Leon?" she hisses, and the gold-skinned guy's head whips around, his face registering absolute horror. He stumbles to get up, though Evie's clawing at him to stay.

"You two know each other?" she says, a look of vexation knotting her brows.

Savannah stands there, momentarily speechless, then slowly shakes her head. "No, we don't. I thought it was someone else."

The guy looks desolate – like he's going to cry. *She's lying,* thinks Daisy. *There's something going on between those two.*

"Don't let me stop you, Evie," says Savannah in a low, hard voice, as she grabs the curly-haired partnerless guy, pulls him into a tight clinch and virtually sucks the face off him. In an instant the gold-skinned guy grabs his clothes and storms out, pushing the curtain aside. Evie sits back, howling with laughter.

"Think we touched a nerve there," Evie says, cackling, and suddenly Daisy feels the skin at the back of her neck prickle. This was no coincidence. Evie engineered the entire situation. She knew exactly who she was hiring for this job.

Someone important to Savannah.

No doubt she's probably responsible for the Zoe porn video. If that's the case, what does she have in store for Daisy?

ZOE

Zoe sobers up in seconds. What the hell just happened? Are Savannah and that hot escort an item? Did Evie set up that whole scenario as another nasty trick to upset her? If so, then Zoe's worried about the explicit Zoe and Zack video. Evie assured her it's been dealt with, but what if she's lying and hoping to use it as a trump card? Typical Evie. She always had to have some kind of hold over her friends, to make sure they didn't step out of line.

Evie stands over Savannah. "Hey, Sav. I had no idea that guy was a friend of yours. I just called an agency and asked for four good-looking hunks. I mean, if I'd known I'd never..."

Savannah holds up her hand. "No need to explain. It's okay."

"We're good then?" Evie flutters her fake lashes and tries to look penitent.

Savannah mumbles a low, "Yup," her eyes fixed on the floor, just as a text comes in from Marcus. *Oh God. Is he here?* But a glance at the message brings the news she's dreaded.

> Some high school reunion. I just checked this out.

A picture follows. A still from the video. A naked Zoe astride an equally naked Zack. She's speechless.

> You're a lying, two-timing bitch.

How can she respond? *You're right. I am exactly that.* Instead, she types:

> It's not what you think. I can explain.

A long pause, then he shoots back:

> Spare the excuses. You'd better hope to hell that whoever's responsible hasn't sent it somewhere your patients can see, or maybe I should keep it. Might come in handy during the divorce negotiations.

Her head is scrambled. She can't process everything that's going on. Too much alcohol is slowing down her reaction time. Maybe she should just quit everything. Forget Marcus and her career. Sell the dream condo. Go find Dr. Zack, and volunteer to work with dolphins in a trendy Monterey research center where they don't give a damn about her sex life.

The only thing that's clear in her head right now is that Evie has something to do with this new development. Evie somehow sent the photo to Marcus, just like she's dealt a stinging blow to Savannah tonight.

Zoe downs the rest of her drink and looks over at the others. Savannah's expression is stony. Daisy's got that wide-eyed, jumpy thing going, which is really spooking her guy. So he gently takes her head and turns it towards him until she dips down and starts kissing him again. *God, she must be making up for years of deprivation the way she's devouring every man in her path.*

On the other end of the white sectional, Evie's having the time of her life with the curly-haired guy Savannah rejected, but why is Daisy trying to hide the fact that she's now furtively taking a video of Evie groping her muscle-bound waiter? Is that why Blair was hiding in her room?

She glances around at the young dancer patiently sitting beside her, waiting for her to take the lead, and feels a swell of sympathy for him. Rummaging in her purse, she pulls out a hundred-dollar bill. "You're way too young to be hanging out with me. Take this and call it a night. You're a nice guy. Stay away from this job."

He shrugs and raises his chiseled eyebrows. "Suit yourself, babe. But you're super-hot for an older woman."

"Thanks for that vote of confidence," she says with a sigh as he tucks the bill into the top of his briefs, mumbles, "Peace, Mama," and takes off. She catches Savannah's eye and nods in the direction of the bathroom, and when they slip out through the velvet curtain Daisy and Evie don't even glance their way.

"Pinch me, please, so I can wake up out of this nightmare?" says Zoe, leaning against the sink. They stand, shell-shocked in the cool blue light of the bathroom.

Savannah shakes her head. "I knew I should've nixed this whole idea as soon as I got the invitation. I didn't need to come here, and that's what pisses me off the most."

Zoe supports herself against the sink. "It's a train wreck. How could I be so naive to think it would be a relaxing break? That's not possible with Evie around. Trouble always follows her. Now I've risked my career and my marriage and I'm still drinking champagne with her in this dumb Vegas nightclub."

Savannah leans her back against the wall. "Why does she have this hold over us? She calls us and we come running. How is it possible she still has that pull after so many years?"

Zoe shakes her head. "I'm a respected doctor, for Christ's sake, and I've behaved like a brainless, horny teenager ever since I got here. Talk about regression. We just stepped right back into our old roles."

Savannah clasps Zoe's hand. "I'm so sorry about that video. I didn't notice anything suspicious last night. I can't think who would've taken it or why."

"Evie tried to convince me they dealt with it, but I can't believe a word that comes out of her mouth. And do you believe that hiring your friend was just a random occurrence?"

"My gut tells me it wasn't, but her explanation makes sense. I know how things work in this town."

"So you do work here? Daisy was right."

Savannah rests her hands on the countertop and leans against the sink. "I do, for now. But I'm leaving soon. My career forces me to move pretty often."

Zoe's interest is piqued. This is the most information Savannah has ever given out. "Where to next?"

Savannah looks away. "Not sure yet. I'm still figuring that out."

Zoe tries to catch Savannah's eye. "Why did you disappear so suddenly, Sav? You know we were so worried about you."

"I had to make a quick decision. I'm sorry I left without an explanation."

Zoe lowers her voice, anxious to maintain Savannah's confidence. "Was it because of Cal?"

"Why do you ask?" Savannah snaps back.

"Just wondering. Only you and Blair were the last ones to see him alive."

Savannah tidies some stray hairs. "He was okay when we left him," she says, in a shaky voice.

Zoe decides she won't push her anymore. She's clearly upset about tonight's incident. "So what do we do now?"

"I was trying to figure that out," says Savannah, sighing. "Do we finish this night off, then opt out of tomorrow?"

"That's exactly what I was thinking. Just play along with everything, thank her at the end of the night and excuse ourselves. I don't want to make an enemy out of Evie. Especially with the possibility of that video still being around."

"I was thinking the same thing. Who knows what the hell she'd cook up if you ticked her off. She's got a long memory."

"Then we're agreed. Tomorrow we'll be on our way. Back to our mature, adult lives and away from Evie's toxic influence."

"Shouldn't we talk to Daisy as well?" says Savannah, smoothing her hair down.

"No way," says Zoe, snapping her purse shut. "Don't tell Daisy anything."

Savannah touches Zoe's shoulder. "Are you saying we can't trust Daisy?"

Zoe can't handle this secret alone, and maybe Savannah is the only person she trusts right now. She takes a deep breath. "I saw Daisy with someone in her room before the party."

"And...?"

"And – I didn't get the best look, but I think it was Blair."

A look of horror wipes the color from Savannah's face. "Does Evie know he's here?"

"I have no idea, but I'm guessing she doesn't."

Savannah falls back against the wall, her face pale and drawn.

"You okay, Sav?"

Savannah nods. "Fine. Don't worry."

But that haunted expression tells Zoe she's anything but fine, and it has something to do with Blair.

SAVANNAH

They plunge back into the noise and clamor of the club, and a dazzling light show. Her phone buzzes again. Leon's already texted her about ten times. She drops the phone into her bag, vowing to deal with him face to face when all this is over. Let him sweat a bit longer. Maybe he'll appreciate her more. For now, all she can think of is the news that Blair is here in Vegas somewhere, and weird things are happening to everyone, including the creepy messages that prove someone's been following her. So maybe it isn't Evie after all, or maybe the two of them are so warped they're playing some twisted game together, and just maybe Blair is conning poor Daisy and has a nasty surprise waiting for her next.

Her head is so mixed up, she can barely put one foot in front of the other, but she has to see this evening through, and now at least she has an ally.

"So what do you think Evie's got planned next?" Zoe shouts above the throbbing bass notes.

"I think it's the freedom karaoke," says Savannah, elbowing her way through the crowds.

"I've never been to a karaoke bar in my life," says Zoe. "Not my vibe."

"Then we'll just let her hog the mic and be the center of attention."

"Yep. She always did enjoy her moment in the spotlight." Zoe grasps the curtain to the private room and pulls it aside.

"That's exactly what I was thinking, but too bad she was always tone deaf."

They walk in to find Daisy's still clinging on to her blond-haired Adonis and looking distinctly drunk.

"Darian and I have the same birthday," she croons, leaning her cheek against his hand. "We discovered we're soulmates."

Savannah feels stone-cold sober as she watches Darian and Daisy collapse into a giggling, smooching heap. Meanwhile, Evie's occupied with her phone, texting frantically, her long nails tapping on the screen. The curly-haired guy chills beside her, but Evie's ignoring him. Her eyes are narrowed and there's an intensity to her expression that makes Savannah nervous. She remembers that look from high school when Evie was cooking up mischief. Maybe she's texting her next moves to Blair.

Evie is a calculating, selfish woman. It's tough to imagine her as a mother. In fact, the very thought of Evie and Blair bringing up a child makes her shudder. Especially considering everything she knows about Blair. Things no one else does. Maybe not even Evie.

At that precise moment, Evie looks up and glares at Savannah. Is she imagining that look of pure hatred burning in Evie's eyes? A murderous expression that sets Savannah on edge. Then just as quickly, the look changes, replaced by a brilliant smile.

"You guys took a helluva long time. You making out in the bathroom?"

Zoe plops down onto the sofa. "Oh – just girl talk. Catching up on lost time."

Evie glances at Savannah then back to Zoe. "Don't tell me Savannah finally bared her soul to you?"

Zoe shrugs. "Nope."

Evie smirks and nods. "Our Savannah is a real mystery woman."

"So what's happening next, Evie?" says Savannah, eager to change the subject.

Evie puts her phone away and stands up, almost knocking the curly-haired guy's head with her purse. He ducks away just in time to avoid a blow to his ear. Evie's oblivious, probably already on to the next crazy idea. "Time for freedom karaoke, and boy do I have a surprise for you all. An amazing band to back us up. I booked a private room at a karaoke bar on the other side of the Strip. Not too far. We'll just hop in a cab and be there in ten."

Daisy's pouting. She's way more drunk than Savannah realized. "Can Darian come along with us? I like him."

Evie laughs. "Sure. My treat. But he'd better put some clothes on."

Darian glances down at his tiny briefs as if he'd forgotten that's all he's wearing. "Oh, cool – I'll go get my stuff."

Daisy leans against him and whispers in his ear, "Meet us by the takshy – I mean tack – tack – oh shit. You know what I mean."

Darian scoots off. He can't be more than twenty-two. Savannah thinks maybe she'll ask him how long Leon's been doing this extra job.

But there's no time to think. Daisy leans heavily on Zoe's arm as they leave the room and make their way through the crowded club. Savannah's eyes are heavy, her head throbs around the temples. This night has been exhausting both mentally and physically. The whole evening frantic and weirdly disjointed. They're supposed to be having fun, but there's a joylessness about the whole proceedings. As if Evie's trying too hard and everything's misfiring. But is it deliberate? That's what Savannah can't figure out.

Fifteen minutes later they walk through the door of the Takeo Karaoke Palace where a hostess directs them to their own private room – cozy and lit with blue neon. Large colorful fans decorate the walls and leather couches are arranged around a stage where a band is setting up.

"I thought it would be great to have live music to accompany us, so I invited an old friend to help out," says Evie, ushering them inside. Zoe first, then Daisy who's clinging onto Darian, then Savannah.

"Almost ready?" says Evie to the long-haired guy adjusting the mic. He looks up and Daisy lets out a piercing shriek. Savannah checks the guy out. He's familiar, older than she remembered and looks like he's wearing a blond wig, but no – she knows exactly who it is. And judging by Daisy's reaction he's the last person she wanted to see.

It's Wade. Daisy's absent husband and Evie's old crush.

DAISY

It's as if someone's poured a bucket of cold water over Daisy's head. Suddenly she's stone-cold sober. Her entire body frozen in disbelief as she looks from Wade to Evie who's giving her a patronizing side-eye.

"I thought it would be a nice surprise to bring him here," Evie says, flipping back her curtain of hair to expose the plunging neckline of her electric-blue dress. "Plus, it gives Wade some incredible exposure. I mean this is just the kind of entertainment mecca he needs to be in, and it could lead to other gigs."

Daisy's brain is foggy. She can't clear her confusion. What the hell is going on? Does Evie know Wade just walked out on her? Does she know he's gone back to live with his wealthy mother? Despite all these important, burning questions, all she can say is, "Your hair? It's – it's..."

Wade is staring at her sheepishly. "Evie set it all up. Got me in with this great stylist and a wigmaker. Gave me a whole new look." His fingers graze lovingly over the expensive gray silk shirt that skims his slight paunch and hangs smartly over perfectly fitted jeans. Polished tan boots she's never seen before, complete the look. He grins, waiting for approval, like a kid who got his candy back.

She glances around. The others have pulled back, probably sensing trouble. Even Evie's watching from afar.

"But you – you left me. What about the note."

He can't even look her in the eye. "I'm not proud of what I did. But I was desperate. Sitting in our kitchen, trying to eat my Cheerios, staring out of the window at the same old street. Nothing to look forward to. That wasn't a life. It was just an existence. I had to get away before it killed me. Before I dragged you down too. So I packed my stuff and walked out of the house. Then Evie called when I was on the way to the bus depot and told me my dad was sick and on his last legs. I was with him when he died and he forgave me. Told me to look after my mom, and that's what I was doing until Evie asked me to come to Vegas. Gave me a chance. I had nowhere else to turn. So I came here."

"You could've called me," says Daisy, feeling a rush of indignation. "What do you think I've been doing day in and day out? Working a shit job, holding everything together while you moped around like a spoilt child. You don't think that was monotonous?"

"I have a real chance here, Daisy. I'm gonna make a fresh start. Evie helped me kick the drugs."

Daisy feels the tide of anger rising inside. "How – after all these years?"

He narrows his eyes. "We were bad for each other and you know it, Daisy. I'm not blaming you entirely for the drug thing, but it suited you to keep a hold over me."

She flexes her hand. She could punch him in the face. "Liar. You're a goddamn liar."

He squares up to her. So close she can feel a fine spray of

spit when he talks. "Face it, Daisy. You were never the same after you lost the baby."

Daisy freezes. *He said it. The awful, terrible thing she cannot bring herself to say.*

But before she can react, someone slings an arm around her shoulders. "Hey, babe," says Darian, smooching her neck. "Who's this rock star?"

Wade looks from Daisy to Darian, his expression morphing from disbelief to annoyance. He laughs. "True to form, Daisy. You didn't miss a moment. Looks like you're getting on fine without me already."

Icy shards stab her heart. "Truth be told, Wade. I was done with you years ago."

There's a moment of ominous silence. "Fuck you," says Wade, turning away and striding towards Evie. Evie places a comforting arm across Wade's shoulders, they whisper together for a few moments, then leave the room.

Zoe and Savannah rush towards her.

"What the hell is going on here?" says Zoe. "What was that about losing a baby?"

"He's lying," says Daisy, panicking. "The drugs have fried his brain."

"You sure you're okay?" says Savannah, patting her shoulder.

"I don't get all this," says Darian, his face creased with confusion.

"Just go get a beer, sweetheart," says Zoe, handing him a twenty. "We girls need to talk."

Darian shrugs and heads over to the bar. Daisy lets out a long sigh. There's no way she's confiding in Zoe, who loved to lord it over everyone with her so-called superior intellect. And Savannah whose cool, detached mystery-woman persona was just a front that hid an insecure woman afraid of intimacy.

"There's nothing to talk about. He's just a dead weight weighing me down and I'm glad to be done with him."

"But why would he lie about you losing your baby?" says Savannah. "Does he mean Ethan? You showed us pictures."

Daisy shakes them off. *Why can't they shut up? Stop with all the questions?* Of course she has a child. She can picture her lovely boy. All the precious stages of his life flash like freeze-frames in her head. Ethan dribbling into his bib, Ethan cooing his sweet, milky breath into her ear, Ethan on his first day at kindergarten, his Elmo backpack strapped across his shoulders, Ethan squeezing her cheeks and begging her to talk funny. Tears prick the back of her eyes.

"I don't know why he'd say that," she says, gesturing to the waiter. She needs a drink. Needs to consider what to do about Wade.

Zoe's about to pipe up again when the band starts up, drowning out her voice.

"Surely she's not going ahead with this damn karaoke?" says Savannah, nodding towards the stage where two guitarists and a drummer have joined Wade.

Daisy has a queasy feeling in her gut, but she orders a double gin and tosses it back, feeling the slow burn in her throat. *So Evie thinks we can still carry on as if nothing's happened. She really must be crazy. Or maybe she's trying to take some kind of weird revenge on me for stealing Wade away all those years ago. Too bad she doesn't know I don't give a damn about him anymore. I just wanna make sure I get what's owed to me.*

Daisy feels her resolve flowing back, bolstered by the knowledge that she can start a new life free from the yoke of Wade on her shoulders and with half the money he's bound to wheedle out of his darling mother. She won't let him worm his way out of that responsibility. Too bad she can't find a way to get all of it. She links her arm into Zoe's.

"C'mon, let's have a good laugh at Evie's tone-deaf performance."

"That's the spirit," says Zoe, settling onto the soft leather couch. Darian slinks back and Daisy pats the space beside her. He flops down and sips a frozen margarita while Zoe shows Savannah pictures of her incredible Toronto house. Daisy takes out her phone to show them Ethan's childhood pictures, when she notices three unanswered texts from the anonymous number. She scrolls frantically through them. The first came in an hour ago:

> Where's your asshole husband?

Fifteen minutes later.

> We know he's in Vegas. Where?

Fifteen minutes ago.

Daisy hears a buzzing sound in her ears, as if bolts of electricity are coursing through her body. Her fingers hover over the screen.

Maybe there is a way to make Wade pay for treating her so badly. Does she even have to stop and consider what to tell them?

ZOE

After an hour of Evie's tone-deaf warbling, Zoe's ready to call it a night. Evie's gone through a host of divorce party classics like Britney Spears' 'Stronger,' Taylor Swift's 'We Are Never Ever Getting Back Together,' Elton John's 'I'm Still Standing' and now finally a version of 'I Will Survive' that doesn't bear any resemblance to the original Gloria Gaynor version. And the crazy thing is, she's so into strutting across the stage like a diva and schmoozing along with Wade at his microphone, she hasn't noticed that her three invited guests are sitting like statues, too dazed to even lift an eyebrow.

No doubt Savannah's upset about her guy; the sexy lap dancer Evie just happened to select from hundreds – maybe thousands – available in Vegas. Seems way too much of a coincidence, and more like another of Evie's spiteful tricks. Daisy's still brooding and chewing her nails, wondering why her husband of nineteen years is up there on stage gyrating like a teen idol with her so-called friend. What exactly is that guy's deal? Walking out on his wife, not telling her where he's headed, and just showing up like an unwanted gift. Then there's his comment about her losing a baby. Did he mean that Daisy had a miscarriage, and then had Ethan, or that Ethan is the lost baby?

But how can she think about Savannah and Daisy's problems when she's got plenty of her own? Now that Marcus has seen the pictures, he wants a divorce. How will that impact her lifestyle? Would he stoop so low to jeopardize her professional reputation and maybe her livelihood by leaking those pics? Maybe she needs to put out some serious cash to hire an image expert. Or do they call them spin doctors? The PR people who deal in crisis management. It'd be worth it. The lakefront condo is hanging in the balance, which reminds her. She wouldn't put it past Marcus to do something spiteful like freezing their accounts or moving money offshore, so she can't get her hands on it until she's spent an obscene amount of money on lawyers' fees.

She really must call her lawyer again, but somehow all her limbs feel heavy, her head so fuzzy she can't seem to focus on one single course of action. Savannah and Daisy look as if they're going to nod off too. They're a sad bunch, and all because of this stupid divorce party. Evie's delivered each of them a major body-blow. Is that why she's looking so damn smug up there?

Zoe checks her phone. No messages from Marcus since the last comment about her career. On impulse she taps in a message:

> Evie set us all up. She's trying to get back at us.

There's a long pause before a reply.

> You guys need to grow up. You sound like a whiny teen, blaming everyone else. You're not in college anymore.

Zoe slips her phone back into her bag. *Weird thing is, he's absolutely right. We've all regressed twenty years this weekend,* she thinks. *And here we are, right back under Evie's thumb. Exactly where she wants us. Ruling by manipulation and coercion. Just like she did with her Truth or Dare games, with the wrestling team, and with Zoe's little scamming sidelines.*

She's had enough of this. She turns to Daisy who's busy texting even though her eyes are heavy with exhaustion. Darian's drifted off somewhere. Probably sick of being ignored.

"I want to get out of here. I don't feel right," she whispers.

Daisy glances up, her face contorted with hatred. "Me too. Let's get as far away from that arrogant bitch as we can."

Zoe looks over at Savannah whose head is drooping to one side. "Ask Savannah if she wants to go. Then we'll just walk out together. Fuck Evie. I'm done here."

Daisy slowly raises her elbow and digs Savannah in the ribs. Her eyes struggle to open, and she squints as if she can't quite make out where she is. "Whaa...?" Her voice trails off, drowned by the ear-splitting finale to 'I Will Survive'.

"Something's wrong," says Daisy, flopping back against the studded leather couch. "I feel weird."

Zoe's first instinct is to reach out and touch the pulse at the side of Daisy's throat. Her heart rate has slowed way down. And then suddenly Zoe can't feel her fingers. Her whole body is slowing down. All she can do is rest her head against the back of the couch and concentrate on breathing. Guitar sounds jangle against her eardrums like glass shattering, and the bright strobe lights make her nauseous. But through the halo of glowing spotlights, she can make out Evie's eyes, suddenly growing larger, watching her, and the last clear thought that comes into Zoe's head is that she's been drugged – somehow Evie's spiked all their drinks – GHB or Rohypnol or... Then everything fades to black.

SAVANNAH

Every inch of Savannah's body aches and the acrid stink of smoke tickles her throat. She struggles to open her eyes, aware of stabbing pains searing her scalp. *What happened?* She runs her fingers across a hard, grainy surface and struggles to raise herself on her elbow, persisting until she's sitting bolt upright against a cold concrete wall on some kind of low wooden bench. She's in a large, empty space with concrete floors. Looks like an old warehouse. A sliver of light filters in below a wooden door up ahead. It's so dusty and stifling she can't breathe. God knows where she is. Her head throbs, but she manages to turn around far enough to see Zoe and Daisy slumped beside her. What the hell is going on? And what's that burning smell?

In the other direction, a large woodstove glows in the darkness. Wisps of smoke leak around the edges of the glass door. Close by, two shadowy figures stoke the fire with logs and a mound of white rags is piled nearby. Is that Evie in the sparkly blue dress?

Zoe begins to stir beside her, moaning as she struggles to pull herself up.

"What the fuck?" she groans. "And where the hell are we?"

"Looks like a warehouse, but I have no idea where," whispers Savannah. Her hands go to her side. "Where's my purse? My phone? Dammit."

"I'm gonna throw up any minute," Zoe whines.

"Hold it a few seconds," says Savannah, reaching for a nearby garbage can and almost fainting from the pain of the exertion. "There, toss your cookies, but don't expect me to clean it up."

Zoe dips her head down towards the bucket and retches so hard it sounds like she's throwing up her innards. "Oh God, oh God – I think I'm gonna die."

"Please don't. You're the doctor. We need you."

Zoe straightens up, her hands searching frantically around her. "Oh Jesus. Where's my stuff? I need to wipe my mouth. It's – it's disgusting."

Savannah closes her eyes for one blissful moment, pretending she's back in the bedroom of Leon's apartment. "Needing a tissue is the least of your worries. Someone's taken all our ID and money."

Zoe clamps a hand across her forehead. "Oh – God. Someone drugged our drinks. That's the last thought I had before everything slowed down and went black. Must have been GHB or Rohypnol. I'd know the symptoms anywhere."

Cold prickles of dread chill Savannah's body. No wonder she felt sick. "You think Evie did it?"

"Who else? Kind of goes along with the entire weekend, doesn't it? But I promise you, I'm gonna sue the ass off her when I get out of here. Either that or turn her in to the cops." Zoe mops at her mouth with the back of her hand.

"We can't do that," says Savannah.

"And why the hell not?" says Zoe, squaring her shoulders.

"You know exactly why."

"You mean the Cal thing?"

Savannah nods.

"I'm tired of even thinking about that." Zoe pauses and glares at Savannah. "Oh, I get it. You have a guilty secret. We never knew what actually happened after you and Blair drove away with Cal. He was okay – a little banged-up but still alive."

Savannah feels sicker than ever. "We dropped him off. No one knows what happened after that."

"I don't believe that for a minute, and sooner or later you're going to have to tell us," says Zoe, angrily flashing her mascara-smudged eyes, "because your damned secret is why this sociopathic bitch is still controlling us and we'll never escape her."

Savannah lowers her eyes. Zoe's right. But she'll never tell. Not yet. "Right now we need to work together to get out of here. I know my way around Vegas. If I could only figure out where we are."

They both look over at Daisy who's sleeping with her mouth open, leaving a dark drool-stain on the wood. Zoe nudges her shoulder. Daisy's face twists in a grimace as she begins to wake. One set of eyelashes is stuck to her cheek like a furry caterpillar. With eyes still closed, she reaches a finger up to feel it and sits bolt upright screaming and clawing her face.

"Get it off me..."

Savannah lunges across and swipes the offending eyelash from Daisy's face. "Cut it out. Look." She holds it up to Daisy, who stares at it with bloodshot panda eyes.

"I think I'm gonna be..." She doubles over as Savannah grabs the reeking bucket and holds it under her head. Daisy retches, with a wet gurgling sound that makes Savannah feel like throwing up too.

All the ruckus has brought Evie stomping across to them.

"What the heck is going on?"

Zoe tries to get to her feet but falters and flops back onto the bench. "Oh, that's rich coming from you. Maybe we could ask you the same question. What the hell do you think you're doing drugging us and bringing us here against our will?"

"And where are our phones and purses?" Savannah chimes in. "Not to mention, where the fuck are we?"

Evie holds out her hands to her sides as if to pacify them. She looks remarkably put together, and yet Savannah remembers her drinking champagne like it was water. "Not feeling so good are we?" She taps one foot nonchalantly on the floor and inspects a fingernail.

"You're kidding," says Zoe, glaring daggers at Evie. "All you can do is stand there, checking your manicure while we've been poisoned. I'm a doctor. And I believe you roofied us and brought us here against our will, which makes you guilty of kidnapping and assault."

Evie inhales deeply and pulls back her shoulders. "Is that your professional opinion, Dr. Ryan? Really? You're not exactly a reliable source, are you? That explicit porno shows your focus might be elsewhere, don't you think?"

"Leopards never change their spots," hisses Zoe. "You always were a spiteful bitch, inside and out, Evie."

"At least I wasn't a cold and ruthless robot, driven by money and ambition and totally devoid of empathy," Evie spits back.

Zoe tries to laugh but grimaces in pain. "That is actually hilarious coming from you, the woman whose daily routine and leisure activities for the past twenty years have revolved around shopping, shopping, and more shopping."

"Really? That's what you think of me?" says Evie, tapping the side of her temple. "That I'm just some airhead who's had an easy ride in my life. Well, I think maybe it's time for a game of Truth or Dare before we do the dress burning. You guys fancy a throwback to old times?"

DAISY

Evie's drugged and kidnapped them and somehow brought them to this filthy warehouse, and now she has the nerve to suggest they sit round like good old buddies and play a kids' game. She's gone so far over the line, it's out of sight. Maybe she's finally lost her grip on reality. Married to Blair for all these years has unhinged her.

And now, Zoe and Evie are locked in a standoff. Two iron wills fighting for dominance. Daisy's head reels as Evie's voice booms into the silence. "Truth or dare? Your choice, Zoe."

Zoe sets her shoulders back, and pulls herself upright. "I refuse to be drawn into one of your sick fantasies. I'm a grown woman. A scientist. I deal in logic, not crazy delusions."

She turns and starts to make her way towards a small exit door at the far end of the room. Daisy watches, open-mouthed, wondering if she should make a move too. But even if she managed to get outside, how would she get back to the hotel without her phone or money?

"You know where we are?" she whispers into Savannah's ear.

"No idea. Just humor her for now."

Daisy nods. "Okay. But I have an idea."

Evie's head jerks around. "Whispering is so ignorant. Didn't anyone teach you that?"

They watch Zoe drag her feet to the door where Tom stands like a brick wall blocking her from the outside world.

"Let me through, you dumb lug. I have important things to do."

She raises a hand to push him aside and, swift as an adder, he grasps her wrist.

"He was runner-up in the Mr. Galaxy muscleman contest ten years ago," shouts Evie. "You wouldn't want him to mess with your surgeon's hands now, would you?"

Daisy's body freezes. Evie's way out of control.

"Besides, I have something of yours." Evie waves a phone in the air. "Don't you need your lifeline?"

Zoe stamps her foot on the concrete so hard she's hopping around in pain. "Damn you and your boyfriend-on-steroids."

If Evie's got Zoe's phone, then she's probably got mine too, thinks Daisy. *What if Evie finds out I've been seeing Blair? Come to think of it, he's probably been trying to contact her. She's probably seen all the notifications already. This definitely won't end well if she has. On the plus side, her location app is on, so he might try to find us.*

Savannah gets up and goes over to Zoe, allowing her to rest her head on her shoulder until she limps back to the bench with the others. Evie's face is impassive, a spiteful smirk twisting the corner of her swollen lips. Daisy has the sudden urge to shove her so hard she topples over like the fake, hollow doll she really is, but she stays seated. Impassive. Saving her trump card for later.

"Give me my fucking phone, you psycho bitch," says Zoe.

Evie shakes her index finger and grins. "Music to my ears.

That's what I was waiting for. The old Zoe. Not that stuffy doctor with a stick up her ass."

"Don't let her get to you," says Savannah, patting Zoe's arm.

"Oh, but I plan to," says Evie, pacing back and forth in front of them. "The fun is about to begin, ladies. We're going to play a game of catchup. Only this time we're really going to bare our souls. No topic is off the cards."

"And then you'll give us our phones back?" asks Daisy.

Evie strokes her chin, looks up to the ceiling in an exaggerated attitude of contemplation. "Oh, Daisy, Daisy. Such an innocent. Butter wouldn't melt in your mouth. Except you're a scheming little bitch."

Daisy gasps as if Evie's delivered a punch to her solar plexus.

"Why are you picking on Daisy like that?" says Savannah.

"Maybe you should ask her why she wants her phone back so badly. Could it be that she wants to send another secret text to my soon-to-be ex-husband?"

"What the...?" says Zoe. "Why is Daisy messaging Blair?"

Evie's eyes are blazing. "Maybe you'd better ask her yourself."

Everyone's eyes are on Daisy. She drops her head, unable to face them.

Savannah is first to speak. "You might as well tell us what's going on, Daisy. Maybe we can help you if you're in a tough situation."

Evie gives a slow, smug grin. "Oh, our Daisy knows exactly how to get herself out of a scrape. Tell them, Daisy – tell them how you agreed to spy on me for Blair in return for an airline ticket and spending money."

"Hey, I sent you money for your ticket as well," says Zoe, eyes flaring with outrage. "Were you actually scamming me?"

Daisy feels tears well into her eyes. "No – no. It wasn't like that. You both offered to help me at the same time. I was desperate. Wade had just walked out on me. I thought I could come here and make a new start. I was going to give the money back once I got a job and set myself up."

Zoe slumps back against the wall, a look of utter disgust twisting her face.

"You're right to be appalled, Zoe, because thanks to our dear, dippy Daisy, my creep of a husband knows exactly where we are, and is no doubt looking for me as we speak. But thanks to Tom, my bodyguard, we've eluded him so far."

Tom waves from the other side of the room, but everyone's too caught up in the drama to wave back.

"You're a rat," hisses Zoe, eyes burning.

"And she sold Wade's rare album collection without even asking him."

"Someone stole it," says Daisy, tears streaming down her face. "I didn't sell it. And so what if I did? He's a jerk and a useless piece of crap. You're welcome to him, Evie. And good luck to you both."

Furious, Daisy buries her face in her hands, but not because she feels guilty. They don't know how she'd tear lions apart to get her own back on Wade for all his apathy and neglect. Evie's too dumb to know that Wade is a wanted man, and Daisy knows the guys who are after him.

When she started dealing with them, she always made sure to pay up on time. She'd seen too many fingerless hands and broken kneecaps to do otherwise. So when she went back to teaching, she put Wade in charge of accounts. Made sure to impress upon him the importance of keeping their suppliers happy, while she concentrated on hustling up business among her new teen clientele. But Wade was a sloppy businessman. Sampled too much of the merchandise and missed more payments than she realized. Now they're after him, and if they don't find him, they'll move to find her.

Right now, the best-case scenario is that these suppliers will show up, demand to be paid and Wade will somehow bank on Evie still carrying a torch for him, and charm her into coughing up enough money to cover his debt. Or maybe he'll ask his dear old mom to help out.

But she has to wait for the right moment to let Evie know about the danger, and it isn't now.

Evie has to play her game first, then Daisy will strike.

For now, she'll keep quiet.

ZOE

"Come on then," says Savannah, breaking the tension. "You wanted a captive audience. We're all here. Let's play."

Zoe glares at Savannah. Why the hell is she encouraging Evie? And what's with the sudden heat? It's like an inferno in here. The back of her neck is drenched in sweat.

Evie moves away from Daisy who's still bent over, cradling her head. "Go ahead, Sav. You seem eager to get something going."

Savannah looks up at Evie. "No, you're the keener. You go first."

Evie narrows her eyes. "Okay. I have nothing to hide. Go ahead."

Savannah sighs and stands up to face Evie. "Okay, truth or dare?"

"Truth," snaps Evie.

The atmosphere is so tense, there's a buzzing sound in Zoe's ears as the two women stake each other out.

"Evie, what's the worst thing anyone's done to you?"

Evie chews her lip and glances at the floor. "I can only pick one?"

"The worst," says Savannah in a low voice that's almost a whisper.

Evie looks away. Her eyes are glossy with tears. This looks bad. Zoe can feel it.

"Okay then, if you insist." She clears her throat and continues in a husky voice. "After my final rhinoplasty, my husband, Blair, slammed me onto the bed, pushed my face into the mattress and raped me from behind because he said I'd become a freak and a gargoyle and he couldn't stand to look at me anymore."

Her face is turned away from them, but her shoulders are shaking. She's sobbing. Everyone is speechless. Only the crackle of the woodstove breaks the silence. Tom stands close by, curling and uncurling his fists.

Zoe feels helpless at the brutality and injustice of Evie's story. She wants to throw up – scream out to everyone that the world's really a crappy place and everyone just tries to pretend it isn't. But she can't give in to that hopelessness. Can't put those feelings into words, can't find the right thing to say. So she just blurts out the first questions that come to mind.

"Why did you cut your face up just because he asked you to? Why did you stay with him? What about you and what you want?" But it all sounds so hollow.

When Evie faces them again, her makeup is streaked with tears. "This – this hatchet job isn't something I wanted. But Blair knew how to get under my skin. He'd tell me my lips were too thin, my nose crooked, my face too wrinkled. Then he started to cheat on me, secretly at first. It got so bad he didn't even try to cover it up. Didn't care that my friends saw him holding hands in a bar with a girl ten years younger than me, or that I saw all the sickening texts that came in for him all times of the day and night. So in the end you convince yourself something's wrong with you. That you're not young enough or pretty enough to hold his interest. Then somehow you can't find the strength to say no to another operation that just might make you perfect enough for him to love you. In the end, you hate yourself so much, you don't care who's cutting up your face or how shocking the results are. And by the time you realize what you've done to yourself, it's too late to fix it."

Evie's story confirms what Zoe already knows. That Blair is a heartless monster. She was his girlfriend long enough to find out. She should know. But she doesn't want to talk about that time in her life. It cuts too deep. She has to steer Evie away from that topic.

"That's a sad, sad story, and my heart goes out to you, but that's no reason to keep us here against our will," she says. "And besides, you're divorcing him, so you won't have to put up with that kind of abuse anymore."

"Don't dismiss Evie's pain like that," says Savannah, turning on her. "You can't just brush years of physical and mental abuse under the carpet and pretend they didn't happen."

Savannah's such a bleeding heart, feeding into Evie's tragedy. Zoe's discovered there's only one way to deal with adversity. Steel yourself against it. Refuse to let it touch you. That's what she did. "In my life I've discovered that wallowing in self-pity doesn't get you anywhere. It just stops you from moving ahead."

Evie's face hardens as she points a finger at her. "And here we have Zoe, the ice queen. Underneath that polished exterior lies a frozen heart. Nothing and no one can touch her. Truth is, she's incapable of showing even a shred of empathy to anyone. I always wondered why you went into pediatrics, Zoe. It's a strange choice for a person who detests children or any living, breathing life-form with a heartbeat – except maybe herself."

Zoe feels hot and shaky, but she won't be goaded into Evie's little mind games. "I'm just a realist. Weakness is for those who don't care about being left behind, and for dependent people – those who don't have the strength to make it on their own."

"Hmm, let me think back a bit. I believe you were extremely dependent on people with money right from the get-go. I remember you didn't have time for a few of our wrestling tournaments because you were too busy scouring online matchmaker sites for wealthy, older men desperate to connect with younger women who were, coincidentally short on cash."

"Hypocrite," says Zoe. "You were into it too."

"I was and I'll admit it, but I never lied about it or tried to cover it up. Not like you, claiming you always had your nose buried in the books. Studying. When you were really checking out the prospects. Trying to hook up with someone who'd be your meal ticket through college," Evie says, hands on hips, surveying them all.

Zoe looks around. Why is everyone staring at her with such accusing eyes? "I – I don't want to play this game anymore," says Zoe, her body suddenly limp and devoid of all sensation.

Evie dangles the phone in her hand. "I still have a copy of a certain juicy video. And you're playing a starring role in it, except you're butt naked. Wouldn't want a little excerpt to find its way onto TikTok now, would you? You can have it if you cooperate, and I get to ask the question since I bared my soul first."

If Zoe had a knife in her hand, she would've stuck it between Evie's ribs by now, but all she can do is imagine fountains of blood spurting from her intercostal arteries.

"So truth or dare, Zoe? What's it to be?"

"I told you I don't want to play this anymore," she says, sliding along the bench, away from all the staring eyes.

Evie waves the phone again. "Truth or dare? What's it to be?"

"Okay," she mumbles through gritted teeth. "Truth."

Evie walks in an exaggerated circle, nodding and stroking her chin. Zoe feels dizzy. As if she's having some kind of out-of-body experience and she's floating ten feet in the air watching herself break down into a blubbering mess. Maybe it's the aftereffects of the drugs, or the fact that she's starving, but right now all she can think of is that beautiful condo and the bright living room with its floor-to-ceiling windows where filmy white drapes shiver in a light breeze from the lake. She can get through this, and if she does, she's going to be there, in that room by next weekend. She just has to hold on to that vision. Evie suddenly stops and turns to her, smiling.

"Okay. What's the biggest mistake you've ever made?"

"Coming here," Zoe says.

"Not fair, Zoe. I mean in your entire life."

Zoe's mind races through everything that she has, everything she treasures. Her career, her patients, her independence, her pride that she made it. She rose from the ashes of a bleak childhood, a rotten adolescence, and a traumatic young adulthood. What's to be lost now by telling the truth? Maybe it might make a difference. She clears her throat. Inhales deeply.

"You want to know the worst thing I've done? I'll tell you. I did go to those country club dances. Evie was right. I was on the hunt for a rich boyfriend. It seemed like the only way I could get to med school. Finally, I found one. His name was Blair Cummings."

Evie slaps her thigh. "Yes, now we're getting somewhere. You didn't waste any time hooking your claws into him after Savannah turned him down. So tell us what happened after you hooked up with my soon-to-be ex-husband."

Zoe tries not to concentrate on Evie's frozen face and the unblinking eyes of the women around her.

Think of the room overlooking the lake. The ripples on the water.

She breathes again and lets them dim out of focus. "He was young, handsome, rich and crazy about me. Said he was bored by all those tight-assed preppy girls with no imagination. We went on a few dates. He was charming, sexy and he didn't push things. I was a willing partner. Guess I naively thought he'd fall for me and we'd get married in a splashy fairy-tale wedding at some exclusive country club with his mom and dad cheering us on. That might have happened if I hadn't got pregnant. When I told him, he acted like I was to blame. Claimed I'd done it deliberately and ruined his future. Said he couldn't possibly have anything to do with the baby because his dad would be furious and cut him out of the family business. Eventually he managed to get some money together, enough to get an abortion at a good hospital. But I – but I..." Zoe feels as if something's blocking her windpipe, choking the breath from her. The solid lump of grief she's buried all these years has grown into a monster and become unmoored. Now it's fighting to come out.

"Take your time," says Savannah, placing a warm, comforting hand on her back.

"I – I took the money." She hesitates, choked by grief and shame. Savannah's hand is warm on her back. "But I – I put most of it in my med-school tuition fund, and went to a cheap, backstreet guy who claimed to be a doctor, but turned out to be a drunken quack. He did the procedure. Got rid of the baby, but the place was filthy. I bled so much and got a terrible infection. I stayed in my room for days, fighting the fever and when it was all over, my uterus was so badly scarred, I've never been able to get pregnant ever since."

It's finally out. The whole story. The shame of it washes over her in a tidal wave. Forcing her downwards until her head rests on her knees and all she can do is let it take her along with it.

"Why didn't you tell us?" says Savannah, placing a hand on her shoulder. "We could've helped you. Taken you to a hospital or something?"

Now Daisy's by her side too. "You went through all that alone? How did we not know about it?"

Zoe rests her head on her hands. "I was too proud. And I felt so ashamed. I just locked myself away. Couldn't face you guys. Dosed myself with Tylenol. Slept a whole lot."

"You could've died," says Savannah.

Daisy rests her head on Zoe's back. "Sorry we didn't check on you. We should've known something was up."

Evie's face is thunderous. She pulls herself up to her full height, her body twitching like she's some skinny praying mantis just ready to strike.

"The story isn't over," says Evie. "Tell us what happened with Blair."

Zoe gulps back the tears. "He said he didn't want anything more to do with me. That's when he moved on to you."

"So I was second – actually third choice as usual. Too bad you didn't warn me about him. Instead, you handed your leftovers to me without so much as a word about how he'd just abandoned you. In fact, you actually told me you were bored with him and you'd met someone else. Not even a hint about what a bastard he was."

Evie's voice is like a knife in Zoe's head. The way she takes Zoe's pain and twists it into a trivial personal slight. "You stupid bitch. You'd never have listened anyway. I could've said he was a blood-sucking, serial-killing vampire and you'd still have dragged him to the altar."

"You're probably right about that. For once I had my eye on

the prize and I actually won it – over you. Too bad it wasn't exactly a jackpot."

"This has gone far enough," says Savannah, intervening. "Why can't we leave all this pain in the past? Where it belongs?"

Evie stamps her foot and swivels to face Savannah. "Sav, Sav, Sav. So typical of you. Always the diplomat. The consummate peacemaker. Never putting yourself on the line. Always the observer watching from the outside. So quiet, so understanding, but behind that icy-calm exterior there's a calculating, tough-as-nails survivor who gets exactly what she wants no matter what she has to do to the people around her. Believe me, I know firsthand."

"You're not still harping on about Blair picking Savannah first?" says Daisy.

"Are you kidding? I'm talking about something way more serious than that."

SAVANNAH

Savannah feels the first fluttering of real panic in her gut as she sits back down and shifts uneasily on the bench. Evie has them at her mercy and they're all too weak to retaliate. Just the mention of Blair brings her heart slamming into her throat. She can't possibly relive what happened all those years ago. Maybe calm reasoning might defuse the situation. She lowers her voice so that Evie has to lean in to listen.

"How about we do the dress burning and call it a night? I'm thinking we all need to have a shower and sleep this off."

Evie's taut face contorts into a malevolent smile. "Very clever. Trying to distract us from the game. We've all bared our souls and now it's your turn. Don't think you're going to wriggle out of this one."

Savannah's skin crawls just thinking about that time. She struggles to breathe and glances around. Three sets of inquisitive eyes are fixed on her, probing her for answers she doesn't want to give.

"So – do you want to tell them or shall I do the honors?" says Evie.

Savannah speaks quietly. Deliberately. "You think you know everything. But you don't. You have no idea." Her head starts to ache. The temperature in the warehouse is rising. The sun must be up and soon it'll be hot as hell in here, especially with that fire burning.

Evie plants her feet apart, squaring her body to face Savannah. "Are you sure about that? I know your speedy little exit from La Jolla involved my husband and a close friend of his. I also know what my husband is capable of."

"So do I," says Savannah, unable to stop herself. "He's a beast with no heart. I'm amazed you stayed in the marriage as long as you did."

"I didn't know enough about him then. I only saw what I wanted to see."

"Then why did you stay with him? You could have left anytime," says Zoe. "If you knew for sure he was cheating, you could have taken him for everything he has."

Evie turns on Zoe. "That would seem so easy to someone like you with your medical degree and your high-flying career and your seven-figure income. But I don't have that kind of leverage. And I learned very early in my marriage that leaving Blair was next to impossible. He's not someone you simply turn your back on and walk out the door."

It's working. Evie is distracted by Zoe's question. Typical. She always did prefer to talk about herself. Savannah breathes a temporary sigh of relief as Evie continues railing against Blair.

"Blair has to have the last word and, believe me, he's a ruthless bastard. He would've hired the best lawyers to uncover every bit of dirt on me, so he could sue me for full custody of our daughter. I'd never have seen her again, and I couldn't live with that. So I put up with him until she turned eighteen and went off to college. Now Blair has no hold over me anymore. But you see, he's still going crazy trying to screw things up for me. Trying to find something incriminating so he can cut me out of a proper divorce settlement. And you're trying to help him do that!" she screeches at Daisy. "What kind of a friend are you?"

DAISY

Daisy's in panic mode. She's not going to let Evie mess things up for her now that she finally has some hope for a better life. Maybe that life involves Blair and maybe not, though after all she's heard from Evie and Zoe, she's already thinking she doesn't want anything to do with him. But she has to make a good show of things. Keep up this naïve and clueless persona they've all come to expect. She doubles over, gulping the tears back.

"I'm sorry, Evie. I couldn't say no to him. He was so persuasive."

Evie's body stiffens like a ramrod. Her eyes blaze. "Bullshit. You probably jumped at the chance to make a few bucks. You've always been a conniving little bitch."

Daisy closes her eyes. She's done taking Evie's abuse. A flood of anger rises inside her, driving her to lunge forward, screaming like a woman in labor as she launches herself onto Evie, clawing at her hair, and pulling her down towards the concrete floor. Thick skeins of hair come away in her hands. Has she torn Evie's hair out from the scalp? But metal clips show she's holding extensions in her hand. Behind her she hears Savannah and Zoe as they pull her away.

"She's not worth it," says Zoe.

"Let her fight it out with her asshole husband," says Savannah. "They both deserve each other."

Evie looks like a wild thing – hair sticking out in ragged tufts where the extensions used to be. Her eyes burn with vengeance. "I might be a bitch, but at least I'm not a murderer."

Everyone freezes and turns to stare at Savannah who backs away, her face frozen in a mask of horror. "She's lying."

Zoe turns to Evie. "What are you talking about? You'd better explain yourself."

Savannah's face is sheet-white. She backs away from them until she reaches the bench and slumps down on it. "Where's Blair?" She's panting, her breath coming in short bursts. "Is he here in Vegas?"

Evie studies her nails and sighs. "According to Tom he is. Last sighted in the lobby of our hotel, thanks to Daisy."

Savannah's eyes dart to the overhead door. "And where is he now?"

Evie grins maliciously. "Why're you so worried about Blair? Does he know something about you and Cal? Maybe something you don't want any of us to know about?"

Daisy glances from Evie to Savannah. Something's terribly wrong with Savannah. Her face is chalk white. She's tapping her foot on the ground at ninety miles an hour. Her eyes are darting everywhere as if she wants to find even the tiniest gap and wriggle through it, out of this hellhole.

Zoe's head darts from side to side in panic. "I don't get it. We all know about the horrific car accident after the – after…"

"You mean after the wrestling incident?"

"Yes," gasps Zoe. "After the thing we agreed never to talk about."

Daisy pipes up, her face still flushed after her attack. "You were part of that too, Evie. You agreed to keep it quiet. So why are you bringing it up again?"

"Maybe because it wasn't our fault. For all these years we thought we killed him, and we lived with all that guilt." Savannah is still silent, while Evie studies a silver-painted fingernail, then points it right at her. "Ask her. She knows what she did to him."

Daisy looks from Evie to Savannah. The two women don't speak, as if they're waiting for the other to draw first. She thinks about Cal. How could she forget him? The tall, muscular football player with piercing eyes and a lazy drawl of a voice. That night after grad he called her a *dirty little drug pusher*, said trash like her didn't deserve the privilege of studying at UCSD. She shudders at the memory of him shoving her hard against the wall and warning her to *stay the fuck away from Wade*. But he'd always been obsessed with Savannah who wouldn't give him the time of day, and Cal was the kind of guy mystified by women who didn't show a lick of interest in him.

Damn, I can't think clearly. It's so hot in this cursed place. She can't think of Cal and what happened to him, because the bastard deserved everything he got.

"You mean what *we* did to him," says Savannah, collecting herself.

Evie sighs, pressing her swollen lips together in a tight line. "Okay – since she won't tell you, I will. After the *accident*, Blair and Sav took Cal home. Blair left Savannah to keep an eye on Cal and when he came back Cal was dead. Savannah had Cal's insulin in her pocket. Guess it comes in handy having access to lab supplies. You know exactly how much insulin to administer to kill someone. Blair broke down when he told me this. Said he couldn't live with it anymore. He only kept it quiet because he was weak and let her convince him not to tell. She seduced him – persuaded him to tell us he died from the wrestling accident. That's when he called us and told us to come over. And we all know what happened then with the car and the cliff. It was horrible. No wonder she ran."

"Lies," mutters Savannah, burying her head in her hands. "That's not how it went down."

"I don't even want to hear your twisted version of events," Evie says, turning as if to leave. "I'm done with this game. And I'm finished with you all – my three *best* friends or should I say *frenemies,* who never really gave a damn about me. In a couple of minutes, Tom is going to stoke up the fire and make sure my wedding dress goes up in flames, but don't breathe too hard. I've heard the fumes can be toxic, what with all that flame-retardant stuff they put on fabrics these days. Oh – and when the sun comes up it may get a little hot in here, but I hear sweating is great for cleaning your pores. Gets rid of all those nasty impurities."

She checks her phone. "I believe Blair might be on the way here. He always has the location app on. Doesn't like me to go too far without knowing where I am. In the meantime, maybe Savannah can entertain you with an explanation of how she's capable of killing a defenseless man in cold blood."

Just then Zoe springs up from the bench. "Hold on now. We've established the main fight is between you and Savannah, so now I want my purse and phone back. I personally have no interest in your sordid conflict."

Evie laughs. "Typical Zoe. Always looking out for number one. Self-preservation has always been your driving force. I think maybe you should stick around. Your friends might be in need of medical help in a couple of hours when this place turns into a toxic sauna."

Zoe's face is flushed. Daisy can hear her breaths coming

short and fast. "She won't stop until she ruins us. I should've known it. She's played us right from the start."

Evie whirls around. "Hypocrite. You didn't need playing. You were always on the make. Scamming our friends to make a bit of cash on the side. Scalping fake tickets. Selling fake designer jewelry. You were money-hungry. That's why you threw yourself at Blair. Got yourself pregnant. That's really something to be proud of," says Evie.

"Too bad you used the same script to catch him," says Zoe. "How did you manage that? Mommy and Daddy didn't put up the money to get rid of it?"

"You may think you're more intelligent than me, Doctor, but you sure don't have the killer instinct. One thing my mom taught me was to be a fighter. Always pull yourself up and deliver the last punch. I knew Blair had gotten you pregnant. I also knew he didn't want his parents to find out. We made a deal; my silence, in exchange for a lovely wedding and entry into the good life."

Zoe leans forward, straining against Daisy's grip. "You've heard that phrase – *be careful what you wish for*. I guess you finally discovered the meaning of that."

"Twisted little scammer," spits Evie.

"Takes one to know one," says Zoe.

"Enough of the clichés," says Daisy relaxing her grip on Zoe. "Where's Wade? What does he know about any of this?"

Evie throws her head back and laughs. "That's the most delicious part of all. I get to finally move on. Put all this crap behind me and be with the person I always wanted in the first place. That's why Wade and I are going far away. Somewhere near the ocean, maybe an island hideaway. Preferably a remote, exotic place. It's not too late for me to find some happiness. Wade and I were always meant to be together. See, when I first met him all those years ago at college, we used to talk about how we'd go to the West Coast. I was going to be his manager. I would've helped him make it in the music business, but you dragged him down, Daisy. Trapped him in your sordid little house by the railway bridge. Fed him all those drugs to keep him under your thumb. But it backfired, because you sapped away all his talent like the bloodsucker you are. Thank God I found him again at just the right time. When he was ready to walk out on you, and just in time for this fabulous party. So we're back together again and we're going to plan our future while we're lying on a beach, soaking up the sun, and sipping something cool and tropical."

Daisy has a bitter taste in her mouth. She looks around at the others, her stomach roiling with panic. She doesn't care about Evie's delusional plans, and she damn well won't die of suffocation in this hothouse. All she knows is, she wants her purse and her phone back so she can call a cab and get the hell out of here. Evie has no idea that some scary dealers might be out for Wade's blood right now, and if they don't find him, they'll be after her instead. Not that Daisy cares about what happens to him. She'd kill lions with her bare hands to protect her new future.

"You think Blair will actually bankroll your crazy dream?" says Savannah, suddenly coming to life.

"He won't have a choice. I have the best lawyers on it."

"He has better," says Savannah. "I can guarantee it. You'll always be looking over your shoulder to see if he's after you."

"Nonsense. We have an agreement."

All Daisy can hear is meaningless jabbering. She needs to make a move, and it has to be soon. "Where's our stuff? Our phones?"

Evie's walking away, but she turns to them. "Just to show I'm not completely unfeeling, I'll leave them at the hotel in Zoe's room. If you actually do manage to escape from here, they'll be waiting for you. But don't try to find me. I have too much on you all. Leave Wade and me alone and I'll keep it to myself. You can all get on with your lives, that is, if you get through today. Ciao, everyone! Have a great life."

Daisy tries to grab Evie's arm. "You need to listen to me now. Wade is in danger."

"Take your hands off me. I'm sick of your lies."

"No – no – I'm telling the truth. Bad people are after him for money. They're dangerous."

Evie shoves her away. "That's a pretty desperate attempt to sabotage my dream. Can't you come up with something more original?"

Daisy heart is racing. Evie's possessed. She's not thinking clearly.

Just then, she feels a rush of air behind her. Next thing she knows, Zoe's rushing forward, yelling at the top of her lungs. "I hate you! I fucking hate you, I've always hated you!" She barrels into Evie, pushing her back against the wall with such force, Evie bounces off and slides down onto her ass, landing with a thump on the concrete floor. She sits, shaken, her party dress hiked up to her thighs, legs splayed out in front of her. But Zoe doesn't stop. She's a wild woman, raging and screaming curses at Evie.

Daisy has to think quick. This might be her opportunity to make a move. From the corner of her eye, she sees Tom moving towards the ruckus. She taps Savannah, who's frozen in horror at the spectacle, and nods towards the door. Holding on to Savannah's arm they back away from Zoe who's in a total meltdown, raining curses onto Evie, who is cowering on the floor, her arms folded over the top of her head.

"What about Zoe?" whispers Savannah.

"We can't worry about her. We have to leave now. It's a life-or-death situation."

Tom crouches down, trying to pull Evie onto her feet, while Zoe stands like a crazed woman, clawing at her hair. She turns as Daisy and Savannah reach the open door. Daisy gets a glimpse of her eyes, ringed black with mascara, her hair like a nest. In one swift movement Zoe winds up her leg and knees Tom in the back, pushing him forward so he topples hard on top of Evie. Then the two of them squirm and struggle like a pair of wrestlers trying to untangle their limbs.

"Wait for me," yells Zoe, running towards the door, slowing down for just a second to snatch up Evie's designer purse that's lying on top of her shredded wedding dress, along with the three other purses lying there.

ZOE

Zoe's in full survival mode now as she clutches Evie's Gucci purse, noting with some satisfaction it's an actual crocodile-top model. Must be worth a few thousand bucks. But she doesn't give a damn about the purse, it's the fact that all their cell phones are packed inside. She tears through the open door. A wall of heat slams into her face, taking her breath away.

"Wait up for me. I've got your phones," she gasps, wondering how she's even able to speak when the surface of her tongue is like dried leather.

Savannah stops dead and Zoe almost runs her over. "You have her purse? Do you see a fob or car keys in there?"

But Daisy's taken a sharp side turn and is running away from the black SUV parked on the street, her eyes trained on the open doorway where Tom or Evie could burst out at any moment. "We don't have time for that!" she screams, her arms flailing in panic. "We need to hide."

But Zoe's determined, scrabbling through the lipstick tubes and pill bottles until *bingo* – a fob. She presses it and the black SUV's lights flash on.

Savannah swings the door open and lunges into the driver's seat. "Daisy!" she yells. "Get the hell back here."

Daisy tears back to the car and scrambles into the passenger side, slamming her door shut while Zoe struggles with the back door. *Dammit – a kids' lock, and the fricking purses are weighing my arm down.* "Open up," she yells, just as Tom appears in the open doorway. Zoe's brain is operating at warp speed. There's no way this big lug of a guy is going to get the better of her. She hasn't clawed her way this far for nothing. "You can't go without me, idiots, I've got the damn fob. Hurry up."

Savannah fumbles with the lock until Zoe hears the welcome *click-click* sound, throws in the purses and swings the heavy door wide open, slamming it against Tom's oversized chest with a sickening thud. His face goes a bright shade of red as he grunts and doubles over, retching and choking.

Evie appears at the door just as Savannah floors the gas, sending the car squealing away around the corner into a narrow back alley. Zoe falls back against the plush seat, panting. She's reached the point where she'd hand over the entire contents of her investment accounts just to get out of this filthy, goddamn city, and away from these damaged, dysfunctional people she left behind sixteen years ago. Hell. She crossed the border into the Great White North to get away, but still they've managed to drag her back into their messed-up lives.

Savannah turns to look at her. "Jeez, you're a warrior woman, Zoe. I'd never have guessed you had it in you. You were awesome – incredible."

Zoe tries to catch her breath, blinking to stop the little motes from dancing in front of her eyes. They're making her dizzy and nauseous. She could kill for a glass of iced water. Anything to get rid of the gross furry-mouth feeling. Finally, she closes her eyes for a blessed few seconds and the wave of nausea passes. She's safe. At least for now.

"I watched all the wrestling drills during your practices. Put myself through the warmup routines. Threw a few pillows around my dorm room. I actually got pretty good at the whole thing."

Savannah glimpses at her in the rearview mirror as she maneuvers around the twisty back alleys. "You missed your calling. You should've joined the MMA. Called yourself The Doctor."

"Hell, yeah. I'd wear a bum-skimming white coat over my bodysuit and walk into the arena with a gold stethoscope draped around my neck."

Savannah's giggling breaks up the tension, but Daisy is uncharacteristically quiet, chewing her nails and gazing out of the window. Zoe digs into Evie's purse to rescue their cell phones, hoping to buck up Daisy's mood. Her own phone is dead. "Dammit. Is there a phone charger in here?" she says, handing them out to her friends who clutch them like lifelines.

Daisy punches frantically at hers, shaking her head and cursing under her breath. She slams it against the dash.

"Hey, take it easy," says Zoe. "What's up? Something wrong?"

"It's Wade," she mutters.

They round a corner onto a street of rubble-filled empty lots punctuated with the occasional dingy motel. This has to be the seedy underbelly of Las Vegas. She'd always known the superficial glitz of the Strip was just a thin veneer, hiding the sad truth. But Daisy's still silent. Looks like she's stewing about something.

"C'mon, Daisy," she urges. "Spill. You ought to feel good about him being saddled with Evie for the rest of his life. What can be worse than that?" But Daisy still doesn't respond.

"What's wrong?" says Savannah. "We can't help you unless we know."

When Daisy looks up, her eyes are brimming. "I – I'm worried they've already got to him. While we were playing stupid games in that warehouse, there's a very good chance someone may have harmed Wade."

"How could he have any enemies? I thought you said he's been moping around the house for the past few months," says Savannah.

"I wasn't exactly truthful with you," says Daisy, resting her forehead on her hand as she leans against the window. "He's been depressed for years about his failed music career. At first, he smoked a little dope to help him sleep and deal with work. But when he lost his job, he sank into a deep depression. The marijuana zoned him out so much, he lay on the couch all day watching soaps. Then he did a gig at some west-side dive and suddenly he found some new friends. They started texting him all the time, picking him up from the house and taking him out. I hardly saw him. He'd show up at home with small amounts of money here and there, but he was acting more jittery, like he couldn't wait to go out again. When I asked him where he got the money, he was vague. Then he became moody, unpredictable. I didn't even like him to be around Ethan. But when our son finally went off to college, he started to pull all-nighters. I hardly saw him."

"So you do have a son," says Savannah.

"Of course I do. Why would you ask that?"

"Just something Wade said back at the nightclub."

"He's a liar. You know that by now. Don't you?"

"Sure," says Savannah, focusing on the road ahead.

Zoe wonders if anyone's telling the truth, and why didn't Daisy mention this drugs thing before? Given her history she wouldn't be surprised if Daisy was the one dealing. "Sounds like he was getting into heavier drugs," says Zoe, wanting to test Daisy a little more.

Daisy runs her fingers through her hair. "I suspected it too. Then I started getting weird texts – maybe once or twice a month from these guys he'd been hanging out with – saying he owed them money."

"D'you think he was dealing?" says Savannah.

"Using and dealing," says Daisy. "That's why he left. He was afraid of what they'd do to him. And now they're hassling me. They want to know where he is."

"Just tell them he's here, Daisy. Or they'll come after you," says Zoe.

"They've already threatened Ethan," says Daisy, sobbing.

Maybe Daisy is telling the truth about Wade and the son who may or may not exist. She sure seems broken up. "Can't you call the cops?" she says.

Savannah glances at her in the rearview mirror. "Not a great idea. Then Daisy becomes *the dealer's wife*. By the time they've processed her through the system, those drug guys will have dealt with Wade."

Zoe leans forward. "He's bad news, Daisy. You have to tell them where he is. Let him deal with them."

"They already know he's in Vegas. They just don't know where."

"Then tell them. Besides, I thought you didn't give a damn about him. At least that's what you told Evie."

"I may not love him anymore, but I don't like to think of someone hurting him. I mean, we've been married a long time."

"And he is the father of your child," adds Savannah.

Daisy turns to look at them, her eyes filled with hurt. "You sound really sure about that."

"What do you mean?" says Zoe.

Daisy flops back against the passenger seat, her eyes squeezed shut. "Oh God. Oh God."

"What's going on?" says Savannah, taking another sharp

turn onto a street lined with pawn shops and luridly painted wedding chapels.

Zoe checks out the surroundings and feels a deep sense of gloom. This is Vegas – all surface glitter, but at its heart, shabby like a cheap carnival sideshow. An apt metaphor for Evie and their friendship. It's time to lance the boil and drain out all the ugly secrets. "C'mon," she says. "Tell us the truth."

Daisy groans and covers her eyes with her hand. "Wade isn't Ethan's dad."

"Then who the hell is? Do we know him?" says Zoe.

"Don't hate me, guys, but Cal's his father."

Zoe's speechless for a few seconds while she processes this revelation. "How on earth do you know that?"

"After Ethan, I tried to get pregnant for years. We went for medical tests, and they discovered that Wade was infertile. He had a severe case of the mumps when he was a kid. Cal was the only other guy I had sex with at that time." She turns to look at Zoe with sad puppy eyes. "I'm so ashamed of myself, coz Cal was such an asshole. He basically screwed me then told me to get lost. Called me a piece of trash. I never told Wade. I had no idea I was pregnant until weeks after the night of the – the..."

"You mean the wrestling incident?" says Zoe, shocked at this new information.

Daisy closes her eyes and nods her head.

The car is silent as Zoe considers this new information. This whole Cal thing has dogged her for so long. Circling her life like a funnel cloud that hovers just out of view, threatening to sweep in at any moment. Destroy everything she's ever worked for. And all because of a stupid dare. She searches back in her memory to that night just after the grad ceremony. She's spent so long trying to suppress the events, she wonders if she can actually remember them clearly, but now that Evie's mentioned it, flashes of memory come to her as the car careens around corners, making her head pound even harder.

It was an impromptu after-grad party in their dorm common room. Everyone was totally slammed. All the stragglers had left except Evie who'd stripped off her grad gown and climbed up onto the table. Even Savannah was drunk. She must've been because she'd actually allowed Blair to rest his head on her feet. It was no secret Blair was gaga over her, but normally Savannah wouldn't have anything to do with him. Unlike Zoe who'd already found out what a jerk he truly was. Wade was lying, half-conscious on a couch but Daisy and Cal were missing. Evie started flexing her biceps and doing deep knee squats, just as Daisy appeared at the foot of the stairs, her gown all creased and her hair a tangled mess. She stomped into the party room, flopped down next to Wade and chugged half a bottle of wine.

Cal followed her, a weird smirk on his face, but stumbling around as if he was drunk or high. He tried to rouse Wade and get him to leave but Wade just moaned and rolled over. Then he spotted Blair draped all over Savannah and the smirk disappeared. That's when Evie started goading him. Calling him a dumb jock and a loser who couldn't even beat her in a matchup. Zoe was sober enough to tell her to shut it but Evie wasn't having any of that. Instead, she jumped down from the table and put up her fists. Started jabbing him in the chest. He backed away, lurching around like some wounded bear. Suddenly he let out a massive roar and pushed Evie down onto the floor, his hands around her neck. She cracked her head against the table.

Everything moved so fast after that.

Daisy leapt to her feet and launched herself onto Cal's back.

Clawed at his face, but he wouldn't let go of Evie. Then Savannah sprang up and was trying to shove Cal away, but his eyes were weird and glassy as if he wasn't fully with it. Zoe remembers the sound of blood rushing through her ears. She had to do something to help or he'd have strangled Evie whose face was turning purple.

Blair was behind him, trying to talk him down but Cal just shook his head as if he couldn't hear. Blair and Zoe joined in, pulling and pushing Cal from all sides. The force of their combined strength knocked him off balance and he went down hard, the back of his head smacking onto the floor. His whole body went stiff for a few moments, then started twitching in the most terrible way as if someone was poking him with a cattle prod. Zoe knows now it was a classic seizure. They all pulled away, stone-cold sober until the twitching and jerking passed and he lay still, blood leaking from the back of his head. But he was still breathing. That's when Blair said he'd take him back to his room and make sure he was okay. Said he'd call a doctor if he had to. He begged Savannah to come with him, and she actually went.

Zoe gasps for breath. Is it the heat, or is it the sudden blaze of light as Savannah leaves the dark back alleys and turns onto a wide-open street that looks very much like the top end of the Strip.

She turns to Zoe. "Back to the hotel?"

"Of course," says Zoe, trying to get her breathing back under control. "I'm out of here as soon as I can pack my bags."

"But what if those dealers are there? What if they didn't find Wade?" says Daisy. "And now they're coming for me?"

"That's why we need to leave as soon as possible," says Savannah.

Zoe's so mad she can barely speak. How can Daisy be so stupid? It blows her mind that she's still mixed up with that whole drug scene, and is now dragging them all into this massive fiasco. It's likely she's the one who got Wade mixed up with drugs in the first place with her college dealer sideline. Zoe's done with all this juvenile shit.

"Personally, I've had enough of this entire weekend. I just want to get the hell out of this town," she says.

Daisy looks longingly at Savannah. "Please, Sav – will you stay with me? Help me?"

Savannah pauses. Zoe hopes to hell she says yes, so her conscience doesn't have to be weighted with guilt that she left Daisy alone to deal with the drug henchmen.

Savannah finally lets out a long sigh. "Okay. I will."

"You're a true friend," says Daisy. "I knew I could trust you."

Zoe feels a slight sting of remorse. "Sorry, Daisy, but I truly have to get back to my patients. Got some life-or-death decisions to make this week."

"It's okay. We can handle it," says Daisy, shooting a frosty glare her way.

"And how exactly are we going to handle it?" says Savannah. "What's our plan?"

Daisy's back to chewing her lower lip. "I haven't figured that out yet. Hey – I've got some juice," she says, texting frantically.

Who the hell can she be texting now? Wade or maybe Blair? And why the hell would she want to help Blair out by spying on Evie? It's all so twisted, and her head hurts again. She wants to be home, gazing over Lake Ontario from the window of her pristine palace in the sky.

Savannah scowls and taps her fingers on the steering wheel. They've run into heavy traffic.

Zoe glances out of the window. They've moved about fifty feet in the last five minutes. "What's going on here, Sav? You know this place. Why aren't we moving?"

"Now of all times," says Daisy, her palms flat against the glass.

"Not sure. Could be an accident."

The wail of sirens sets Zoe's nerves on edge. "Maybe they've already found Wade."

"Shut up, shut up," hisses Daisy.

A fire truck whooshes by them, turning quickly into the street next to the Strat Hotel. "Looks like there's a fire – or maybe someone had an accident on the Big Shot."

"What the hell is that?" says Zoe.

"You get strapped into a seat and catapulted one hundred and sixty feet into the air at forty-five miles an hour. Lots of puking and heart problems associated with it," says Savannah, grinning at her through the rearview mirror.

"Sounds like torture," says Zoe.

"Isn't there an alternate route?" says Daisy, drumming her fingers on the side window.

Savannah suddenly screeches into the far-right lane, throwing them all against the side of the car. "Sorry, just remembered a shortcut."

They turn into a busy four-lane road, then make a quick left at another set of traffic lights onto a narrower street. Savannah weaves the car expertly around corners, as Daisy turns to her. "We may never see each other after this, so we need to know, Sav. What happened with you and Cal? You know everything about us. The least you can do is tell your truth. Did you really poison Cal?"

What the hell is Daisy thinking? Who cares at this point

about all that old history? They just need to get the hell out of here as soon as they can, without running into some crazed drug pushers trying to collect a bad debt. Hell, she'll write them a check if they want it, but it's probably cash they're looking for and heaven knows how much they're after.

But Daisy persists, leaning towards Savannah, whose white-knuckled hands are gripping the steering wheel. "Tell us, Sav. What happened? Because whatever you did, he probably deserved it."

SAVANNAH

Savannah feels a steady throbbing in her head. She's run so long from the memories. From the fear. She can taste it. Sharp and metallic on the roof of her mouth. "I can't talk about it."

"You don't need to tell us, Sav. Just concentrate on the road. On getting us out of here." Zoe speaks with an uncharacteristically soothing voice. She must be switching into doctor mode.

At first, Savannah feels like she's choking, her breaths are so shallow. But somehow, she finds her voice, all the while trying to focus on the busy traffic. She takes a deep breath – lets her mind travel back to grad. "I didn't want to go with Blair, but I couldn't say no. Not after what had happened. We should've called for an ambulance, but Blair said there'd be too many questions. They'd assume we caused the fall and he couldn't afford to get into trouble with his parents or Cal's. Evie was still shaken and Daisy – you were hysterical. So we dragged him, half-conscious, back to his room. Got him onto his bed and Blair said he had to leave for a while. Told me to keep an eye on him in case he had a bad concussion and then – and…"

She grips the steering wheel and almost swings the car into

the lane next to her. Nausea rises, bitter in her throat. "I can't do this now. Not if you want me to get you back to the hotel safely." Her shoulders heave as she tries to stifle the hurt and fear she's bottled up for so long.

Zoe squeezes her shoulder. "Take a moment. Just breathe. We'll finish it later."

"Really? We were just getting to the interesting part," adds Daisy.

Zoe shoots a withering look at her. "Sometimes you can be such a cold, unfeeling bitch. Can't you see what kind of pain she's in? Sav, you don't have to tell us now. We can wait."

"She needs to tell," says Daisy. "She's been carrying this around for far too long."

Suddenly the shining towers of the Aria loom above. Savannah steers them into the back parking lot.

"My God. We made it," she says, slumping back against the driver's seat, thankful they've arrived so she doesn't have to explain the rest of her miserable story.

"You have to finish what you started," snaps Daisy.

"Dammit. We don't have time for your morbid curiosity," says Zoe. "What does it matter now after all this time? We need to get our stuff quickly before Evie or those dealers get here."

Savannah pockets the fob as they make their way towards the back entrance. She wonders if there's a service elevator somewhere so they can avoid the long snaking walk through the casino to the guest elevators. Her prayers are answered when a nearby side door opens and a woman in a chef's jacket steps out and lights up a cigarette.

"Over there," she whispers. "Follow me and try to look like you work here."

"How do we do that?" says Zoe, glancing down at her ruined party dress.

"Watch and learn," says Savannah, striding towards the open door. She nods at the woman who steps into their path.

"No guests through this door," the woman says, her face impassive.

"We're housekeeping. Had a rough night and we can't be late. Gotta get into uniform quick."

The woman narrows her eyes until Savannah reaches into her purse and slips out a twenty. "Housekeeping," she repeats.

The woman pockets the money and steps aside.

"Service elevator?" asks Savannah.

"Turn left. Middle of hallway," the woman whispers, taking a long drag of her cigarette.

Savannah leads the way into a dank series of hallways that stink of stale cooking oil and tomato sauce. Halfway up the left-side passageway is a grimy-looking elevator. She presses the button, setting off a whiny, cranking noise.

"So seedy," says Zoe. "Makes you wonder what's going on in that kitchen."

"All the hotels are like this. That's the reality for workers here," says Savannah as the elevator clunks to the ground level and the door squeals open to reveal a bare interior with stained floors. They step inside. Zoe covers her nose.

"Ugh – it stinks of rotten milk in here."

"Guess you've forgotten how bad your dorm room smelled," says Daisy. "Mold and old socks I recall."

Zoe frowns. "Why did you bring that up? I managed to block that memory, and now you're triggering all my old trauma."

"Sometimes we need a reminder," says Savannah. "So we don't entirely forget who we are."

"Don't act so self-righteous. We still don't know if you're a murderer yet," snaps Daisy.

"Stop fighting. This is not the time," says Zoe, fixated on the numbered buttons. *Fourteen, fifteen, sixteen.*

"Oh God," says Daisy. "What if the elevator doors open and they're waiting? What if they're torturing Wade and he tells them where we are? Oh God, oh God. What if they've already got to Ethan? I need to check my phone. I need to call Ethan."

Daisy begins hyperventilating, her body shaking as if she's about to start screaming. Zoe lunges forward, clapping a hand over Daisy's mouth. "Shut it, Daisy. You can't have a meltdown in an elevator. You need to calm down. I have Bromazepam in my room."

"I thought you were leaving," says Savannah.

"Guess I can look after Daisy."

"Good," says Savannah. "We may need medical help."

Everyone goes silent. Savannah prays they can simply pack up and leave. She's already cataloguing suitable destinations on the West Coast for her new life. Leon will have to understand. This whole business with Evie has gone too far now. She can't saddle such a young, promising guy with the kind of secrets she's carrying. Maybe she's always known it, and that's why they haven't gone any further sexually.

The elevator clunks to a halt on the twenty-second floor. Evie's place is two floors higher. They all hold their breath as the door swishes open way too slowly. Collectively they exhale. The hallway outside is empty.

"So, do we stay in here and check Evie's floor or get out here and give Daisy something to calm her down?" says Savannah. She holds the *door open* button.

"I need something – like now," says Daisy. "And I have to plug my phone in and make some calls. Call Ethan for sure." Her face is set in a frozen mask and her breath comes in short, sharp gasps. She sways against the elevator wall as if she's going to pass out.

Zoe places a finger near Daisy's pulse. "I think she's having a panic attack.

Savannah exhales. *Might as well take the plunge.* "Okay, Zoe, you take Daisy and settle her down. I'm gonna get rid of Evie's bag. Throw it back in her room. And maybe I'll just take a quick peek in there."

"Are you sure?" says Zoe, leading Daisy out into the hallway. Savannah follows her.

"I won't go in if I hear someone in there. I'll probably just go back to Leon's place," says Savannah, feeling the dull thud of her heart. She's not looking forward to facing him after last night's fiasco. "Just give me Evie's key card."

Zoe opens the purse and roots around, pushing aside lipstick tubes and pill bottles. The key card is in a zip pocket. She holds it out to Savannah and shoves the purse at her.

"See you around, Sav. I'm gonna leave as soon as I'm packed and I don't need to know the whole sad story of that night with Cal. It's behind us now. No sense in dredging it all up again."

"I appreciate that," says Savannah. "I always respected you, Zoe. You know that."

Zoe nods and squeezes her hand. "Take care," she says, heading down the hallway.

Savannah stands outside the elevator and lets the doors close, trying to decide what to do, when a message *pings* onto her phone. It's anonymous. Cold fingers crawl across her skin when she reads it:

> Want to know who's been sending you those creepy messages? Come up to my suite and I'll tell you.

Is this some kind of sick joke? How could Evie have beaten them back here? It's not possible. It must be someone else, and she has a good idea who. But does she really want to find out?

She presses the elevator button and soon hears the *clank-clank* of the doors opening. Eyes fixed on her phone, she gets in and presses number twenty-four, but instead of moving upwards, the damn thing lurches downwards towards the main floor.

DAISY

Zoe clutches Daisy's arm as they head towards her room.

They move as one, stumbling along the hallway. Daisy feels weak, as if a fist is blocking her windpipe and she can't breathe. At least not until she gets to plug in her phone and make a few calls.

Zoe stops at Daisy's door. "Let's hope the key works."

Daisy unhooks her purse from Zoe's arm. If she doesn't get inside her room quickly, she's going to pass out. She makes a futile attempt to find the key card. "I can't – I mean I don't..."

Zoe snatches the purse back and tears through the contents, finally coming up with the card. She waves it in front of the reader and the green light flashes. Daisy feels such a swell of relief, she could crawl in on her hands and knees and kiss the floor.

"Go in and rest. Lie down. I'll see if I can find something to calm you down. And just in case I have to make an emergency call, don't move from there without telling me," says Zoe, suddenly all business.

"Don't worry. I'm going to be calling Ethan right away."

Zoe bustles away to her room next door. She won't be back.

She's too much of a survivor to waste any more time getting away. She'll have her bags packed and be out the door ASAP. But that's okay, she'd only interfere with Daisy's plans.

She slips inside her room and holds the door open for a moment to check that no one else is around. But the hallway is quiet. Not surprising this early. A riptide of relief washes over her as she fixes the chain lock and rushes over to the work desk where she plugs in her phone, her heart slamming against her ribs. The screen lights up, stacked with messages, missed calls and notifications. *Oh God. What if one of them is Ethan begging for help?* She scrolls through, madly checking for his name, and gulping for air. If she keeps this up, she's going to pass out. But there's nothing from him.

She knew there never would be, so why is she so disappointed?

Grief is like the hidden part of an iceberg. A great, cold mass that occupies the center of her heart. She's numb. Drained of emotion.

She plunks herself down in the leather chair, her legs splayed out in front of her. *Get a grip,* she tells herself, reaching into her purse for her meds. Haldol, Thorazine – the doctors have tried them all. Some work, some just dull the edge of reality. But often she'll miss them on purpose so she can indulge herself in the fantasy of Ethan and all his heart-melting little milestones. His first smile, first tooth, first day at kindergarten, holiday concert where he sings like an angel in the front line of the chorus, first date, graduation day with his handsome young face beaming at her from under the blue mortar board. She scrabbles at the bottom of her purse, in the secret zip pocket where she keeps the small plastic envelope with her only picture of Ethan. She takes it out and studies it. He *was* real. If only for a few days. There he is – a tiny preemie with a miniature wrinkled face and blind kitten eyes.

Wade was gutted when they lost him. Cried like a baby and rocked the tiny bundle until they had to take it from his arms. She'd lain dry-eyed facing the wall, telling herself it was Cal's baby. Call it a gut feeling, but she just knew it. Of course, that's why he'd tried to break up her and Wade by calling Wade's parents and telling them their son was seeing a common little drug dealer. Blair told her all about it. Even said they'd threatened to cut Wade off from the family if he carried on seeing her. Then Cal turned on her that night at grad. Pretended to make love to her, then ruined her life. Left her with Wade, a penniless loser.

She didn't even have to think about it when Blair came to her the night of Cal's accident, begging for help. Seems he couldn't find Cal's seizure medication and was worried about him passing out in his sleep. She'd calmed him down and settled him onto her sofa while she tinkered with her secret drug stash – by then, a mini-pharmacy hidden in the false bottom of her suitcase. It was so easy to add a whole lot of insulin to the phenytoin oral meds she sent Blair back with. Let someone else take care of Cal. That bastard deserved everything he got. Too bad she didn't know about the baby until later. Then she regretted taking him down.

Now she checks the phone calls. Her gut does a somersault. Wade called just over an hour ago. What the hell did he want? To tell her he was running away with Evie so they could start the next chapter of her charmed life? So she could swap one wealthy husband for another? Not if she can help it. Daisy will make sure she gets half of what she's always been entitled to for putting up with that lazy asshole for so long.

Her heart pumps like a sledgehammer as she calls his number. She feels like her head is encased in a huge jar and the ringing sound is coming from somewhere outside it. There's a sudden click but it's only voicemail. But the message starts up, then mysteriously cuts out.

What the hell does that mean? Did he deny her call? Or, worse still, does someone else have his phone?

Now all kinds of scenarios flash across her mind like trailers from bad action movies. The ones where the baddies gun people down like moving targets, spurting fountains of blood, or cut people up like they're ripping open a sack of potatoes. She's frozen to the spot, unable to move and barely able to breathe. And only yesterday she was here with Blair having the greatest sex she's had in years – possibly ever – on the heavenly pillow-topped bed.

It's inevitable that she and Blair would end up together. It was just a matter of when. That's what he'd told her last night when they'd gone over the plan together. How she'd make up the story about the drug debts. Get Evie and the others riled up. But did he know about Evie's intentions to kidnap them? And why hadn't he mentioned that Wade had reunited with his mom and likely his massive inheritance? *Is Blair still lying to me? He'd better not be.*

The shrill ring of the phone is like a knife in her gut. She's afraid to look. Afraid to know what's going on. Finally, she glances down at the screen. It's him. Blair. Her skin prickles. *Where is he? What's happening?*

Her breath comes in short, staccato bursts as her finger hovers over the *reply* button.

ZOE

Zoe took the liberty of packing her bags. Now they're lined up neatly by the door. Ready for a speedy evacuation of this tacky hotel and a vulgar city Zoe will never, ever set foot in again, even for the most prestigious medical conference. She sits back on an easy chair. Tries to collect herself, calm her racing heart.

It won't do Daisy any harm to wait a little longer for the pills. Besides, hopefully Sav will go upstairs and scout out the situation. She always liked to play the hero. Guess she never had Zoe's fierce drive for survival.

She tries to ignore the tiny voice nagging at her for handing over Evie's key. Sav is taking a huge risk going upstairs alone and possibly meeting up with a bunch of vicious drug dealers hungry for money and revenge. But she volunteered. No one strong-armed her. She went willingly to collect her things, oblivious to the potential risks. That's the logical way to rationalize the situation.

She checks her phone now charging on the TV table. Strangely there's nothing from Marcus. Maybe he's accepted his fate and decided it's time to move on, which would be the mature thing to do. She couldn't take any more messy emotional scenes. But there is one from Zack asking if she'll be around later tonight. Sadly, she won't, but maybe she'll invite him to Toronto and they can christen her new bed in the brand-new condo. It's a tantalizing prospect.

There's also a couple of missed calls from Phyllis, her lawyer. She definitely needs to get back to her, though 8.15 in the morning might be stretching it a bit, even for Phyllis who's a bit of a party animal. She has to be prepped to get the maximum settlement possible from Marcus now that there won't be any trouble from Evie. She'll make sure of that right now.

She takes out Evie's phone from her own purse. Thank God she had the wherewithal to snag it when they were in the car. Now she can start the process of erasing everything and restoring the phone to factory settings, making sure all videos and other files are gone from the cloud.

Now Evie will have nothing to hold over Zoe's head. Seems like all that stupid guilt they've been carrying about the past has been a total waste of time and nervous energy, because if Evie's telling the truth, then Savannah is the one responsible for his death and not the rest of them. But Evie's only going on what Blair told her, and he's a compulsive liar. He lied to Zoe for all those months they were together. Always promising he'd take her home for the holidays to meet his parents and then coming up with the flimsiest of excuses, like his mom was having surprise guests from out of town or the toilet in the guest bathroom was leaking and had to be repaired. Didn't make a difference that she'd packed a suitcase and waited hours for him to pick her up, only to be let down at the last minute.

Another message is from Jaz saying the vendor will include all the furniture – every gorgeous stick of it, including accessories and pictures. It's a no-brainer. She can simply walk out of the house she shares with Marcus and move right into the condo without lifting a finger, except to transport her clothes, and even those she can do without. Mostly they were picked according to Marcus's taste in trashy glamor.

She'll arrange to have drinks with Jaz again. It'll seem surreal talking to him about normal things like down payments and furnishings and possession dates, considering the bizarre night she's just survived. What she wouldn't give for a bar stool right next to his, a chilled Radler and a plate of sweet potato fries with spicy mayo.

A massive shopping spree glitters on the horizon. She'll get a stylist. Put herself in the capable hands of an expert who'll select a tasteful but luxurious professional look. Lots of cashmere, linen and eco-friendly fabrics. Not a hint of polyester, Lycra or man-made crap. Heck, she'll even hire a trainer. Maybe do some of that Thai boxing. Get back some of that physical strength and swagger she had in her twenties. Kick some ass out there. Be a little more like Evie used to be.

Until Blair got his hooks into her.

A surge of emotion makes her drop the phone onto the table. *What is she doing?* Why should she care about Evie? Evie was always the one with attitude. The strong one who didn't give a damn about what people thought of her. Who set herself out to show that a woman could be just as physically tough and assertive as a man.

She has every right to be pissed at them all. Why didn't they warn her about Blair and what a rat he really is? She could easily have told Evie her story about the abortion. At least given her the chance to consider her options. And Savannah is carrying a secret about Blair that may be even more shocking. She should've confided in her friends. Not run away from them. Knowing Blair, he only married Evie to keep tabs on everyone and make sure the secret never came out, and somehow during those years, he destroyed Evie. Slowly and insidiously working on her. Whittling away all her self-confidence with cruelty and persistent abuse until she became just a shell of the strong woman she once was.

Zoe's seen plenty of abused women among the parents she regularly meets, and most of them don't have bruises. She's learned to recognize that miniscule flinching movement when the husband raises his voice or talks over his wife as if she isn't there. The timid, faltering voice as if she has no right to ask questions about her own child and her immediate silence when her husband completes her sentences or says, *"Don't mind her, she doesn't know what she's talking about."*

Her blood boils with all that injustice, and the thought of Blair getting away scot-free with everything he's done, and still doing, now he's working on luring Daisy into his messed-up world.

Terrible thoughts slam into her head. *What if he's up there in Evie's suite? Savannah might be in danger.*

Maybe it's time to get Daisy, then the two of them can go together and rescue her. She shoves her phone into her pocket, gets up and edges the door open, and looks out into the silent hallway. The only sound she can hear is her own beating heart as she makes her way to Daisy's room. Strangely, the door is ajar. She inches it open and peers inside. Daisy's suitcase is on top of the bed, clothes spilling out of it as if she's left in a hurry. The bathroom is empty. The counters cluttered with hairbrushes, bottles of lotion and makeup containers.

Maybe she heard from Savannah and went up to help her, or maybe Blair is up there now. She stands in the open doorway, and in a split second decides she's going up there too, and not looking back as she heads towards the elevator, but her phone rings. It's Phyllis. *Damn.* She has to answer it. Surely Daisy and Sav can wait just a few more minutes.

SAVANNAH

As the elevator finally starts to climb upwards, Savannah steels herself. She's not afraid to face anything or anyone. She's always been cool and fearless in a crisis. Truth is, Daisy, Zoe, and even Evie are weaklings compared to her.

Every weekend when she was a kid, her dad took her out into the countryside for gun practice. They shot at tin-can targets and eventually moved on to small animals. She was a skilled marksman by the time she was ten, and had a black belt in karate by the end of the following year. She pretended to be an inexperienced newbie when Evie recruited her for the wrestling team, but it was clear from the beginning that Savannah was always the anchor of the team, with the flexibility, speed and strength only a dancer possesses. And the other girls didn't have a fraction of her determination.

So while Zoe and Evie were swanning around the Phi Delta Kappa house scouting rich, spoilt frat boys, Savannah was at the gym where the resident judo coach schooled her in advanced martial arts techniques. He even offered to introduce her to the scout for the women's Olympic team, calling her a natural fighter with just the right balance of athleticism, strength and sheer ruthlessness.

That training saved her life.

The night of the accident still triggers so many memories. Panic at the state of Cal when they finally got him to his bed. All her first-aid training told her he needed medical help and they were foolish to ignore the signs of concussion. The drowsiness, clammy skin, trembling hands. But Blair convinced her they'd all be in trouble because they'd caused the accident, and maybe he'd just snap out of it if he rested. So while he went to get food and coffee to sober them up as well as painkillers for Cal who was bound to have a crashing headache when he came to, Savannah stuck around to keep an eye on him.

She'd wandered into the neighboring bedroom and, feeling sleepy, settled onto the bed just for a short nap. She'd woken a while later, her arms screaming with pain. Her eyes opened at the sound of Blair's voice; his face pushed so close to hers she could feel the warmth of his breath. Sickened, she turned her head away, noticing the glint of steel around her wrists.

"Your ice-queen act is such a waste of a beautiful body. I've always wanted you and you know you want me," he'd said.

She shudders at the memory of his hands all over her. Stroking her face, creeping under her shirt, sliding into the waistband of her jeans, fumbling with the zipper. At first, she'd been so disoriented, so buzzed with the after-effects of the booze, it was all she could do to thrash from side to side to turn her body away from him, but his wiry arms had enough strength to pin down her shoulders so she couldn't move. She tried to scream, but he grabbed a towel and shoved it into her mouth while he told her he'd always wanted her over all the other girls.

Her heart races at the memory of her utter helplessness. She was totally at the mercy of this creep who treated her as if she was less than human, as if he owned her and could do whatever he liked. She gasps at the sudden thought that Evie has put up with Blair's cruelty and abuse for so many years. Evie's right. They should have warned her. The sudden realization is like a punch to her gut, but she pulls herself together and focuses on what happened next.

She'd called for Cal, but Blair just laughed and slapped her face with one stinging blow. He told her that Cal was gone. He'd taken care of him. That Cal had always had the hots for her, but didn't deserve her. That's when he climbed onto her and straddled her body, told her he'd been waiting for so long to have her, and couldn't wait another moment. He unzipped his pants, but her fear soon turned to anger and outrage. A white-hot wave of adrenaline coursed through her blood, giving her the strength to flip onto her side, destabilizing him so that he rolled off her, freeing her legs, which she immediately clamped around his neck in the deadly choke-hold her martial arts teacher had taught her.

"Unlock the cuffs, asshole," she'd screamed, squeezing his throat until his face turned purple, "or I'll cut off your blood supply."

It took only a few more seconds of him gasping and choking before he begged her to stop. She released the pressure a little – enough to allow him to drag himself over to the bedpost and release the handcuffs. He fell back on the bed panting for breath as she pounced on top of him and yanked his arms upwards, surprised at the weakness of his body.

"Don't put up much of a fight, do you?" she said, cuffing him to the bedposts.

"Fuck you," he said. "Wait till the others get here. I'll tell them you killed Cal and left me here like this."

"Then what? You'll call the police? I don't think so. You're so obsessed with saving yourself, that's the last thing you'll do. We're all mixed up in this together now."

"But I'll always know the truth. He was alive when I left him in your care, and when I came back he was dead. I'll always have that on you, Sav. You'll never know another moment of peace."

Now the elevator door swishes open onto the empty hallway. She sniffs the air. It's clean – just the watery ozone scent of pumped-in oxygen. She pads along the carpeted corridor towards Evie's suite, one of only two doors on this floor. Outside the open door she stops and waits, alert for any noise coming from inside. A few seconds of silence pass. The only sound being the elevator doors swishing shut, and the faint cranking sound of the gears as it moves downwards. She moves the door open, ever so slowly, her gaze flickering to the red exit sign close by so she can be ready to bolt if anyone appears.

The cavernous great room is tidy and filled with sunlight. Housekeeping must have cleaned it up after Friday's party, only the display of high school photographs remains on the walls. But as Savannah moves closer, she notices that someone's taken a black marker and slashed it across many of the pictures, scribbling in a wild, frantic rage. Her heart drums softly in her ears. The place is way too quiet. There's no sign of intruders, or of Wade.

All three of the bedroom doors are ajar. She looks from one to the other and suddenly feels like she's in a bizarre game show. *Which door should I enter first?* Slowly she moves towards Evie's bedroom.

The room is pitch-dark. Drapes are pulled shut. She blinks until her eyes become accustomed to the darkness. Someone is lying on the bed – not moving, probably sleeping. She goes to open the drapes a little so she can see who it is. Creeping closer, she recognizes Wade, but his eyes are wide open, blank and sightless, staring up at the ceiling, and he's lying on a white bedcover that's soaked in his own blood. She stumbles backwards, tripping over a long, serrated knife with the hotel insignia on the handle. She fights for breath, clinging to the heavy drapes and stifles the scream that threatens to rip out from her throat.

She has to get back downstairs and make sure Daisy doesn't see this. Then they'll need to call the cops. She knows for a fact there are no security cameras in the hotel hallways so they'll just have to go by Daisy's text messages. *Poor Wade.* Such a gruesome end to a sad, wasted life. The drug dealers must have finally gotten to him.

The creak of the main suite door sends a charge of fear through her. Without another thought, she grabs the knife and disappears behind the drapes. She holds her breath at the sound of footsteps padding through the adjoining room and a voice that is unmistakably Blair's calling for Evie, then Daisy. A wave of anger surges through her. He's the guy who ruined her life and made her a fugitive, forced to run from one place to another to escape.

The footsteps reach the bedroom. The door creaks open. Someone walks right by her and stops. She holds her breath, heart pulsing in her ears. *Too loud. Too loud.* But when she looks down the blood rushes to her head. Her toes are sticking out from below the drapes. Before she can pull them back, someone throws the curtains aside and Blair stands, facing her, holding a gun. She drops the knife as Blair backs away, his face a tightly-stretched caricature of the Blair she remembers.

"Freeze or I'll blow your head off. What did you do to Wade?"

She stops dead as Blair's arm raises and stiffens until she's staring right into the barrel of the gun.

"I found him like this. Someone must have gotten here before me and killed him."

Two small curves appear around his mouth. The rest of his face is a taut mask. The pale-faced, pretty boy is long gone, leaving the true reflection of the sick, twisted man he is. "You're a liar, Sav. Deep down you were always just a delinquent street kid. Never could rid yourself of the stink of the back alleys. You killed Cal, now here you are, carving up Wade just to get back at Evie."

Savannah stops breathing. She knows what kind of a coward he is. *He's a pussy. He won't dare pull the trigger.* At least she hopes he hasn't changed. She shakes her head and inches forward. "Not true. Cal was still alive and sleeping when I went into the other bedroom and passed out."

"Don't lie, Sav. Admit you did it."

"You're deluded, Blair. Remember how you cuffed me to the bed and tried to rape me, then told me you'd taken care of him. How exactly did you do it? How did you kill him?"

His arms shake. The gun wavers in the air. "Wasn't me. I'm no murderer. Why don't you ask your drug-dealer friend, Daisy, how she spiked his meds?"

"Why would Daisy do that?"

He laughs. "You have no idea what she's capable of. She was mad at Cal because he screwed her then dumped her."

She shrugs. "So why did you make everyone believe I might have finished him off? Then you put him in the car and convinced the others to help you roll it over a cliff."

His eyes look wild. Panicked. "We had no choice. We had to protect ourselves. You should be thanking me. The cops would have come after us. Instead, they decided it was misadventure. Another college kid mixing prescription drugs with alcohol. Besides, he was too burned up to find any real conclusive evidence."

"You're a heartless, rotten coward. Letting everyone do your dirty work for you. Making them believe they were responsible for what happened when it was really you who killed him."

He waves the gun. "Yeah, well, you're the one who'll need backbone to survive when you're locked up in jail for Wade's murder."

"I don't see any cops here," whispers Savannah, advancing towards him and noting the flicker of fear that crosses his eyes.

"Don't come any closer. I'm going to call them right now," he says, trying to hold the gun steady and grab his phone from his pocket.

"You're a liar, Blair. You'd never do that."

"I would – you'll see," he says, backing away so fast he bumps up against the bed, causing his arms to splay wide enough to allow Savannah to lunge at him, knock the gun from his hand and wrench his arm behind his back. Together they stumble towards a purple velvet couch at the foot of the bed. Blair's body feels strangely light and bony, as if she could crack his spine with one snap, but he wriggles and groans, sweat making his skin slick and slippery. With a final surge of strength, she places her free hand on the back of his neck and smashes his head down onto the wooden arm of the couch, knocking him out cold. He slumps onto the floor, his cheek pressed against the cushions. Blood screeches through her veins as she looks down at this man who's ruined the better part of her life.

But her entire body freezes at the sound of the other bedroom door opening.

"What the hell did you do to him?" screams Daisy, a ghoulish sight in her blood-spattered dress.

Savannah eyes the gun lying on the floor, but before she can make a move, Daisy lunges forward and grabs it. She holds it out, her hands shaking.

"I heard everything you said. Is it true? Did he actually rape you?"

Savannah's chest heaves as she struggles to breathe. She nods. "He tried. I fought him off. He said he'd taken care of Cal. Did you help him, Daisy? Is that why you're here? And did you kill Wade?"

Daisy shakes her head. "No, it's not true. Blair called me to come up here. Said he was going to tell me the truth about Wade and his inheritance. When I got here he was standing over Wade's dead body, with a knife, cursing Evie and saying crazy things like he never wanted her to be happy. There was so much blood. I couldn't look at what he'd done." She doubles over, clutching her gut. "What'll we do now, Sav? They'll find us here and think we killed Wade. They'll believe Blair. I know they will."

Savannah looks from Wade's corpse and back to Blair. If he survives, he'll never leave her alone. He'll plague them all forever. But to kill him in cold blood? That's stepping over a line she can't cross, no matter what the consequences might be.

But now Daisy's glaring at her, one foot tapping on the floor. "C'mon, Sav. You were always the cool one. What should we do?"

Savannah backs away, shaking her head. The room feels like it's spinning. Pinpricks of sunlight explode into her line of vision. Is she going to faint? Is Daisy telling the truth? Did Blair kill Wade or did she?

"Okay," says Daisy. "There's only one way to go."

Daisy moves so fast, and yet Savannah feels like she's watching her in slow motion as she takes a tissue from the ornamental box on the nightstand and picks up the gun. She puts it in Blair's hand and places it inside his open mouth. Savannah's about to lurch forward and stop her as Daisy releases the safety, shoves a pillow over his head, and pulls the trigger. She gasps as Daisy jumps aside to avoid the splatter of blood and allow the lifeless body to slump to the floor.

"Don't just stand there. Help me clean the prints," says Daisy as she wipes down the knife and places it in Blair's hand, wrapping his clammy fingers around the handle then letting it drop to the floor beside him.

Savannah's head reels as she looks from one blood-soaked body to the other. "You – you killed him."

"I had to do it. He'd never have left us alone and you know it. Don't you know that he's the person who's been sending you those threatening messages all this time?"

"How do you know about them?" says Savannah.

"He told me. Boasted about it the other night. Said he had to get you back for leaving him with Evie." Her eyes seem off focus as she taps the side of her head with her index finger. "I know what we can do. Just to make this scene perfect."

Savannah watches her as she moves with robotic precision. This must be some imposter who's come in and replaced the real Daisy. It's like the sci-fi movie where the evil clone takes over the real, living, breathing original. This is not the ditzy sweet girl Savannah knew. This girl is ruthless. Determined. Rummaging through drawers, wiping the prints away as she goes. Savannah feels sick. *Has she lost her mind?*

"Paper. Lots of it. Perfect," squeals Daisy, waving it in the air. "And a pen."

Daisy takes the pen and dabs it in the pool of blood near Wade's head, scrawls some words on the paper and places the note next to him, making sure to handle the edges with tissue-covered fingers. She's just wiping fingerprints from the pen when the suite door opens again and footsteps pad across the floor.

"Quick, behind the drapes," says Daisy, yanking Savannah by the arm.

They gaze in horror through a crack in the drapes as Evie runs into the room and leaps onto the bed calling Wade's name in a breathless, frantic voice.

"Wade, my love…"

A stomach-curdling scream pierces the air, followed by a loud thud as Evie hits the floor.

ZOE

Zoe makes her way towards the elevator, relieved by Phyllis's assurances that she'll have no trouble getting a very generous divorce settlement, but the buzzing of her phone yanks her back to reality. *Damn, it's Savannah. Shit – this is the fourth time she's called in the last five minutes.* The insistent noise stabs at her conscience and a little voice in her head repeats, *You are not a heartless, unfeeling person. You are a doctor, therefore you should be brimming with empathy, poised with your doctor's bag, and ready to help your friend. Damn you, Savannah.* She sighs in resignation and clicks the *accept* button.

"Where the hell have you been? You need to get up here, pronto," says Savannah in a weird, breathy voice.

This sounds bad. Damn. Why didn't I follow my instincts and leave? Now it's too late. "What's happened? Did you find Wade?" There's a weird whining sound in the background, like a small animal in pain. "Who's making that noise?"

"I can't explain, just get up here," says Savannah in a sharp, no-nonsense voice that borders on threatening. "And bring some of those sedatives."

"Okay," says Zoe, "I'm at the elevator."

The line clicks off and Zoe is afraid, and a little pissed off at Savannah's bossy attitude. She sure didn't sound like the cheery, carefree Vegas showgirl she makes herself out to be. But maybe that's all a front to hide some dark and guilty secrets. You don't take off and leave your hometown and friends at a moment's notice, then completely disappear, unless you're trying to escape some serious shit. And she was always the quiet type. The dangerous ones are always quiet. Maybe she really did kill Cal.

Besides, what gives Sav, a mere show dancer, the right to lord it over Dr. Zoe Ryan? But now's not the time for injured pride, she'd better get the hell up there right away.

Up on Evie's floor it's silent, and there's no sign of Blair. There's actually nowhere for him to hide. No secret closet doors or shady alcoves – only the exit stairwell halfway along the hallway. Zoe feels a weird sense of foreboding when she approaches the wide-open door of Evie's suite, and hears a pained, whimpering sound that gets a whole lot louder when she strides into Evie's suite, crosses through into the main bedroom and stops dead in her tracks at the sight that greets her and the smell of death.

It's a scene she's watched many times on Netflix, only this time it's real. Absolute carnage. Bloodstains spattered across the pale-gold drapes. Blair's body slumped on the floor, a mass of shredded bloody flesh that was once his face, pressed against the carpet. Another lifeless body on the blood-soaked bed, and Evie huddled on the floor sobbing, her shoulders heaving, her face smudged with saliva and snot. Savannah stands above it all, her face a ghastly white color, her eyes inscrutable, and Daisy's huddled over on a chair, covering her face with her hands.

Zoe should be used to scenes of death and blood, but she's so shaken all she can manage is a croaky, "What happened?"

Savannah takes a deep breath and runs a hand through her hair. "I – I found them here."

Daisy looks up. "Blair called me and told me to come up here. Wade was dead. I think Blair did it with that knife." She points to the bloodied weapon on the floor next to Blair.

"And Blair?" says Zoe, her stomach churning. *This is bad. Really bad. Maybe I'll never get home now.*

"Looks like he shot himself after he left that note."

"Blair killed himself?" says Zoe, eyes flitting towards the hastily scrawled note lying across the mound that was Wade: *You want him, you can have him.*

So spiteful and obviously addressed to Evie. Could Blair really have done this? Sounds more like something Daisy would say.

"So you're thinking it's a murder-suicide?" She makes some hasty calculations. Moves over to the body on the bed and takes a look. She can't – absolutely can't touch that cold corpse. *Poor bastard,* she thinks, gazing at Wade. *A loser in life and in death.* But to her professional eye, it looks like this guy's been dead a whole lot longer than fifteen minutes, the way the blood has dried. She turns to the foot of the bed and looks at the thing that was Blair. Blood is still wet, sticky and congealing around Blair's face. She looks up at Savannah and, for the first time, feels a sense of suspicion. And trepidation. She doesn't want to mess with either of these women. Savannah's hands are streaked with blood and Daisy's clothes are covered in it.

"Definitely looks like it," says Savannah.

"You're absolutely sure?"

Savannah's eyes flicker momentarily away from Zoe's gaze. "What else could it be?"

Zoe narrows her eyes and chews on her lower lip. *Looks very much like Wade had already been dead a while and Blair died sometime in the last five minutes.* But she can't put her suspicions into words. There's a neatly tied-up scenario here that's best left just as it is, if she wants to get out of this situation unscathed. She tilts her head and nods slowly. "You're right, Sav. What else could it be?"

Savannah holds her gaze. "So what do you suggest we do now?"

Zoe feels like they're in a standoff. Her brain ratchets through all the possible scenarios until she finds the most airtight solution. One that will satisfy any coroner worth their salt, and one that will allow her to remove herself from this entire situation. "I think you should all wash your hands. Wipe everything down. Don't touch anything else. Leave everything as it is and wait a little longer before we leave. But first I'm going to give Evie a sedative that will calm her down and put her to sleep. Let the cleaning staff discover this mess."

"Good plan. She's had such a shock," says Daisy, in a tone of hollow empathy. "I'll hold her still for you."

Zoe fills a glass of water at the sink and tips in some of the Rohypnol she found in Evie's purse. It'll put Evie to sleep very quickly and also affect her memories of what exactly happened here. She bends over Evie as Savannah cradles her head.

"You've experienced terrible trauma, Evie. Drink this and you'll feel better." Evie mumbles as she sips the drink, but Zoe's sure she's saying Wade's name. "We need to give her at least fifteen minutes before it works."

"I'm not sticking around that long," says Daisy. "I think Evie is grown-up enough to deal with this situation on her own. Besides, housekeeping will be here within the hour. Do you want to be here when they arrive?"

Zoe takes a good long look at the two women. After this, she'll never see them again. She'll be out of the country within a couple of hours, and once she's crossed the border, she'll erase all memories of this cursed weekend from her memory. In fact, if anyone ever asks her about it, she'll shrug and say she left early to deal with a real estate emergency. With that in mind, she pockets the water glass. "You read my mind, guys. The exit door is just to the right of the hallway. I think it's best we take that way out."

"Good thinking," says Savannah, as they walk towards the bedroom door.

Zoe watches as Evie tries to stumble to her feet, then her legs give way and she flops to the floor. "Oops. I hope I didn't give her too much."

"Guess we'll never find out," says Daisy, shrugging as they stride out into the empty hallway and disappear through the glass exit doors.

EIGHT MONTHS LATER

DAISY

Daisy sits on her sixth-floor balcony, overlooking the rolling waves of the Pacific. It's spring in Seattle and the trees are in bloom. Her laptop is open in front of her. She's fifty thousand words into her new novel, and is keen to get another thousand down before supper.

This new free and easy lifestyle suits her just fine, and she's managing just fine with the money from the sale of her house, the proceeds from Wade's life insurance policy, and a generous settlement from his family inheritance.

There was also an unexpected bonus payment from the drug dealers. Seems Wade was becoming a real liability. Talking too much, gambling away a whole whack of drug money, and trying to blackmail them by claiming he had a buddy who was a cop. Those dealers were so grateful when Daisy said she'd help them out. She remembers the last text she sent them that final morning in Vegas.

> My friend will meet you in the lobby of the Aria. He'll take you to Wade, no questions asked.

Once she knew Evie wouldn't be there to rescue Wade, the

plan went like clockwork, though she's never been sure exactly when Blair arrived on the scene. Too bad he thought she'd dreamed up the drug dealers. Guess that's what happens when you've led such a protected life. The sight of Wade lying there scared him shitless. But the murder-suicide story was an unexpected surprise. Very creative. And her hands are relatively clean, her conscience clear.

He had to go.

So, the upshot of it all is that Blair and Wade are gone, and everyone is happy. Evie's living it up in her new villa in the Bahamas, coasting on the windfall of Blair's money while trying to restore her self-respect and heal her battered soul.

Savannah lives just down the coast in Oregon with Leon. She's opened a dance studio and he's landed a great job with a corporate law firm. Most importantly, Sav doesn't have to run anymore now there's no secret stalker trying to mess with her head.

They haven't heard much from Zoe, although the last word was that she'd divorced her banker husband, become a pediatric surgeon and hooked up with some hotshot real estate agent named Jaz.

She focuses on the line of gulls cutting across the sky, and the pristine white triangles of sailboats coasting on the horizon. Life can't get more perfect than this. Can it?

Footsteps echo in the hall. A key clicks into the lock, and a tall, burly man enters. Dark-haired, tanned, with a muscular physique. This guy turned out to be a great cook, as well as a dab hand with a toolbox, and an incredible lover. She's utterly spoiled.

Daisy knew she could win Tom away from Evie. All it took was a couple of hours of making out, that Friday night of the divorce weekend, and Tom was hers. Didn't take long to shift his loyalty, though he never let on to Evie the whole time. And at the warehouse, he deliberately fell on top of Evie, lying there long enough for Daisy, Zoe and Sav to escape.

Zoe slamming the car door against his chest was not part of the plan, but Tom was a real trooper, even though he had to hustle to get a cab back to the hotel in time to bribe the doorman to stall Evie by pretending Wade was waiting for her at reception, while he directed the drug dealers upstairs to her suite. He's a big guy, so they knew he wasn't someone to mess with. He showed them the way as if he was seating them at a prime table in a restaurant. They handed him a big tip, and he disappeared downstairs to deal with Evie, who was waiting there, fuming. The rest is history.

"Picked up a fantastic sea bass," Tom says, placing a package on the kitchen counter.

Daisy stretches and grins. Maybe she can knock out the extra thousand words tomorrow morning.

"There's a bottle of Pinot Grigio chilling in the fridge. Want to pour some?"

"Anything you say, babe," he says, smiling and busying himself with the glasses.

Daisy closes her eyes and silently thanks Evie for inviting her to the divorce party.

Turns out Evie wasn't the only one who needed to make a fresh start.

They all did.

THE END

A MESSAGE FROM M.M. DELUCA

Thank you so much for reading *The Divorce Party*. I hope you enjoyed reading it as much as I enjoyed writing it!

If you'd like to keep up to date with any of my new releases, please sign up for my newsletter. Your email will never be shared, and I'll only contact you when I have news about a new release. Sign up by visiting the website below:

https://www.marjoriedeluca.com/

If you have the time to leave me a short, honest review on Amazon, Goodreads, or wherever you purchased the book, I'd very much appreciate it. I love hearing what you think, and your reviews help me reach new readers – which allows me to bring you more books! If you know of friends or family that would enjoy the book, I'd love your help there, too.

You can also connect with me via Facebook, Goodreads, Instagram and Threads. I always love to hear from readers.

A MESSAGE FROM M.M. DELUCA

Instagram: https://www.instagram.com/mmdelucaauthor/
Facebook: https://www.facebook.com/marjorie.deluca.3
Goodreads: https://www.goodreads.com/author/show/20984340.M_M_DeLuca
https://www.threads.net/@mmdelucaauthor

Thank you again, so very much, for your support of my books. It means the world to me!

ACKNOWLEDGEMENTS

Many thanks go to the incredible publishing team at Bloodhound Books, most notably Betsy Reavley for believing in my book and making it a reality. Also, a big thanks to the other team members who helped make this an incredibly smooth and exciting journey: editorial and production manager, Tara Lyons; editor, Ian Skewis and proofreader, Shirley Khan. Mel, cover designer from Better Books, and marketing team, Hannah Deuce and Lexi Curtis. I really do appreciate your support.

I also want to thank my generous fellow writers who read the early chapters and encouraged me to continue: J.A. Corrigan, Joel Nedecky and Arianne Richmonde.

Finally a big thank you to all the readers out there who've supported me on this journey. It's your love of reading that keeps me striving to produce the best work I can. I couldn't have done all this without you.

ABOUT THE AUTHOR

M.M. (Marjorie) DeLuca spent her childhood in Durham City, England. After graduating from the University of London, she moved to Canada, where she worked as a teacher and a freelance writer. She studied Advanced Creative Writing with Pulitzer Prizewinner Dr Carol Shields.

She's the author of five gripping suspense novels: Amazon bestseller, *The Perfect Family Man*; Bookscan Top 100 bestseller, and Apple Books Top 100 bestseller, *The Secret Sister*; critically acclaimed historical suspense, *The Savage Instinct*, and her latest psychological suspense novel, *The Night Side*.

She lives in Winnipeg, Canada with her husband and two children.

ALSO BY M.M. DELUCA
(NOT PUBLISHED BY BLOODHOUND BOOKS)

The Savage Instinct
The Secret Sister
The Perfect Family Man
The Pitman's Daughter
The Night Side

A NOTE FROM THE PUBLISHER

Thank you for reading this book. If you enjoyed it please do consider leaving a review on Amazon to help others find it too.

We hate typos. All of our books have been rigorously edited and proofread, but sometimes mistakes do slip through. If you have spotted a typo, please do let us know and we can get it amended within hours.

info@bloodhoundbooks.com

Printed in Dunstable, United Kingdom